Plea Bargain

Plea Bargain

A NOVEL

LARRY AXELROOD

Cumberland House
Nashville, Tennessee

Published by
   Cumberland House Publishing, Inc.
   431 Harding Industrial Drive
   Nashville, TN 37211-3160
   www.cumberlandhouse.com

Cover design: Gore Studio, Inc.
Text design: Mary Sanford

Library of Congress Cataloging-in-Publication Data
Axelrood, Larry, 1960–
  Plea bargain : a novel / Larry Axelrood.
    p. cm.
  ISBN 1-58182-273-1 (alk. paper)
  1. Attorney and client—Fiction. 2. Trials (Murder)--Fiction. 3. Chicago (Ill.)—Fiction. I. Title.
  PS3551.X45 P56 2002
  813'.6—dc21
                           2002010894

Printed in the United States of America
1 2 3 4 5 6 7—08 07 06 05 04 03 02

To Anne Sherman, for everything.
To Jack and Claire for making
every day an adventure.

ACKNOWLEDGMENTS

Nothing is easy. There are so many people who have helped me in so many ways. My wife, Anne, daughter, Claire, and son, Jack, for their love and support. My father and mother, Jack and Helen Axelrood, for their guidance and unwavering belief in me. Special thanks to my brothers, Mike and Barney, and to my sister, Lisa.

In no particular order, Pete Vernon, Jimmy Linn, Rick "Elvis" Mottweiler, Tim Joyce, Jim Epstein, Chris Donnelly, Tom Romano, Kevin Milner, Roe Conn, Rick Kogan, and Tom Molitor for their friendship and advice.

Sheila Klee and Lauren Presta for helping get it right. Stacie, Julia, Teresa, Mary, and Ron at Cumberland for championing my work.

PREFACE

The shiny black Lincoln Town Car seemed out of place amid the wreckage of abandoned warehouses. It glided slowly over the cracked pavement of a driveway that led to a building with row after row of filthy, broken windows. The car traversed the length of the building and headed around to the back, where it slipped through a pair of open warehouse doors and parked in the middle of the cavernous space.

The driver got out of the car and looked around casually. Cracking his knuckles as he adjusted and fit his fingers snugly into his black leather gloves, he walked back to the doors and, tugging on the rusty chains that dangled from each of them, pulled one, then the other door closed. They met with a boom that echoed through the building.

After dusting off his stone-white trousers, the man in the black leather gloves reached into his pocket and pulled out his keys. He strode confidently back to the car and popped the trunk with the remote; it flew up and bounced open. Hands on his hips, he surveyed the contents, took a deep breath, and leaned in. With great effort and in a single motion, he yanked out the lifeless body of a young man, holding it firmly under the arms. Were it not for the dead man's shoes, which snagged abruptly on the lip of the trunk, the removal would have been smooth and clean. But this break in momentum caused him to lose both his balance and his grip, and the body thudded head-first onto the concrete. It hung from the trunk, twisted at an awkward angle.

After studying the corpse for a minute and trying to figure out which end to work, the man decided on the feet. He grasped each ankle and pulled again. The body dislodged and remained facedown on the concrete. Choosing not to drag the corpse across the floor on its face, he flipped it over—a small act of kindness. He pulled the body quickly over to a corner of the warehouse and into an office that was empty except for a few metal drums, a pile of empty boxes, and debris. The body lay faceup on the floor while the man fumbled through some trash to retrieve a five-gallon can of gasoline. Gripping the can by the handle, he walked back toward the corpse, and when he reached it he tipped the can forward as he kicked the man's hands palm-side up.

The corpse's hair grew dark as the gas slicked it back, and the man half expected the corpse to blink or flinch when the liquid hit its eyes. When he was sure the body was saturated, he tossed the near-empty can back into the junk heap and removed his gloves, finger by finger, stuffing them into the front pants pocket of the corpse. The air was thick with the noxious fumes. He reached into his shirt pocket and pulled out a book of matches, then stepped outside the office and lit a match, tossing it toward the body. There was a slow whoosh, and the man shielded his eyes as he peered around the corner just in time to see the dead man disappear into the flames.

That done, he walked hurriedly back to the warehouse doors and pushed them apart, tucking his hands into the sleeves of his shirt like a turtle's head. He poked his head outside to take a quick look around before dusting himself off and returning to the car. He slammed the trunk down and got in. Then he backed out carefully, surveying the burning building as he did; put the car in drive; and sped away.

As he drove from the industrial district into the residential neighborhoods, taking as circuitous a route as possible, he kept his eye on the rearview mirror. Assured no one was tailing him, he pulled into a gas station—one of the large anonymous chains with a mini Pizza Hut inside. The pumps were busy, but he wasn't interested in gas at the moment. Instead, he pulled up to one of the vacuums, popped the trunk, and got out of the car. Leaning over the trunk, he reached into his front pants pocket and pulled out a plastic bag, the contents of which he had collected days earlier from this particular machine. He opened the baggie and shook out the debris, spilling a mixture of dog hair, lint, sand, grass—and whatever else might have been sucked from the hundreds of cars previously cleaned here—onto the carpeted floor of the trunk. Then he deposited three quarters into the vacuum. He vacuumed up everything he had just laid down and then continued through three more quarters just for good measure. Satisfied with his housework, he slammed the trunk down again and removed a handkerchief from another pocket. After he'd glanced casually over to the pumps, he wiped his fingerprints off the trunk and nonchalantly continued to shine spots along the car as he made his way back to the driver's seat.

He drove from the gas station to the expressway and took the Stevenson toward the city, then he looped onto the Kennedy and headed for O'Hare. When he arrived, he veered off to the rental car return area, found his agency, and exchanged the Town Car for a receipt. Then he hopped onto the bus that would shuttle him to his terminal.

The bus driver wore a nametag that identified him as one of the rental car company's owners.

"What airline?" the driver asked with a smile.

"United," the man replied.

The driver pulled the doors shut.

"No luggage?"

"Nope," the man answered, taking the seat across from and just below the driver. "I dropped it ahead. My wife is at the terminal waiting for me."

"Smart move," the driver said, pulling away.

It was only then that he began to relax. Leaning his head back against the window, he closed his eyes and sighed deeply.

Plea Bargain

Darcy Cole had finished his morning swim, taken a steam, and was sitting in his bathrobe having breakfast at a table by the pool. He was reading an article in the *Tribune* about a trial in federal court. Finally, he put the newspaper down and paid attention instead to his oatmeal and toast. His once salt-and-pepper hair had given way to a full head of gray. He was still lean and healthy from his daily swim, and for the first time in years he was invigorated by his work, enthusiastic even.

He finished his breakfast, showered, dressed, and walked out of the club. It was less than twenty feet from the club to the side door of his office building. He shot through the lobby and into an empty elevator. He rolled into the office and greeted Irma with a big smile.

"Good morning, Irma. How's life?"

She smiled back. "It's busy," she said, handing him his messages. "Start returning phone calls, will ya?"

"What would I do without you?" Darcy said as he snatched the messages out of Irma's hand without pausing and made his way into his office.

Irma Rosales had been with Darcy for over a decade. She had started as his secretary and had gradually taken on the role of office manager. Darcy worked with Kathy Haddon and Patrick O'Hagin, lawyers who had recently become Darcy's partners. Kathy had been a law clerk to Darcy while she was in law school. She began by doing research and writing briefs. Before long Darcy was dependent on her. She had an excellent grasp of legal issues and was a tireless worker. Her sense of humor and gentle presence gave some balance to Darcy. Patrick had only been with Darcy for a few years, since his forced departure from the United States Attorney's Office where he had been a prosecutor. Now Irma, Kathy, and Patrick served as Darcy's surrogate family.

Seeing there was nothing urgent, Darcy tossed the pink message slips onto his desk. Darcy dealt with crises more than he liked. He often represented powerful, successful people at the most desperate point in their lives.

Just a year ago he had been the target of a hit by a disgruntled mobster client. He had survived, but his car had been blown up with Patrick's lover inside.

He had tried three high-profile cases in a row, leaving him tired and stressed. He swiveled in his chair to look out over the lake—crisp, blue water with low waves. It was a bright, beautiful day. He enjoyed this break. A peaceful, almost routine day allowed him to reflect on his life and relax, but he knew it could all change with one phone call. In the distance, he could see a barge trudging its way up north, and nearer, a number of sailboats worked their way along. He loved to watch them cut gracefully across the water. He had no interest in owning a boat, but he certainly did admire them.

Darcy was startled by a knock on the door, and turned around to see Kathy Haddon standing in the doorway.

"Good morning, kiddo. What's happening?" he said, beaming.

Kathy managed a weak smile and then shut the door as she came in and sat in a client chair across from Darcy's desk.

"Can we talk about a couple of cases?" she asked.

Darcy sat up a bit straighter and looked across the desk at her. "Of course," he said.

"On Alvarez, we have a motion to quash the search warrant and a motion to suppress the wiretap. Neither of which is going anywhere." She tossed copies of the motions onto Darcy's desk.

Darcy read them in silence. "You did a nice job," Darcy began, "but there aren't any federal judges suppressing wire-taps." He smiled.

She had a pained look on her face as she blankly looked out the window. Darcy knew something was wrong.

"Okay, kiddo, what's wrong?" he asked.

"I'm worried about Jim. He's up to something."

Darcy was shocked. "Your husband? I don't believe it."

"Two Thursday nights in a row he's been out late, and when he comes back he smells like a bar."

"Why are you worried? He smells like a bar two Thursdays in a row. He goes out with his friends and stops for a cold one. So what?"

"I don't know. I'm getting weird vibes," she said. "Sometimes my work is hard on him."

"Well, do you want to do more from home? Do you want to cut your hours? Do you want to take another day off?"

Kathy managed a tired smile.

"I appreciate it. You're so considerate in that way, but I think ultimately it comes down to the fact that he just doesn't earn as much as I do."

Darcy smiled. "Well, I can't help you there. Unless, of course, you want me to pay you less."

Her smile turned genuine. "No, the pay I have is just fine for now, thank you very much. It is a shame though," she said. "People don't value teachers."

"Teachers don't get paid very well, that's for sure," Darcy said. "And it's such an important job. Anyway, I think you should talk to him."

"Yeah, you're right. Thank you, Darcy." She smiled. "Thanks for your time."

"My door is always open to you, kiddo. You know that," Darcy said.

"I know, and I appreciate it."

* * *

Harry Feiger sat in the waiting room at the law firm of Cole, Haddon and O'Hagin, wearing a black-and-gray herringbone sport coat with gray slacks, a blue shirt, and a blue-and-black tie. His initials were monogrammed on his left sleeve near his Hamilton wristwatch, and a black Mont Blanc pen poked above his shirt pocket. Bypassing an old edition of *Cosmopolitan,* he had opted for a *Newsweek,* which he was absentmindedly thumbing through. The door to the offices opened and Irma beckoned to him, smiling.

"Mr. Cole will see you now."

Harry dropped the magazine on the table and stood up.

"Thank you," he said.

"Follow me."

She led him through the hallway past Patrick O'Hagin's office, which was closed, then Kathy Haddon's office, which was open but empty, and finally into a large office where Darcy Cole sat behind a massive, tidy desk. Darcy rose, walked out from behind the desk, and warmly shook Harry's hand.

"Mr. Feiger, nice to see you."

"Thank you, thanks for seeing me. Please, call me Harry."

"Why don't you sit down," Darcy said as he motioned Harry toward a client chair.

Irma quietly walked out and shut the door.

"Do you remember meeting me?" Harry asked.

Darcy gave him a puzzled look. "I recognize your face, but quite honestly, I don't remember when we met."

Harry smiled. "Oh, it wasn't that memorable. We were in Branch 57—one of my rare trips to felony preliminary hearing court."

Branch 57 was a Felony Narcotics Preliminary Hearing Courtroom. "I'm sorry, I don't remember," Darcy said.

"No reason you should. But let me get to what brings me here today." Harry leaned forward and rested his forearms on Darcy's desk.

"I'm in trouble," he said quietly, looking at his mono-grammed cuff.

When Darcy showed no reaction, Harry smiled. "But I guess you've heard that one before, huh?"

"Why don't you tell me what's up," Darcy said calmly, encouraging Harry to continue.

"Okay, then," Harry said. "My practice is primarily misdemeanors and traffic court. For a long time, I was doing hooker cases in Branch 40 when it was really active. Most of the clerks, state's attorneys, and public defenders call me Hooker Harry. I'm not really proud of that, but it doesn't bother me either. After all, I was making a pretty good living. I never wanted the high-profile stuff like you have."

Harry loosened his tie and looked around the room. "Everything we say here is covered by attorney-client privilege, right?"

Darcy nodded. "Of course it is, whether you retain me or not."

"I understand, but sometimes lawyers talk. One of the reasons I came to you is that I hear you're discreet, and that I can trust you."

"I'll keep that in mind," Darcy said. "I assure you, what you say here stays here."

Harry continued. "When I got out of law school, I took a job at the Corporation Counsel's office. I was in traffic court for a while, but it didn't take me long to realize that a guy can make a lot of money doing traffic cases and misdemeanors. I went from traffic court to a court call where I watched the state's attorneys disposing of the misdemeanors. One hundred, one hundred fifty a day, and they're still done by three o'clock. So I said what the hell, quit the job and hung a shingle.

"Through some coincidences, I started representing a lot of working girls. I'd grab two, maybe five hundred from the broad or her pimp. Then I'd collect her bond slip and dispose of the case. You wouldn't expect it to be much of a practice normally, but hell, I'd have three, four, sometimes ten cases going in the same courtroom on any given day. I was pulling in good money and, except for the bond slips that came back in checks from the county, it was in cash, and all from representing the least credible people on the planet.

"One day as I stood in the hallway outside court, a guy in a suit walked through the courtroom door, right up to me. You could see him shaking.

"'Are you a lawyer?' he asked me. I told him yes and asked what I could do for him.

"He told me this tired tale about how he'd got caught soliciting a prostitute who was really a policewoman, and how they'd agreed to give him supervision. He was asking me what he should do. I explained to him that supervision was not a permanent conviction and that he could file a petition to expunge, which would erase all evidence of his arrest—any fingerprints, photographs, and negatives would be returned to him, and he could do whatever he wanted with them.

"'Is that legal?' the dumbshit asks me. So the lightbulb goes on above my head. I kind of lead him to believe that I'm doing something slick, something not exactly kosher. He's eating it up. At this point I'm selling the sizzle instead of the steak. The last thing I want him to know is that an expungement only requires someone to fill out some forms and pay a fee. So maybe I'm playing it like a scam but it's really legit. After all, all I'm doing is an expungement.

"He must have asked me ten times if I was sure it would destroy the entire record of the incident. After I assured him, he pulled out his checkbook and asked me to do the expungement on the spot. Not really thinking, I shot him a fee of five hundred bucks, and he just started writing. I gave him my card so he could put my name on the check, then I went back into the courtroom and looked at his file. I talked to the state's attorney, told him I had been retained and they agreed to dismiss the case. Seems the policewoman wasn't in court that day anyway. I got the information I needed to do the expungement from the court file, and it was as easy as that.

"I didn't think much of it. The guy would call me periodically while the expungement was pending. Finally, when I got everything back, he came to my office. I told him I would mail it to him, but he insisted on picking it up in person. I gave him his package and he reached in his pocket and pulled out five hundred-dollar bills and gave them to me. I asked him what it was for.

"He said, 'This is for your discretion. I really appreciate it.'

"He left that day and I haven't seen him since."

Darcy looked puzzled. "This is what brings you here?"

"No, that's how I got the idea that brought me here."

Harry leaned back in his chair, let out a sigh, and continued.

"The next time I was in court taking care of my girls, I looked around for prospects and saw a guy wearing a suit. You can tell the marks from a mile away, clean-cut guys wearing suits. They're always sitting alone without a lawyer nervously looking around. So I talk to this guy and find out he had been arrested for soliciting a policewoman. I immediately grabbed the file, got all of his information and pulled him out into the hallway to talk.

"I explained to him that in certain situations, people could get upset if their police reports or mug shots from such incidents were to get into the wrong hands. I had his rapt attention as I continued my sales pitch. After about ten minutes, he agreed to pay me twenty-five hundred dollars to make sure no one would ever find out about his arrest.

"That's when it started. I was very careful: I picked my spots and approached only the really nervous guys. It wasn't illegal but I'm acting like a miracle worker for these guys. If they thought I was bending the law to help them, I wasn't going to clear things up. Soon, word of my services got around."

Harry leaned back and continued.

"Look, I'm not proud of what I did, but I was very careful not to extort. The bottom line is this: I was making money hand over fist, and all in cash. These guys didn't want any evidence linking them to me. I bought a really expensive shredder for my office, and let them come and run their own documents through. You could see them get this rush of relief when the history of their mistake vanished before their eyes. Well, the business took off, and then got crazy; I was paying clerks to let me know when they would have high-volume hooker arrest dates."

"How long has this been going on?" Darcy asked.

Harry exhaled loudly.

"Hoo boy, probably four and a half years now," he said.

"Obviously, something broke bad on you," Darcy said.

Harry nodded. "An FBI agent came by and gave me a grand jury subpoena and wanted to talk to me. I told him I would as soon as I lawyered up."

"So what do they want?" Darcy asked.

"Well, I'm sure one of my former clients or somebody I've approached dropped a dime on me. It is a pretty weak extortion case, but I'm not going to minimize. There's a lot of potential exposure."

"Do they have your office records?"

"No. I shredded everything about it."

"What about your financial records?"

"They can seize them, but that won't do them any good."

Darcy raised an eyebrow. "Is that right?"

"Believe me, I'm very thorough," Harry said, looking confident.

Darcy turned and looked out the window for a moment.

"Harry, if I'm going to be your lawyer, you'll have to be honest with me and tell me everything."

Harry leaned toward Darcy.

"Well, here's the thing. If they want my law license, they can have it. If they want me to plead to an extortion count, I'll do that. If they want me to do six months in a halfway house, I'll do that, too. But I'm not going to talk to them. I know the Feds will want me to come in and confess all my sins."

"You mean you think they'll want you to do a proffer," Darcy said.

"Yeah, and I don't want to do it," Harry said.

"Why not?"

"Well, there's more about me they don't know than they do," he continued. "I'm positive that they'll never be able to find all the guys I've done this for, and most of them would deny it anyway. Even if they get three or four of them, it's not going to amount to much. You're talking extorting ten thousand dollars from four guys, if, in fact, it is extortion. I looked at the guidelines on this, there isn't a lot."

"Do you do much federal work?" said Darcy.

"None. But I've read the federal code and understand the federal guidelines. My criminal history is zero, and the criminal element offense for this is minimal. Now I do know there's upward departures and downward departures, and enhancements. I'm not going to pretend I know everything; that's why I'm here. And I have a bigger problem than that."

Darcy leaned back. "Go on."

"About ten years ago, I realized that there are ways to ensure a bright future, especially when you have a cash business. In 1991, I vacationed in the Cayman Islands."

"Nice beaches," Darcy said. "Great diving."

"Do I look like a beach guy?" Harry laughed.

"I went down for a banking seminar, and after that, I opened an account and formed a corporation. My corporation consists of a three-by-six-inch plaque on a wall, among hundreds of other plaques in a bank off the main drag in Georgetown on Grand Cayman. For years my reported income fluctuated between a hundred ten and a hundred forty thousand dollars. The truth is, I was sometimes making three times that much, but like I said, it was a cash business. Most of my time was spent running around to different places buying money orders that I'd make out to my corporation and mail off to the Cayman Islands. Most often I was sending between three and five hundred, sometimes less, but I'm doing this a couple of times a week. The corporation's mail was delivered to my personal banker, where they'd endorse and deposit the checks into my account. Once a year I'd fly down, spend a day at a brokerage house and make investments for the corporation.

"The bulk of the money went to mutual funds and blue chip stocks. I don't have to tell you what that's been like the past ten years. There is no way the government knows about it. There's no way they could trace it, and there's no way they could prove it. So, yeah, I am prepared to take a little hit on these extortion cases, but there's no way I am talking to them. I can't talk to them. If they find out about my Cayman Island account, I'm screwed. They'll nail me for tax evasion, money laundering, you name it, and I'll never be able to spend the money."

"What do you want me to do?" Darcy asked.

"I want you to protect me," he said. "I want you to walk me through this. They don't know how many people I did expungements for—I assume they could find out, but there's nothing illegal about doing expungements. It is only illegal if people are forced to do them, and these guys were happy to pay me the money. So I don't know how much of a case they have against me.

"I'm fifty-one years old, and like I said, if they want my law license that's fine. Three years ago I became a licensed real-estate agent in Florida. I could take a hit and still keep that license. My corporation bought a house in Naples. If things get hairy, my wife is going to leave me and move down there. I'll pay rent to the Florida corporation that owns the house in Naples. The Florida corporation's property management company is managing it for my Cayman Islands company. So when my wife leaves me and I'm paying rent on her house down there, I'll be in effect paying myself, and, of course, deducting it from my income taxes. If I have to do some time, I'll do it and then move to Florida where my wife and I will reconcile."

"It is a nice plan," Darcy said, "but I don't know if you're going to pull it off. What if they know more than you think?"

"They don't," he said. He reached into his pocket and pulled out an envelope. "But now you know everything about me," he said. "Will you take my case?"

"Of course," Darcy said. "All you have to do is pay me and cooperate with me."

Harry pulled a certified check out of an envelope and put it on the desk.

"I know you charge a good buck," he said, "but this is going to be a plea. There's no way I want to go to trial."

He slid the check to Darcy.

Darcy looked at it. It was for twenty-five thousand dollars.

"I assume that will cover it from start to finish," Harry said.

"That'll do it," Darcy responded, "but I'll need some more information from you."

"Remember, Darcy, I'm not looking for the world on this. Whatever pill I have to swallow, I'm ready. I just want to get this over with and get on with the next half of my life."

Two

The shades were pulled. The room was dark. Al Maggio sat on the edge of a tattered sofa over a coffee table, chopping up chunks of white powder on a small mirror. His gun, a Smith-Wesson .38, was to the right of the mirror on the table. The TV was on, providing the only light he needed.

Maggio finished breaking up the lumps, then guided the powder into three straight fat lines. He held one nostril closed as he picked up a two-inch length of plastic straw and took a line into the open nostril. He repeated the process on the other side. He split the last line between nostrils, then cleared the mirror of residue with his finger, which he swiped across his gums.

He sank back into the couch and tossed his head back, trying to work the coke into his system. As he felt it drip into the back of his throat, he smiled, satisfied, until he glanced at his watch. Shit, he thought to himself, time to go to work.

He stood up uneasily, bent down for his gun and put it in his shoulder holster. Then he felt for his badge, which was in its place, clipped next to his beeper on his belt. He picked his jacket up from the floor near the front door and stopped to look in the mirror before he walked out. His eyes were red and watery. They sagged and appeared to melt into his lower face. Whiskers grew unevenly over his pockmarked skin, and his thinning hair was greasy in some places, and straw-like in others. He brushed away remnants of white powder from his nose hairs and grabbed a half-empty fifth of vodka from the hall table below the mirror. As he tipped the bottle back and took a long gulp, he closed his eyes on his reflection.

Maggio was almost forty-nine years old and had been a cop since he was twenty-one. Before that, he'd done a stint in the army at his father's strong urging; it was either join the army or get a job. So Maggio took the easy way out and ended up an MP stationed in Germany—as far away from his old man as he could get.

Halfway through Maggio's tour of duty, his father had a massive coronary and died, leaving an estate of bad suits, a piece-of-crap car, and four hundred bucks. Maggio's uncle, a podiatrist, took care of the funeral arrangements, so all Al had to do was make the interminable trip home, pay his respects, and return to Germany to finish out his time. His father was laid to rest in a grave next to his wife's—a woman Maggio barely remembered. The only thing about his mother he couldn't forget was that when he was nine years old, she took the train downtown and managed to jump off the fire escape of an old eighteen-story high-rise. She crashed into the alley below, leaving him and his father to fend for themselves.

With his father gone, Maggio returned to Chicago to land one of those cushy city jobs. When it became clear he didn't have enough clout to get into Streets and Sanitation, he applied to the police department. Within a month he was at the academy.

Maggio proved to be an aggressive cop, making lots of arrests and endearing himself to the other rookies. He was quickly promoted to the tactical unit and spent most of his off hours in bars with the guys, drinking and talking shop. Nine years after joining the force he became a detective, and he felt he couldn't have scripted his life any better. But there was one thing he had overlooked during his climb up the ladder—an investment in his personal future. He had seldom dated and never saw himself as a family man. He had all the family he needed at the station. Meanwhile, his partners got married and had kids, and spending their evenings in bars with Maggio was no longer an option or an inclination. But Al kept going. And he kept drinking.

As the years and his drinking progressed, Al alienated most of his friends and partners. He became antisocial and belligerent, and no one wanted to be around him. On the job, he stayed drunk on vodka and functioned with the help of cocaine, and he was smart enough to make sure that he never gave anyone probable cause to make him piss in a cup. Now he was two years away from full pension benefits.

After he pulled his banged-up Taurus into the lot at Area Three Headquarters, he trudged up a flight of stairs to Homicide and tried to catch his breath on his way to his office. Usually the waiting room outside the detective bureau was empty, but today one of the two chairs was occupied by a young, attractive blonde. She glanced up at Maggio, then immediately stood up, letting the magazine in her lap fall to the floor. She was clearly nervous as she gathered it up and put it on the table next to her chair.

"Are you Detective Maggio?" she asked, extending her hand.

"Yeah," he replied cautiously. Her hand was limp and cold. "What can I do for you?"

"I need to talk to you, please."

Maggio motioned to a desk in the open area. "Why don't we talk here?"

The woman hesitated. There were three detectives working at desks nearby. "Uh, is there someplace a little more private, please?" She spoke with an accent that Maggio couldn't place and she used the word *please* with insistence rather than pleading.

Maggio directed her to a small conference room down the hall, letting her walk ahead so he could size her up. She was dressed well but simply, in a tight black skirt and white sweater set. Maggio wasn't sure what he found more attractive—her slim and shapely legs or her gold and diamond Rolex.

They took seats opposite each other across a rickety table that rocked whenever Maggio rested his arms on it. The woman kept her hands in her lap.

"First of all," he said, "why don't you tell me your name."

"I'm Anaka Vanderlinden," she said. "My boyfriend is missing and I fear the worst." Her full lips began to tremble.

"And who is your boyfriend?" Maggio asked. No one he knew would be with a woman of this caliber.

"Please, you don't know him, but I was given your name and told you could help find him."

"All right, then, why don't you explain the situation as clearly as you can."

"His name is Jacob Orloff, and he's an Israeli national. He's also a courier for the Israeli Diamond Merchant Association. He transports diamonds from Tel Aviv to Amsterdam, London, New York, Chicago, and Miami, and travels with large amounts of stones and cash. We arrived in Chicago and checked into a hotel on Michigan Avenue. Jacob wanted to sleep while I went shopping. When I returned he was gone, but his clothes, wallet, and cell phone were on the bureau. That was three days ago, and I haven't talked to him since. You have to help me, Mr. Maggio, please."

"Why did you come to me about this?" Maggio asked. This was so far from his usual cases that he was almost amused.

"I called Jacob's family in Israel and told them what happened, and they put me in touch with a man named Avi Joseph."

Maggio didn't have to think twice. "I don't know an Avi Joseph."

"Yes," she said. "But he seems to know you. He told me to come here and said he'd contact you afterward."

"Is that right?" Maggio said skeptically. "Well, I'll tell you what, I don't do missing persons."

Anaka folded her hands on top of the table, and gazed desperately at Maggio. It looked as though she was wearing her boyfriend's stash of diamonds on her fingers. He began to soften.

"Okay, how old is the guy?"

"He's twenty-seven," she said, picking up her purse from the floor beside her. She produced a photo.

He was handsome with short dark hair, brown eyes, and a square jaw.

"What I need from you are personal items—his wallet, address books, anything like that you can find."

"Sure, I can do that," Anaka said enthusiastically.

"Also, try to recall everything you've done since you arrived in Chicago—including the details of any conversations you had with Jacob."

"Sure," she said, nodding.

"Give me a call when you've gathered everything, and we'll go over it together."

Maggio patted and fished through his pockets for a business card, knowing full well there weren't any there; he hadn't carried business cards for years. Then, after demonstrating a bit of annoyance for further effect, he nonchalantly ripped a small square off a piece of paper and wrote down his pager number and slid it across the table.

"We'll get started as soon as I hear from you."

Anaka thanked him, and he walked behind her to the waiting room. As she left, he looked at his reflection in the glass of the door.

* * *

Maggio dropped his walkie-talkie and official police department notebook on the table so the waitress could see it. It was one of those Greek restaurants on Lincoln Avenue that gave discounts to cops; Maggio never ate at any other kind. In fact, Maggio seldom ate at all. Between the coke and the booze, he consumed just enough food to keep him from falling on his face.

As he waited for his gyros platter, he kept his eye on the entrance. When the guy walked in, Maggio knew instantly. It wasn't that the man looked any different from everyone else in the restaurant—he was big and ethnic-looking, with dark hair

and a mustache. No, Greeks, Arabs, Israelis, whatever, all
looked the same to Maggio, sounded the same too. But there
was something different about this guy, the way he carried himself. He was simultaneously guarded and confident, as if there
was nothing that could surprise him and nothing he couldn't
handle. Maggio immediately thought of his days in the military
when he worked with the special forces. Arrogant assholes, he
thought; they busted their ass so they could wear some silly
beret. But what Maggio didn't admit to himself was that, in
fact, he had always envied them.

The man glanced quickly around the restaurant, then
walked directly to Maggio's booth and slid in across from him.

"Looking for something?" Maggio asked.

"Yes, I'm looking for you, Mr. Maggio," he said with a
slight accent.

"And you're Avi Joseph?"

"That's right."

"What do you want with me?"

"I want your help," he said.

"Yeah, why should I help you?"

"Because I'll make it worth your while."

"Yeah? How do you know what my while is worth?"

Avi Joseph checked his watch and glanced around the
restaurant.

"Let's put our cards on the table, as you Americans say.
Shall we?"

"Okay. Let's start with why you're talking to me. What
makes you think I can help you?"

"Here's what I know, Mr. Maggio. You've got twenty-seven,
almost twenty-eight years on the job. You're two years away
from your full pension. You're a drug addict and alcoholic.
You're one drug test away from losing everything. No one
wants to work with you, so you work all your cases alone and
have no one looking over your shoulder."

Maggio looked at him. As a veteran cop with military experience, Maggio came to one conclusion: Avi Joseph had to be a
spook. Maggio knew all about spooks, how they lived and

worked in the shadows, changing identities like most people change underwear. Maggio's mind was working. This guy could get him bounced from the job. On the other hand, solving this case could lead to something good, maybe a cush job with the Israeli government after retirement, maybe some reward money. He decided to go cautiously. "Been doing your homework, huh? But what do you need a homicide detective for if the guy's gone missing?"

"Because he wouldn't go missing unless he were dead."

"So, you don't think it's possible for a twenty-seven-year-old kid with a bag of diamonds to take off for Tierra del Fuego?"

"No, I don't. Not this one."

Three

Maggio thought his brain had exploded, but when he opened his eyes, he realized that someone was banging on his door. He lay there for a minute, trying to remember where he'd put his gun. As usual, it was on the coffee table, with the vodka bottle, hand mirror, razor blade, and TV remote. As the pounding continued, Maggio swung his legs off the bed, hoping the momentum would carry him up. It worked, except it felt like he left his head on the pillow. He staggered to the door and peered through the peephole at Avi Joseph, who was staring right back at him. Maggio unchained the door and let it swing open. Avi stepped in and looked around.

"This is Chicago's finest?" he said with little expression.

"Hey, you came to me, remember?" Maggio said, smoothing his hair back in the hall mirror.

"Yes, I did," Avi replied, walking over to the couch and surveying the top of the coffee table. "You're definitely the man we want."

Maggio cleared a space on the table as Avi took a manila envelope out of his briefcase and handed it to him. Maggio opened it and spread the contents out in front of him. There were a half dozen photos, including one of a young man in a military uniform, and assorted documents.

"This must be our hero," Maggio said, arranging the photos as best he could in chronological order.

"Detective Maggio, I understand that you're unconventional, but this matter requires your serious attention."

"Right," Maggio said sarcastically, looking around for his cigarettes.

"So here's the thing. There's a man named Marcus Tatum."

"You mean the pawnshop king?" Al asked with a chuckle.

"He owns quite a bit of property on the south side of Chicago. Your government believes that he is involved in cocaine trafficking and money laundering through his pawnshops. From my investigation, I believe that Jacob and Mr. Tatum had some business dealings."

Maggio looked amused. "Now why would a diamond merchant have business dealings with a pawnshop king?"

"All right," Avi said. "Here's how it works." Before he began, he looked around the room. "Can we open a window? It's a little . . . stuffy in here."

"Can't," Maggio said matter-of-factly. "They're painted shut."

"Let me explain," Avi continued. "The diamond business is somewhat of a throwback—checks aren't accepted currency. Diamond dealers are only interested in cash. That means a young man like Mr. Orloff, a courier, might deliver a briefcase full of diamonds—three hundred thousand, maybe half a million dollars worth. Then, he'd have to turn around and fly back with this cash, or make a deposit here and transfer it back by wire. If he sold all the diamonds on a Monday, no one would be concerned if the money was not deposited until Thursday, or if he waited until he returned to Israel to deposit it. . . . Do you see where I am going with this?"

"Over here we call that a float. He had a lot of cash and he had a few days to play with it. Am I with you so far?"

"Yes. Very much so."

"And what you're saying is he could hook up with a scumbag like Marcus Tatum and use the money to buy dope. Use

Tatum's contacts to turn around and unload the dope, and in a day or two double that money, right?"

"That would be one way of looking at it, yes."

"Then he could deposit half a million of the diamond money in the diamond account and the other half a million in his own account."

"Yes, that would be correct."

"So what's in it for Tatum? Why is he hooked up with Jacob Orloff?"

"Tatum has the connections. He brings the buyers and sellers in narcotics together. And by fronting the money he gets a twenty, thirty, or fifty percent return in a matter of hours. It's a classic middleman operation. However, if Mr. Tatum doesn't have the means to acquire a sizable amount of money through his pawnshops, he can bring in a partner, Orloff. Let's say they do half a million dollars and within a day or two they cut and sell it for eight hundred thousand dollars—there's three hundred thousand dollars in cash to split between them."

"So what you are thinking is that Marcus Tatum got tired of giving all of this money to this guy and popped him."

"A bit ineloquently stated, but accurate," said Avi.

Maggio needed a drink or perhaps to chop up and snort a line but he couldn't do that with Joseph sitting there. So he settled for a cigarette, which he lit and inhaled with one swift move.

"So where do I find this Marcus Tatum?" Maggio asked.

Avi let out a slight laugh. "Well, Detective, I know that you are a skilled investigator. I suggest you watch TV and look for the Marcus Tatum Pawnshop King ads. He does his own ads. He'd be the large black man wearing a crown."

Maggio finished his cigarette and stubbed out the butt in an ashtray. "Long live the king!"

* * *

After Avi Joseph left, Al Maggio sat with the photographs and documents, wondering if he should even have gotten involved in Jacob Orloff's disappearance. Ultimately he felt he had no choice. Avi could ruin him. There was a feeling deep inside of him, something he hadn't felt for years—that he could be a good cop, a good detective once again. The international angle was intriguing; the level of the players impressive—particularly Anaka Vanderlinden—and, of course, there was the money. It wasn't that he had aspirations of living the high life—material possessions never really meant that much to him—but he did have a certain habit to feed, and the cash from this job would take care of that for quite a while. As he pondered the latter point, he glanced at the coffee table—the smudged mirror, empty vial, and almost empty bottle of vodka. He reached for his pack of cigarettes and lit one with a shaky hand. He'd have to pick up some blow on the way to work, but he only had eighteen dollars in his money clip. Time for a drive through Logan Square.

He skipped a shower—feeling entirely too awake as it was—splashed some water on his face, and jumped in his Taurus. He drove to the area where the Latin Kings were throwing a lot of coke, around Wrightwood and Kedzie. It didn't take him long to spot Hector, a kid he had "negotiated" with in the past. Hector was on the curb with his head inside a pickup truck when Maggio pulled up behind it. By the time the kid realized what was happening, Maggio had him up against the Taurus and was patting him down. When he was sure Hector had something worth grabbing, he handcuffed him, threw him in the backseat and drove to an alley where he knew there was an old half-standing garage to hide in.

"What the fuck, Maggio?" the kid said, familiar with the routine.

Maggio ignored him while he parked the car and turned off the engine. He got out, opened the back door, and pulled Hector out by the handcuffs.

"Goddamn," Hector said, trying to pull away from Maggio's grip.

"Let's see what you got today, Hector," Maggio said, rifling through the kid's pockets.

He pulled out a small bundle of coke packets. "Hey, man, I'm just holding those for someone," Hector protested.

"Yeah, for me. Now, what else?" Maggio patted him down again and pulled out a wad of cash—50's, 20's, 10's, 5's—in no particular order. "Payday!" Maggio said gleefully.

"Why don't you get a fucking job, Maggio?" Hector grumbled, disgusted.

Maggio slapped him hard across the face. "What did you say?"

Hector said nothing this time.

Maggio went through all of Hector's pockets one more time, but didn't find anything else. He took Hector's beeper and laid it on the ground. He used the heel of his cowboy boot to try and smash it, but the beeper was too strong.

"What the fuck you doing, man?" Hector said, furious.

"Say another word and I'll shoot your fucking head off."

Hector looked away, his lips still moving.

"Hector, do you believe in Santa Claus?" Maggio asked.

Hector was wary and looked at him, waiting.

"Here's what I'm gonna do for you, Hector. I'm going to give you a choice. Either I could arrest you or I'll smack you and send you home to the Kings. You can tell them that you got busted and I let you go. What'll it be?"

"You gonna let me go?" Hector asked. "What the fuck, let me go."

Maggio looked around, then hauled off and punched Hector in the stomach. Hector buckled over, groaning in pain. Maggio then punched him in the face, knocking him back. Hector dropped onto the gravel floor of the garage. Maggio bent down and released the handcuffs. Then he pulled his gun and rested the barrel on the bridge of Hector's nose, pointing it between his eyes.

Hector didn't move.

"You can go!" Maggio said.

Hector dragged himself slowly backward across the dirty floor and stood up, keeping his eyes on Maggio. He backed out of the garage and took off running. Maggio laughed. He put the coke and wad of money in his pants pocket. He looked around and saw no one. He got back in the car and pulled out of what was left of the garage. He had coke. He had money. He was ready for work.

* * *

Darcy Cole was studying the chessboard across from his old friend, Seymour Hirsch. Once a week Darcy walked down the hall of his building to Seymour's office where they played chess, drank Scotch, and talked. Seymour was a short, thin man with a gentle manner and warm personality. It was Seymour whom Darcy trusted with his inner thoughts. That cramped, cluttered office had become a sanctuary for Darcy.

"I bet you're a crack poker player," Darcy said softly.

"Now, Darcy," Seymour said in his calm, fatherly way. "It's no use trying to read my expression. Your clients might give their secrets away with their eyes, but not me. You'll have to read my mind. Sharpen your intuition, and you'll be a better lawyer."

Darcy knew he was about to lose the game. He moved a rook. Seymour immediately slid in his queen, forcing checkmate.

"Damn," Darcy said loudly.

"Thank you, sir," Seymour said with a smile, and finished off the Scotch in his glass. He stood up, but had to steady himself on the edge of his desk.

"You okay, old man?" Darcy asked.

"Yeah, sure," Seymour replied. "I just have to stop drinking in the middle of the day—making me old before my time."

"Try drinking older Scotch," Darcy said. "I've heard it makes you feel younger."

"Nah," Seymour said dismissively as he opened the office door. "Beating you soundly every week makes me feel younger. Till next week, my friend."

Darcy watched as Seymour sat down slowly at his desk, a little slumped over, a little tired. Darcy walked back to his office thinking of Seymour. Seymour was well respected in the legal world, and Darcy never knew him to compromise his integrity.

In contrast was the man sitting in Darcy's waiting room; Harry Feiger was only one of the myriad of lawyers gone astray.

"Hello, Harry," he said, feeling sympathetic.

Harry extended a sweaty hand and Darcy shook it quickly. Harry sat in the client chair across from Darcy.

Darcy went to call Patrick O'Hagin in to join them. They walked back into the office together.

"Harry," Darcy said, "This is my associate, Patrick O'Hagin. He'll be assisting me on your case."

"Nice to meet you, Harry," Patrick said. Patrick had a mop of unruly black hair. His fair skin and blue eyes gave him a boyish look. He had on a white button-down oxford shirt, which had the top button undone, with a blue-and-red tie pulled down a bit.

"Hey, how you doin'? So, guys, where are we at?"

"Well, Harry," Darcy began. "We have a pretty good draw. The Assistant U.S. Attorney is a guy named Carl Stringer."

Patrick cut in. "I know Carl," he said. "He and I have known each other for years. He understands the value of each case."

"I just hope he has a sense of humor, you know?" Harry piped in with a chuckle.

Darcy and Patrick exchanged glances.

"It's not his humor we're interested in," Darcy said. "At this point we're interested in his motivation for going after you."

"I think my grand jury subpoena is a clue," Harry said sarcastically.

"Actually," Patrick countered, "I talked to Stringer. He doesn't think you pose a threat to society, and he's not even sure a crime has been committed. As far as the subpoena goes, we're not sure if you're the target or just a potential witness."

"A witness to what?" Harry asked, confused. "I was the one shaking people down."

Darcy leaned in slightly. "Harry," he said, "let's use different terminology. You're an aggressive lawyer, and sometimes your actions can be misconstrued. But you're also an advocate, and you're out there trying to protect the civil rights of your clients. Let's look at it that way."

"Okay, then," Harry said, sitting up straighter. "Do they have me or not?"

Darcy sighed without trying to hide it.

"That's the question, Harry. At this point they're not playing it as if they've got you. They're playing it as if they want to take a look at you. And that's more than we'd hoped for. The last thing we want to do is give them any more than they have. So we're going to sit and wait."

"But what could they be looking at other than I was . . ." Harry stopped midsentence. "Other than the fact that I aggressively protected my clients' civil rights." He smiled, as if proud of himself.

Patrick took over.

"Harry, we haven't heard anything since we talked to the U.S. Attorney about getting you in for a proffer."

Harry almost leaped out of his chair.

"Darcy," he said, wide-eyed, "I told you I absolutely cannot proffer!"

"Relax, Harry," Darcy said. "We just told them we wanted an immunity letter or a proffer letter to see what they would say, to see where you are. But we haven't heard anything, and we take that as a good sign."

"Well," Harry said, slicking back his hair again. "I trust you guys know what you're doing, and I'll do whatever you say. I don't want to proffer."

"We can use the proffer to see what they have against you," Patrick began.

"We can end the proffer at anytime so we can use it to make them show us their cards."

Harry rose slowly. "Be careful," he said.

Patrick stood to show him out of the office.

"Try not to worry, Harry," Patrick said, opening the door. "We'll get it done right."

Harry stood and shook Darcy's hand. "I appreciate that," he said. "We attorneys need to stick together."

As he walked out, Darcy considered that comment. Harry, Darcy, Seymour—each representing a different part of that vast spectrum called lawyers.

Al Maggio parked his car outside the nondescript warehouse that was home to the Organized Crime Narcotics Division of the Chicago Police Department. He climbed out of the car and walked intently up to the secured doorway. He flashed his badge to the attendant, who buzzed him in. Then he followed the corridor to an open office area where he waited for someone to notice him. A cop with a goatee and a ponytail motioned him over. He wore his police star in a leather case hanging from a chain around his neck.

"What can I do for you?" he said.

"Yeah, I'm Al Maggio, Area Three Homicide. I need some information."

The detective stood up.

"Mike Luzinski," he said as they shook hands.

"Good to meet you."

He pointed to a chair and Maggio sat down.

"I need some information on a guy. I think you'll know who he is. He's supposed to be a bigtime mover. His name is Marcus Tatum."

Luzinski smiled. "Oh, yeah, we've been up his ass with a microscope and haven't been able to nail him on anything. What d'ya got him for?"

"I like him on a murder," he said.

"No shit, him or one of his minions?"

"I'm not sure," Maggio said.

"You got good information?"

"It's pretty good information, but I don't have a witness. That's why I need some background on the guy."

"Who did he pop?" asked Luzinski.

"Ah, just some dude," said Maggio, hedging.

"Well, it's not like him to do his own dirty work," Luzinski said. "Normally he just lays out an order and it gets followed. He's got a pretty good racket going. He's layered pretty well, and he's got a lot of legitimate businesses."

"Sounds like a ghetto success story," Maggio said.

"I guess you could say that. Basically, he uses his legitimate businesses to launder drug money. He's tied up with the black gangs. He supplies a lot of them with their dope—Black Gangster Disciples, Vice-Lords, Four-Corner Hustlers, Traveling Vice Lords, you know, the whole all-star lineup. Our working theory is that the Mexicans are buying it from the Colombians, then bringing it in, but they don't deal directly with the black gangs. So Tatum acts as a conduit. He buys it at one price, cuts it, gets the volume, then turns around and sells it for more. We don't think he touches the stuff himself but that he has a crew working for him. The way we figure, he's doubling or tripling his money by being the middleman on the deal. So he's doing well. The key is, he gets the kind of cash he needs, turns around and sells, and lets the dirty dough soak through his legitimate operations. He's pretty good. We've been on his ass, the DEA, but no one's been able to touch him."

"So do you have a file on him?"

"You bet your ass. I could give you access to almost all of it. You can't get near the informant information, you understand that, of course."

"Absolutely." Maggio nodded. "I'll take whatever you could give me."

"Follow me."

Luzinski led him out of the office and down a different corridor. After forty minutes with Mike Luzinski and his files, Maggio believed he knew everything there was to know about

Marcus Tatum. He knew where most of his property was—his pawnshops, Laundromats, the Rib Shack. He was looking at an urban success story, albeit a dirty one. Marcus Tatum had millions of dollars worth of legitimate assets, apartment buildings, pawnshops, jewelry shops, restaurants, grocery stores . . . he had it all.

Now Detective Maggio had a suspect and he knew where to find him. It was time to pay Mr. Tatum a visit.

* * *

Alan Jacobs was the kind of man who thrived under Mayor Richard M. Daley's reign in Chicago. The Daley administration was known for its enthusiasm for developing the city. Everywhere you looked new structures were going up, old buildings were being renovated, and people were getting rich— Alan Jacobs was one of those people. He looked at the warehouse from the outside and envisioned loft apartments, hundreds of them, with their own parking spaces. Fifteen, maybe twenty minutes from downtown. It was a large parcel of land at a good price. He was running the numbers in his head. The only thing left was to see if the structure was worth saving or if he would have to start from scratch.

The broker who met him there to show him the property had no idea of Jacobs' plans. Otherwise, he would have worn a nice suit instead of the gray polyester number he had on, Jacobs thought. A wide paisley tie rested in the middle of his basketball-shaped belly that stretched the seams of a dull yellow shirt. Jacobs, who was short on hair himself, was disgusted by the broker's bad comb-over job. But he was determined, and if this broker was the one who was representing the seller, he had no choice but to deal with him.

"This place has a lot of potential," the broker said with an affected enthusiasm. "I've had a lot of people look at it."

"Is that right? Then why has it been on the market for four hundred and ninety-two days?" Jacobs couldn't resist.

Jacobs liked the brickwork on the building. He gazed up to admire the strong, steel-supported roof. He followed his sight lines along the inside of the warehouse until it led him to the office, where he noticed something unusual.

"Was there a fire here?" he asked.

"Not that I know of," the broker answered. "I didn't notice anything the last time I was here."

They walked toward the office; the paint on the walls was black and had melted from the heat. Jacobs walked to the threshold of the doorway and looked in. He saw something that made him stop but he couldn't quite make out what it was for a moment.

"Oh, my God," he said, "Call the police."

Jacobs retched twice but didn't throw up. The broker seemed unfazed; he was already on his cell phone calmly talking to the police. After the call, they both stood in silence waiting for the police to arrive.

* * *

Al Maggio was at his desk at Area Three Headquarters reviewing the paperwork he had gotten from the narcotics boys. Marcus Tatum was going to be a tough one to crack; he had insulated himself well. He probably never got his hands dirty. Maggio was studying Tatum's associates, looking for a weakness, when Avi Joseph appeared at the counter. Maggio closed the file and walked over to him.

"What are you doing here?" he asked.

"I have information for you," Joseph replied. He was nattily dressed in an elegant European-cut dark blue suit, a light pinstripe shirt with French cuffs, and a rich silk tie.

Maggio was wearing a pair of Dockers, which desperately needed cleaning, and his blue button-down shirt and bad tie did nothing more than pull it all together for an unadulterated grungy statement.

"Yeah, what do you got for me?" he asked.

"They found a body. Area Four detectives are working it as a death investigation. They don't know what the cause of death is. It was found in a warehouse. I think perhaps you should contact the morgue about the John Doe."

"What makes you think it's our boy?"

"What makes you think it isn't?" Joseph rejoined.

He handed Maggio an envelope.

"These are Jacob Orloff's dental records. I'm guessing I'm right and that you're going to need these. Let me know how your investigation progresses."

Maggio looked at him. "How can I contact you if I need you?"

"You can't, but I'll be in touch with you." With that, Avi Joseph walked away.

Maggio called the morgue and learned that they had, in fact, received a John Doe from a West Side warehouse. The autopsy was scheduled for the following morning. Apparently, the body was badly charred. They didn't even know the race of the victim. Maggio signed off. He'd go to the morgue tomorrow.

* * *

Maggio's breakfast consisted of two lines and a vodka chaser. He got dressed and posed for his reflection in the mirror. Passable, he thought, and that was the best he could hope for. He whipped the beaten-up Taurus into a spot at the morgue, entered the building, and flashed his badge to the gentleman at the reception desk.

"May I help you?" the man asked. His nametag read "Alex." He was well groomed and pleasant enough.

"Yeah, I'm Detective Maggio. I'm here on a John Doe that came in yesterday from the southwest side."

"Yes, sir. You'll have to go to the third office on the left. The doctor there will talk to you."

"Thank you," Maggio said, having already reached the designated office before Alex finished his instructions. Maggio knocked once, opened the door, and walked in. He introduced himself to the doctor, who was a petite Asian-American woman. As quickly as she told him her name, Dr. Kim, he forgot it. He asked her for information on the charred, warehouse John Doe.

"Cause of death is undetermined," she said. "I mean, the

only thing I know for certain at this point is that he did not die of smoke inhalation; his lungs would indicate that he was dead before the fire. The body was badly damaged, and it will take some time to identify him."

Maggio pitched the large manila envelope onto her desk. It landed with a gentle plop.

"This might help," he said.

"Whose are these?" she asked, peering into the envelope.

"We've been looking for a guy who's gone missing, and we think this John Doe is him," he said. "Could you check these dental records and see if we're right?"

She gave a tired smile. "I don't do the dental matchups. We have a forensic dentist who does that. I will walk them down to him, though."

"Can I wait here?" he asked.

"I don't know how busy he is," she said, "or even if he's in."

"Why don't you find out for me and let me know, okay?"

"Will do," she replied.

* * *

Avi Joseph was leaning against his rental car in the County Morgue parking lot when Maggio walked out.

"I've got some bad news for you, my friend," Maggio said. "The dental charts match."

Joseph's expression did not change. "I assumed they would."

"I talked to the Medical Examiner. She said that she couldn't give me a cause of death, at least not yet. So for the moment, it's undetermined."

"What does that mean?"

"Well, until she classifies it as a homicide, it's just a death investigation, and I don't do death investigations."

"You'll do this one," Joseph said sharply.

"Yeah, yeah, you made that clear. Okay, I'm going to need you to contact the family. We need somebody to claim the body. I need a victim to bring to the State's Attorney's Office, and they need that next-of-kin shit."

Maggio fumbled through the pockets of his jacket, looking

for cigarettes. He pulled one out and blazed it up. "I'm sorry about your guy getting smoked," he said.

"I'll pass along your condolences," Joseph said flatly. "What do you plan to do now, arrest Mr. Tatum?"

Maggio took a long drag on his cigarette and blew the smoke through his nose and mouth. "Arrest him for what? I got bupkus."

"You could pick him up. I'm sure you could get the information you need out of him."

"I'm not so sure," Maggio said. "If Tatum did kill him, I am sure he went to great lengths to cover it up. He probably feels pretty safe. It's going to take more than a little intimidation to get anything out of him."

"Well, Ms. Vanderlinden can attest to Tatum being the last person her boyfriend was with."

"Wait a minute," Maggio said, "she told me he went out for a walk and never came back. She said she had no idea where he was going."

"I think she was in error. Why don't you interview her again? I'll have her stop by your office."

Maggio finished his cigarette and flicked it away into the parking lot.

"Why don't you just grab Tatum yourself? Have him confess to you and bring him to me? Or better yet, why don't you just pop a bullet in his head, jump on a plane, and go back to Tel Aviv or wherever the hell you're from?"

"It's a thought," Joseph said, unperturbed. "In the meantime, why don't you continue your work?"

A surge of anger flooded Maggio's body, and he exploded at Joseph, shoving his finger hard against his chest.

"I don't work for you, asshole! You got a homicide, get it assigned to somebody. You want me to work this shit, you better start showing me some respect," Maggio fumed. "You remember something, you're the one who came looking for me—I didn't ask for this frigging case."

Joseph got back in his car and drove away with no further conversation.

* * *

Marcus Tatum's flagship pawnshop was at the corner of Sixty-third and Cottage Grove. While it had the obligatory saxophone in the window, the store dealt primarily in gold, diamonds, and other precious stones—all things worth a lot but lacking history, at least as far as could be documented. The Marcus Tatum pawnshops had no use for items with serial numbers or anything easily traced.

Maggio showed his badge at the outside of the first of two doors he had to be buzzed through. Once inside, he was met by a light-skinned African-American woman in her early twenties. She was leaning over the counter reading a book.

"May I help you?"

"Yeah, I'm looking for your boss, Marcus Tatum."

She gave a faint smile. "Mr. Tatum isn't here very often. Why don't I take your name and number and my manager could call you back?"

"I don't want to talk to your manager, honey. I want to talk to Marcus Tatum."

"I'm not your honey," she said. "If you have no business in the store, why don't you please leave?"

"Don't sass me, babe! Because I'll start pulling serial numbers."

She smiled. "Do you have a warrant?"

"Screw you with a warrant."

"Okay, I just wanted to know because," she said, pointing to video cameras, "you're being recorded now and so are your belligerent attitude and lack of respect. It will be handed over to your supervisors. If you leave now, we'll forget about this whole ugly transgression on your part."

"Where did you learn how to talk?" he asked.

She was taken aback.

"Would that be a racial comment?" she asked.

"No, no, don't get your undies in a knot, honey. I'm going."

He reached in his pocket and pulled out a card that was bent in two places. He'd found one for this particular occasion smashed at the back of his dresser drawer.

"You tell your boss to give me a call when he gets in."

"I'll have my manager call you," she said, "or perhaps our lawyer."

"Screw your lawyer and your manager too. You give this card to Marcus."

With that, he walked toward the door and gave it a push— it went nowhere. Then he heard the buzzer and looked over his shoulder. The woman had a grin on her face, a grin Maggio had seen more often than he cared to remember—the grin of superiority—the one that says I know I'm smarter than you are.

"Well, screw you too," he said to himself, and walked out.

Five

South Shore was once a predominantly Jewish section of Chicago, and within that section, there was an elite enclave known as "Pill Hill." It got its moniker because of the large population of doctors who occupied the luxurious houses there. While Pill Hill was no longer the bastion of well-to-do doctors, it still stood for affluence in what was now the comely and mostly black community of South Shore.

Maggio sat in his car a block away from Marcus Tatum's house. He had been there for over an hour, using binoculars to stare at the Mercedes in the driveway. Its license plate that read "BIG T" pissed him off no end. Finally, a side door to the residence opened and out strode a very large man. Marcus Tatum was about six-foot-three and was well over three clicks, pushing three-forty, Maggio guessed. He was dressed for the warm weather in linen pants and a silk shirt. He had on a thick gold Rolex with a diamond bezel and several rings of various shapes and sizes on his fingers. Without an apparent care in the world, he strolled to his car. He hit the keyless entry and slid into the driver's seat. He backed the car to the end of the driveway, but then slammed on his brakes when Maggio blocked him in with his car.

Maggio jumped out and stuck a gun into the side of

Marcus Tatum's head through his open window. "Okay, here's your choice, big man," he said. "I could splatter whatever brains you have all over the dashboard or you can get out nice and slow with your hands behind your back and come with me down to the station."

Tatum looked at him.

"Who the hell are you?"

"I am a Chicago Police detective, and you're under arrest."

"For what?"

"I'll tell you about it later. Now get your ass out of the car."

Tatum looked at him.

"Fuck you. You got a warrant?"

Maggio smacked the butt of his gun into the side of Tatum's head. There was a loud cracking sound as the gun crashed into his skull. He let out a yelp of pain.

"Shit."

"Now get out of the car, asshole, or I'll shoot you."

Slowly, Tatum began to move. He stepped out cautiously and kept his hands to his side, not wanting to set off the freak standing in his driveway with a gun. Maggio grabbed one of Tatum's meaty wrists and cuffed it, pulled it behind his back and cuffed the other wrist.

"Okay, asshole, you're getting in the back of my car."

Tatum looked at the Taurus.

"You got to be shitting me. I'm not going to fit in that thing."

"In there or in the trunk, asshole. It's your choice."

* * *

Marcus Tatum was deposited into a plastic orange chair in a small interview room at Area Three Headquarters. Maggio removed Tatum's left handcuff and hooked his right side to the metal underframe of the chair. The chair groaned under Tatum's weight. Maggio then grabbed a second pair of handcuffs and secured his left side.

"What the fuck?" Tatum said. "I ain't going nowhere. I'm waiting for my lawyer."

"Keep talking about a lawyer and I'll smack the shit out of you."

A broad smile came across Tatum's face.

"The double handcuffs mean you're too big of a pussy to come straight to me man-to-man."

Maggio hauled off and delivered a punch to Tatum's ribs. Tatum expelled a blast of air but showed no pain. He waited a few seconds to regain his composure and then smiled again.

"That's the best you can do, punk?"

"You're going to tell me what I want to know," Maggio said. "I don't give a shit if I have to kill you to get it."

"Look, bitch, you don't scare me. What do you think you're gonna do? Why don't you just cut the shit? My lawyer's on his way, and this ain't going to be over."

Maggio spun and punched him again as hard as he could in the ribs.

"You ain't dictating shit," Maggio screamed. "I'm running this show. So let's get something straight right now. You're going to tell me what I want to know or you're going to die right here on this chair. And I ain't your bitch."

He punched him one more time for emphasis and then got up. "I'm going to get a few things and I'll be back."

Maggio stepped out of the room and closed the door. Tatum could hear him sliding the latch to lock him in.

This motherfucker is crazy, Tatum thought.

Maggio returned a few minutes later carrying a photograph, a white plastic garbage bag, and a black metal rod. Maggio held the photograph of Jacob Orloff in front of Tatum.

"Take a good look."

Tatum looked at the photograph, expressionless.

"You know this guy?"

"I'm not saying shit 'til my lawyer gets here."

"Wrong answer. Try again. You know this guy?"

"I want my lawyer," Tatum replied.

The rod was about eight inches long and made of solid metal. It hurt like hell when Maggio slapped it against Tatum's shin. Tatum clenched his jaw as he tried to suppress the pain.

"I want my lawyer," Tatum repeated.

Twice more Maggio struck him on the leg with the metal rod. Tatum was seething. Maggio held the photograph in front of him again.

"Look at it. Do you know this guy?"

Tatum looked at the photograph and said nothing. Maggio walked to the corner of the room and looked back at Tatum.

Tatum stared Maggio down, giving him his best "fuck you" look. The room was five-foot-by-eight. It had two plastic chairs in it. Tatum was on one, and the other was across from him.

"Let's get something straight," Maggio said. "You have a choice. You either tell me what I want to know now, or you can die trying to keep it from me. But I am going to find out what I need to know."

In his loudest voice Tatum started screaming, "Help! Help! Help!"

Maggio lunged across and smacked him in the throat with the metal rod. He stuck the rod in his pocket and opened the white plastic bag. He threw it over Tatum's head and began twisting it down around his neck. The plastic bag drew in tight at Tatum's nose and mouth as he desperately gasped for air. Maggio watched Tatum struggle through the white plastic bag as he kept a count in his mind. He watched Tatum's head bouncing back and forth desperately searching for air. Maggio loosened his grip and pulled the bag off. Tatum sucked for air and was unable to speak. Mucus flowed from his nostrils.

Maggio leaned in close to him. "Yell again, and I'll put the bag on longer. Now, you're going to tell me what I want to know or this is going to get worse. Do you understand me, Marcus?"

Marcus nodded. He had began pulling himself back together and regained eye-to-eye contact with Maggio.

"Yeah, I know the guy. That's the Jew," he said finally.

"Very good," Maggio said. "Tell me about this Jew."

"We did some business together. What else do you want to know?"

"I want to know everything. I want to know what business you did, and how you did it. I want to know the last time you saw him. I want to know how to get in touch with him. I want to know everything about this guy. You understand me?"

Tatum nodded.

"Start at the beginning. How did you meet him?"

Marcus hesitated slightly and Maggio pulled the bag out.

"Okay, okay," Tatum said. "I met him at the jewelers' building—you know, over on South Wabash. I got a dude there that I move Rolexes with. I got some boys that come to me with Rolexes at my pawnshops. I pay them a nickel on the dollar and then I turn around and sell for fifty cents on the dollar to my man."

"Come on, I don't give a damn about your penny-ante shit. What happened?"

"I was in there selling some watches. The Jew was in there, too. So my man introduced him."

"Who's your man?"

"Some dude," Marcus said.

Maggio reached in his pocket and slammed the metal rod into Tatum's side. He was aiming for the kidney. He hit his mark.

"I don't want to have to play pitch-and-catch here, Marcus. I want you to tell me everything. You got that?"

"All right, all right. Damn. The guy's name is Irv. He buys a lot of shit from me—you know, the shit that I get from the pawnshops. Gives me a good deal. Gives me fifty cents on the dollar and he sells for seventy-five cents on the dollar. You know what I'm saying?"

"Yeah, I'm really interested. Tell me about the Jew. You know his name?" Maggio asked.

"Yeah, he told me Jacob some shit but I don't remember his last name—Jacob something."

"Very good," Maggio said. "Go on."

"So we just started talking and pretty soon me and Irv were done with our business and this Jacob dude said we should go some place and talk. So we went to get something to eat."

"What did he want to talk to you about?"

"Well, it wasn't any accident that he was there. Irv told him when I was going to be there and must have told some things about me. I got the impression that he was looking for someone just like me to expand his business in Chicago."

"Go on," Maggio said.

"See, the Jew had an idea. He told me that he had access to a lot of cash and that he wanted to do a quick turnaround and make some money on it. So I said, 'All right, I'm listening.' He told me he understood that I could move some coke. I told him, 'Hey, cowboy, you got the wrong man.' He just smiled, so I said, 'What the fuck.' I knew he knew what was up. So we talked about this and that, and we ended up working out a deal. He'd front me some money, and then I'd give it to the Mexicans to get some coke at a discount. Then I'd give it to my boys, they'd step on it twice, and we'd turn around and sell to the Disciples or Vice Lords, and then they'd step on it and sell to whoever they wanted—Hustlers, Dragons—you know, the smaller gangs. The Mexicans would deal with the Latin Kings and the Latin Counts, but they wouldn't do shit with the brothers. So I had to step in and take care of my people."

"Yeah, I know. You're an upstanding businessman and a credit to your race," Maggio inserted.

"Do you want to hear this or not?" Marcus replied in a derisive tone.

Maggio smacked him again in the kidney. "You're working for me now. You got that? Now you're my bitch. So give me my props."

Marcus rolled his eyes, smarting from Maggio's bullshit as much as the blow to his kidney.

"You hit me again, I'm not saying shit 'til my lawyer gets here," he said.

Maggio put the rod back in his pocket.

"That's better," Marcus said, taking a deep breath.

Maggio jumped toward him and threw the bag over his head, counting again. Marcus was sucking for air desperately—his head bouncing back and forth looking for an opening. There was none. When Marcus starting convulsing, Maggio took the bag off. Marcus coughed and hacked. Finally, after a few moments, he was able to get his voice back.

"Let's get something clear," Maggio said, stressing each syllable. "I am running this, not you. Do you have that? Tell me the rest of your story. Now."

"I cut a deal with the Mexicans. I get ten keys at twenty a pop, two hundred thousand cash up front. They give me pure shit. Each brick is perfect. No playing around. So me and this Jew go meet the Mexicans. Give them two hundred large. They give us the bricks. I give it to my boys. My boys step on it and turn around and sell it, bring back the cash. Me and the Jew split things fifty-fifty—his money, my contacts, my workers. I had to pay my workers out of my half. The Jew walked away with his in cash."

"How often would you do it?" asked Maggio.

"At first, once a month or so. He'd call me and let me know when he was coming to town. Then the cat got greedy. He would be in twice a month, then every other week, then before you know it, it was every week. We were at our limit."

"What do you mean, at your limit?"

"Well, there is only so much coke the brothers can sell. You know what I'm saying? They got to cook it up and sell it for crack or flake it out and give it to the white boys from the suburbs. Ten kilos in a week is a lot of shit. Don't forget, they're stepping on it a bunch of times too."

"How about the Mexicans? They have any trouble bringing you stuff?"

"Well, it was getting harder, man. Every week. You know, they got their problems too," Marcus answered.

"So when was the last time you saw him?" Maggio asked.

"About a week ago. We did our deal. We split the money, and I haven't heard from him since."

"When should you have heard from him?"

"I should have heard from him yesterday or today," Tatum said. "But of course, I'm not around to take calls today, am I?"

"No, you're not. So what would you do with your money?"

Tatum groaned. "You know I put it through my businesses."

"So you're laundering the money through all those businesses."

Tatum gave him an incredulous look. "No, that little-ass barbecue at Sixty-third and Racine really is making eight hundred thousand dollars a year selling rib tips and chicken wings."

"What does he do with his?" Maggio said, ignoring him.

"Hell, I don't know," Tatum said. "He had to do some serious banking, though, because he was also dealing with the jeweler straight up with real business. You know what I'm saying?"

Maggio nodded. "So he had a banker helping him."

"I don't know."

"Did you ever meet any of his people?"

"His people?" asked Tatum. "He had one guy that was with him all the time watching his back. A guy named Danny, Danny Litwin. I've seen him once in awhile with some straight-up hot bitch."

"What did she look like?" Maggio asked.

"Ah, you know what I'm talking about, man. She was fine. She looked like the kind of chick that ain't spent a day working just 'cause she's so fine."

Maggio nodded. "You know her name?"

"He told me. It was some whacked-out German name. I don't remember."

"Was it Anaka?" Maggio asked.

"Yeah, yeah, that's it," Tatum said. "You met the bitch, huh?"

"Yeah, I met the bitch," Maggio said. "So how did you reach him?"

"He had a cell phone. I'd call, and if he wasn't there I'd leave a message. Sooner or later he'd reach me on my cell phone or my beeper."

"When he beeped you, what number did he use?"

"The cell phone."

"What area code was the cell phone in?"

"Chicago," Tatum said.

"You still got that number?"

"I got it in my cell phone."

"Where's that?"

"In my car."

Maggio paced quietly around the little room for several minutes, and then moved in for the kill. He spoke calmly and deliberately into Tatum's face.

"Now, I'm going to ask you something, Marcus. You were looking for the big score, isn't that right?"

"What are you talking about?"

"Well, this is what I believe happened. I believe that you got together with this Jew, did a deal with the Mexicans, and then took the Jew someplace and whacked him."

"Are you crazy? Kill the goose that laid the golden egg? As long as the Jew was around, I was going to be cranking money left and right. Why would I whack him?"

"Because then you would get all the money."

"Look, bitch, you are out of your fucking mind. I kill him, and I'm done dealing with the Mexicans. I can't pull any kind of cash out of my business without the IRS on my ass. You think I don't know DEA has been watching me?"

"You killed him," Maggio yelled. "You killed him, took him someplace, and you burned him up so we couldn't find him. But you forgot about something. We got dental charts, we got DNA. You ain't fooling nobody."

Tatum looked at him. "Man, you are one crazy fuck. I wouldn't kill him. He was my best money."

Maggio looked at him. "So he was going to cut you out

and deal with the Mexicans straight up, and then you were out of the money and he was going to take it all."

Tatum had a scowl on his face. "He couldn't deal with the Black Gangster Disciples by himself. They would shoot him in the head, take his money and the dope."

"So it's back to you," said Maggio. "You killed him."

"Look, if this is what it's about, I didn't kill the cat and I don't believe he's dead. You got him someplace."

"Yeah, we got him." Maggio pushed a Polaroid photo into Tatum's face.

"Is that him?" Tatum asked.

"Why would you ask that?"

"Because I don't believe he's dead. He's too smart, he's too slick. He never went anywhere without Danny, who was packing large. You know what I am saying?"

"You're saying I'm lying to you," Maggio said.

"You don't listen. This cat ain't dead. 'Til I see him, he ain't dead. And I ain't saying shit 'til my lawyer gets here. I'm through with you," Tatum said. "That picture don't mean shit. It ain't him."

Maggio exploded. He took the rod out of his pocket and he smacked Tatum in the ear. He hit him two or three times near the jawline and started pummeling him in the back and side near the kidneys and the ribs.

"You are going to admit to it," Maggio said. "You are going to admit to it right now. You're signing a confession."

Tatum spit at him. "Fuck you."

Maggio snapped and started bashing him with the rod and his fist everywhere.

Tatum was screaming, "Help me, help me."

The sound of footsteps rushing across linoleum could be heard outside, and then the door burst open. Two detectives reached in and pulled Maggio up off Tatum. They grabbed him by the arms and dragged him out.

"Cool off, man! Cool off," the shorter detective yelled.

The other detective shut and locked the door on Tatum.

They both pulled Maggio into an adjoining interview room and shut the door behind them.

"Are you completely insane?" the taller detective said to him. "You could have killed that guy with us sitting out here. Are you nuts? Don't you know anything? What are you, a rookie up here?"

Maggio's head cleared slightly. "Yeah, you're right. I lost it in there. The guy spit on me."

"You want me to take over?" he asked.

"No, no, I'll straighten it up," Maggio said. "I'm going to finish with him and get the paperwork rolling. I'll get him out of here."

"Shit, man," the same detective said. "What are you going to do about this guy's injuries?"

There was a silence in the room. Maggio looked at him.

"Well, if he's got to go to the hospital, he's got to go to the hospital. There's nothing I can do about it."

There was another pause.

"Look," the shorter of the two said. "We always take them to Masonic or Swedish Covenant. Maybe if you swing him by Northwestern, have him treated, and bring him back to the lockup, no one will know."

Maggio nodded. "What about you guys? You gonna generate paper on this?"

The tall one said, "We didn't hear anything, we didn't see anything, we weren't here. But when you're done with this guy, take him out for a ride. Do you know what I'm saying?"

Maggio understood. He put the rod in his pocket and went back to the room. The plastic bag was on the floor. He picked it up, folded it and stuck it in his front pants pocket.

Marcus was in agony. Blood dripped from his ear. He was favoring one side, the side where he had been pummeled.

Maggio went outside. He sat at a table and took out some forms. He then handwrote a confession for Marcus Tatum. It detailed how Marcus strangled Jacob Orloff, whom he knew as "the Jew," over a drug debt, and that he dragged his body to a warehouse where he poured gasoline on it and set it on fire. Maggio added language indicating that he, Marcus Tatum, had not been threatened or physically harmed while in police custody and that he went with the detective initially voluntarily, and that he was giving a confession of his own free will, without any threats or intimidation. Then he went on to add that he had been treated well, been able to use the bathroom, allowed to smoke, and given food and beverage while with the detective.

He went back to the room with the confession and walked up to Marcus.

"All right, Marcus, I've written everything out and you're going to sign this."

"Kill me," Marcus yelled at him. "Just kill me, 'cause I'm not signing shit."

"Marcus you're going to sign this."

"Fuck you," Marcus said.

Maggio got close to Marcus, standing right in front of him. "You're gonna sign this."

With all the strength he could muster, Marcus suddenly kicked straight up, striking Maggio in the balls. He then leapt to his feet with the chair by the handcuffs still attached to him. Then he did a knee drop into Maggio's face, screaming "Motherfucker, motherfucker," over and over again.

Marcus got up and was about to repeat it when the door burst open. The same two detectives burst in and threw Marcus down into the chair, banging him hard against the wall. Maggio sat stunned on the floor. He was in agony, but he still held the statement. The two detectives helped him to his feet. Maggio looked at them.

Maggio stood across from Tatum, careful to stay out of his reach.

"All right, you got your shots in," Maggio said. "Now how do you want to play this? You want me to take you out and cap your ass, or do you want me to send you to jail?"

"Do whatever you're gonna do," Tatum said, "but I tell you now, this ain't over."

"All right, Marcus, you're going to jail," Maggio said.

"Fuck you," said Tatum.

Maggio uncuffed him.

"Stand up and turn around."

Marcus did as he was told. Maggio cuffed Tatum's arms behind his back and put the other pair of handcuffs in his belt holster. Blood dripped from Tatum's ear, but it began to dry as he walked gingerly down the stairs to an unmarked police car parked just outside the door of the police headquarters. Maggio took off, driving east.

Six

Darcy was on his second cup of coffee, reading a file, when he heard a knock on his door. He looked up. "Yes?"

"Family members are here for a gentleman named Marcus Tatum," Irma said.

"And who would Marcus Tatum be?" Darcy asked.

"Marcus Tatum was arrested for murder. The case is pending in Branch 66 and his family wants to talk to you about representing him."

"Oh," Darcy said. "And how many people are here?"

"Wife and mother, Mrs. Tatum and Mrs. Tatum."

"Well, that'll be easy to remember," Darcy said. "Show them in."

Darcy rose from his desk and shook hands with each of the Mrs. Tatums before guiding them to the client chairs across from his desk. Then he walked around and sat down, opened a leather notebook, and pulled out his pen.

"Mr. Cole, thank you for seeing us. My name is Dorothy Tatum. This is my daughter-in-law, Teesha. Teesha is married to my son, Marcus. You may have seen Marcus on television."

"I'm sorry," Darcy said, "I don't watch TV that often. What show is he on?"

"He does commercials. He's the pawnshop king."

Darcy shook his head.

"So what brings you to see me?"

"He's been arrested. They are claiming that he has committed a murder."

Darcy said nothing.

"I can tell you that he did not commit the murder. I can also tell you that he was arrested by a policeman who took him to the station and beat him. Beat him badly, and claimed that my son confessed to this crime. My son, however, would not sign the statement the officer prepared. Marcus told me that he didn't confess to anything. My son is a very successful man, Mr. Cole. He has a number of businesses and is well equipped to pay your fees. He told me to talk to you and have you meet with him at the jail where you two can discuss your fees. He will then instruct me by telephone to pay you those fees by certified check, which I am to deliver to you personally the following day."

Darcy was impressed.

"How about you, Mrs. Tatum?"—turning to the younger woman—"has your husband talked to you about this?"

Teesha smiled in a broken sort of way.

"He did speak with me about it. But I'm deferring to my mother-in-law in this matter. She is far more proficient than I in my husband's business affairs."

Dorothy removed a piece of paper from her purse. On it was typed the division of the jail and her son's inmate identification number. She also had visitor's information, which Darcy didn't need; attorneys were allowed to visit their clients whenever they wanted to.

"I'll go see him tomorrow," Darcy said.

"Thank you, Mr. Cole."

The two women stood up to leave. They shook hands and Darcy showed them out. Darcy liked the manner in which the Tatums spoke, the way they dressed, and their carriage. They made a very nice change from clients like Harry Feiger. He looked forward to working with them. He hoped his client would measure up to the women in his life.

* * *

Division Eleven was one of the newest parts of Cook County Jail. The sprawling complex went from California all the way to Sacramento, from Thirty-first Street down to Twenty-sixth Street. It was an enormous complex, a tribute to the national commitment to incarceration. A short, fat, gray-haired Hispanic man in the blue Sheriff's Correctional uniform took Darcy down in an elevator. Darcy glanced over at his nameplate, Mendoza.

"Mendoza, huh?" Darcy said. "You ever play baseball?"

The guard looked puzzled.

"You know, the Mendoza line? Guy hit .200 in the majors."

Blank stare.

"Ah, never mind."

They got out of the elevator and went through a couple of doors into an area that looked like the bowels of an alien spaceship. There was a tall tower going straight up to the ceiling with guards inside monitoring the movements in the hallways.

"Your guy is in AB," Mendoza said as he led Darcy off a central hallway down one of the spokes.

They went through two locked double doors, after which Mendoza pointed Darcy to a small room with two chairs in it.

"I'll go get him," Mendoza said. "Have a seat here."

Darcy leaned back in his chair and closed his eyes. He tried to clear his mind and relax. When he heard footsteps, he looked up. Mendoza was back with a very large man. Darcy stood up and stretched out his hand. "Marcus Tatum?"

"That's me," Marcus said. "Mr. Cole, thank you for coming."

They shook hands and sat across from each other. Darcy looked him up and down. "So, where do you want to begin?"

Marcus looked Darcy in the eye. "Well, here's the story. This lunatic cop comes and grabs me in front of my house. He handcuffs me, takes me down to Area Three and beats me. He uses a stick, then he puts a bag over my head until I pass out, and then he puts the bag over my head again. He tells me he's going to kill me unless I cop to a murder."

"Well, did you?" Darcy asked.

"Hell, no. I said, kill me. I don't give a shit. I'm not confessing to anything, especially a murder I didn't do."

"So why did he pick you on this?" Darcy asked.

"I don't know. That's the truth. I don't know why he chose me, but I did know the guy he was talking about. And I'll tell you this," Marcus said, "I'll bet you whatever you got that dude ain't dead."

"Why do you say that?" Darcy asked.

"I'm telling you, if you knew this guy, he was like CIA and shit."

"What does that mean?"

"This guy was slick—like James Bond slick. You know what I'm saying?"

Darcy shook his head. "No. I don't have a clue what you're saying. Why don't you start at the beginning and tell me everything."

"Okay, okay, here it is. This guy meets me. He's an Israeli. I called him 'the Jew.' His name was Jacob, I don't know his last name. He sought me out. I don't know who tipped him off to me, but he knew that I was a player and he wanted to get next to me. You dig?"

"I'm with you so far," Darcy said.

"Anyway, this guy says to me, you know, woowoo and this and that."

"Wait a minute," Darcy interrupted, "that doesn't mean anything to me."

"Okay, okay. I'm sorry," Marcus said. "I'm just excited. I'll slow it down. You see, here's the thing. I have a bunch of businesses and true enough, some of them I use to report income I get elsewhere. You understand?"

Darcy nodded.

"And, well, sometimes I make some deals with some people on some things that are illegal."

Darcy smiled. "Mr. Tatum, everything you tell me is covered by attorney-client privilege. I can't reveal our conversation to anyone, and it doesn't do you or me any good if you don't tell me the truth. It's like going to the doctor and not telling him that your dick hurts when you're pissing fire. If you don't tell him you've got VD, he can't give you the shots to make you better. So, if you're too embarrassed to tell your doctor, he can't treat you. And, if you can't tell me the truth, I can't help you. You understand?"

Marcus smiled. "True enough. True enough. All right, here's the story: I buy Rolexes off the street. I pay almost nothing for 'em. I turn around and I sell them to this guy in the jewelers' building on South Wabash. He gives me about fifty cents on the dollar, and then he turns around and sells 'em for seventy-five cents on the dollar. It's all cash. Everybody is making money except for the fool who lost them. But then again, they're insured for full price and the insurance company is giving them the check. So no one is really losing on the deal. Anyway, I'm there talking to my man and the Jew is there. My man introduces us and we go someplace to talk. He tells me he has a lot of cash and he wants to make more. So we work out a plan. We get a discount price on dope from the Mexicans. We step on it and sell it for an inflated price to the gangs. The Mexicans won't deal with the brothers. They'll deal with me."

Darcy let the contradiction pass and Marcus continued.

"So we're making money hand over fist. Me and the Jew are splitting fifty-fifty. He's fronting the dough, I'm using my connections, and I have my workers doing the work. There's no risk to the Jew. There's no real risk to me. So we're making big cash. I got a barbecue place in Englewood that's reporting eight hundred thousand dollars a year in income. I keep my accountants hopping. You know what I'm saying?"

Darcy nodded. Marcus was on a roll and Darcy didn't want to interrupt him.

"Anyway, for some reason, this detective, Maggio, snatches me and brings me up to Area Three. He's got a bad-ass attitude. He's telling me I'm copping to the murder of the Jew. I told him I'd never kill my golden goose. He's laying golden eggs all over the place for me. Shit, I'll have my own island soon. Anyway, he won't hear it. He's smacking the shit out of me—putting the bag over my head until I pass out. And then he writes up a confession and tells me to sign it. I tell him to go fuck himself and I kick him in the balls. Next thing I know, he's on the ground. I'm still handcuffed to a chair and I'm knee-dropping the mother-fucker trying to kill him."

"The cop?" Darcy asked.

"Yeah, the cop."

"You're charged with trying to kill a cop?"

"No, I'm charged with killing the Jew."

Darcy was perplexed. "So the Jew is dead?"

"That's the thing," Marcus said. "They say they got a body, but it's all burnt up and shit. They don't know who it is."

"So the police have a body they think is the Jew and they think you killed him. Is that it?"

"That's it," Marcus said, taking a breath.

"So what's the evidence they have against you?"

"Well, the only thing I think they have is the bullshit state-ment I didn't give."

Darcy leaned back in his chair. "That's it? Don't they have a witness? Who told them to go look for you in the first place?"

"I have no idea," Marcus said.

"Okay, well, who told this detective to come see you?"

"I don't know, but every time the Jew was with me he had this bodyguard with him. And that motherfucker was even more CIA than the Jew."

"What does that mean, CIA?" Darcy asked.

"You know, Central Intelligence Agency. The spooks, you know, the dudes that Tom Clancy writes about."

"Oh, okay, I got you," Darcy said. "But why CIA? You think it has something to do with the government?"

"Not our government."

"Which government?" Darcy asked.

"Israel, man. These cats were like Secret Service—Mossad and shit."

Darcy looked puzzled. "You think these two Mossad agents were dealing dope with you."

"No," Marcus said. "It was that one dude, the bodyguard, he was like Mossad."

"So where is this one Mossad agent—the bodyguard?"

"I don't know, I never saw the dude before, and I haven't seen him since our last deal."

"How would you get hold of the Jew?" Darcy asked.

"I had a phone number for him, Chicago phone number, 312 area code, cell phone. When he wasn't there, I'd leave a voice message. He would call me. I don't know where he'd call me from though; he traveled a lot, back and forth like crazy."

"Back and forth from where?"

"Israel, London, Amsterdam, all those places. Everywhere they sell diamonds. He'd go back and forth to Miami, too, and New York."

"So when you would call him and leave a message, he'd call you back at some point?"

"Yeah, and he'd tell me what day he would be in so I could set it all up. He'd tell me how much money he'd bring. We'd do ten kilos at a time. Two hundred thousand dollars in cash—twenty thousand a brick. Now, that's sweet. We could turn around and sell them for twenty-six a brick without even stepping on them. If we stepped on 'em two or three times, we'd go thirty bricks at twenty-five thousand. You do the math."

"When you got the cash, what would you do?"

"I'd give him back the two hundred large up front, and then the overage we'd split fifty-fifty."

"In cash?" Darcy asked.

"Yeah, in cash."

"Where would you do this?"

"I got places," Marcus said. "You know, I got businesses and we would do it some safe place."

"So could somebody else involved in the deal have killed him, one of your workers?"

"Hell no. I would never let those niggers know about this Jew boy."

"Why is that?" Darcy asked.

"Shit, if they knew this Jew was coming with hundreds of thousands of dollars in cash, they'd pick his bones clean. Then

I'd be out of the equation. I'd be out of the money and the business. You know what I'm saying?"

"So whose body do you think they have?"

"I don't know," Marcus said. "But I'm telling you, it ain't the Jew. He's too damn smart to be picked off. He dealt with me and only me. Every time we met, it was under his terms and conditions and he always had a bodyguard. You know what I'm saying?"

Darcy nodded. "Go on."

"Every time we planned to meet, he'd be there first, somewhere I couldn't see, to watch for me to come, and then he'd just appear. I'd come alone with my suitcase full of his money plus his share of the overage. He'd just take the suitcase and leave. The dude played it as safe as can be. One time we met in a bagel store across from the police station on Chicago Avenue. I sat down with the dude as police kept coming in and out buying coffee and shit. It was whacked. Ain't no way this guy got smoked. So you do some kind of test and you'll find out that whoever they got all burnt up in the morgue ain't this boy."

"How do you know he got burned up?" Darcy asked.

"Man, that detective wrote out this thing telling me I killed him, said I strangled him and shit. And then I poured gas on him and burnt him up, talking about some warehouse and shit. Please, I ain't stupid. I wasn't going to sign nothing."

"Well, tell me. Did they take you to the hospital after the beating you got?" Darcy asked.

"Yeah, that's the thing," said Marcus. "They were all hush hush and shit. But they took me to Northwestern Hospital. Passed two hospitals on the way over there—took me all the way over to Northwestern. They brought me in under some other name."

"They didn't use your name?"

"No, they were trying to cover their asses, I know that."

Darcy was pensive. "How are we going to get these medical records?" he asked.

Marcus smiled broadly and leaned back in his chair. Darcy

thought it was mostly for effect, dragging out the pause before he answered Darcy's question.

"The doctor who saw me there was named Amy Wagner. I'll never forget her. I told her what happened and that they had used a fake name for me. She told the cop to step outside, but he wouldn't. So then she told him to handcuff me to the bed and that he'd have to leave. And he did. I told her everything. She had some dude come in and take photographs of me. She said she would keep a copy of all the records. Man, I had something wrong with my ear, a cracked rib, a collapsed lung, and bleeding from a lacerated kidney or some odd shit. She has all that. She knows everything. She was all into it because she said there was no reason for me to be there in the first place. She said normally, the only police prisoners they get are from the Eighteenth District over on Chicago Avenue. So she knew something wasn't right. She was real cool. She's waiting for someone to get in touch with her."

Darcy smiled. "Okay, I'll send an investigator out to see this Dr. Wagner."

Darcy looked at his pad. He checked all his notes and asked a few personal questions for purposes of drafting a bond motion.

"Okay, now all we have to do is talk money."

"Yeah, not a problem," Marcus said. "I want you to do this."

"I'll tell you what, Mr. Tatum, I'm not sure how much work this is going to be. If everything you say pans out, we may not even get to trial. I mean after all, maybe it'll be motions only. Normally, I would charge somewhere between fifty and a hundred thousand dollars for that . . . but we don't know what's going to happen. If everything you told me is true, it sounds like the key is either a motion to suppress the statements or to quash the arrest. If we win the motion to quash the arrest, the statement goes out automatically. So we've got two chances to eliminate the statement, and if we do that, there may not be a trial."

Marcus nodded. "Hey, I'll pay you whatever. Let's just get

this done. Money's not an issue. I don't want to be the richest man sitting in the joint."

Darcy smiled. "Okay, let's get this going then."

"I'll get a cashier's check for fifty thousand dollars to your office tomorrow."

"Okay," Darcy said. "I'll have a contract drawn up."

"Forget the contract," Marcus said. "If you need more money, just tell me. Just win this. A hundred thousand dollars—shit, I could make that on the streets in a week."

Darcy smiled. "Marcus, if I'm your lawyer, you have to follow my advice. And my advice to you, at the moment, is don't commit any crimes."

Marcus broke up laughing. The meeting had come to an end.

Al Maggio sat at a table in the food court at Water Tower Place shopping center. He had a cup of coffee in front of him. He had taken two sips of it and then watched it go cold. He was angry. He hated this cloak-and-dagger stuff. He had told Avi Joseph he needed to talk to Anaka Vanderlinden. Joseph set it up for Water Tower—the worst possible spot in the world for Al Maggio. All these rich, happy people running around spending money made him sick.

He watched the suburban housewives loaded up with packages. Each package represented a line of coke to Al. From where he sat, he could see the elevators on his left and the escalators on his right. He scanned them constantly as he waited for Anaka to show up. She was thirty-five minutes late when he saw her appear on the escalator. Spoiled bitch, he thought to himself. She was impeccably dressed, wearing a short-sleeve blouse and linen pants. Her hair was pulled back and she wore what he assumed was an expensive necklace. Without the slightest flash of recognition in her face, she made her way toward Maggio and sat down at the table across from him.

"I'm glad you could make it," he said sarcastically.

"Well, I'd like to do anything I can to help."

"Yeah, I'm sure you're really worried,"' Maggio said.

She gave him a disapproving frown. Maggio pulled his tattered notebook from his battered briefcase and opened it onto the table.

"Okay, sweetheart, why don't you tell me where I can reach you?"

She gave him a cell phone number.

"Where are you staying? Give me your address."

"No, I don't think so," she replied.

"Give me a fucking address where I can reach you," he said, clearly irritated.

"Mr. Joseph said I didn't have to give you an address."

Maggio exploded. "Listen, you bitch—"

He then realized everyone at the surrounding tables had turned to look at him, and he piped down.

"Listen, you bitch," he repeated in a forced whisper. "I'm sick of you assholes trying to tell me what to do. Now, you're going to tell me what I want to hear. Do you understand me?"

"Or what?"

"Or what?" He was exasperated. "Look, I'm gonna walk out of here in a second if you don't tell me what I need to know."

"Detective Maggio, you can do whatever you want. Mr. Joseph has explained to me that you are working for him on this case."

Maggio slammed his hand on the table.

"That bastard. I'm not working for him. Listen. Screw you. Screw your dead Jewish boyfriend. Fuck your—" He stopped in mid-sentence.

She was shaking. "He's dead?" she asked. Tears began to well up.

"Oh, please," Maggio said, "Joseph didn't tell you that there's a John Doe at the morgue that we think is your boyfriend?"

She began to cry and fold into herself.

Maggio was even more aggravated.

"I don't believe this," he muttered.

She looked up. "You have no compassion whatsoever, do you?"

"Compassion," he said. "Look, you people seek me out and throw this Sherlock Holmes crap at me. Now, I need to know what is going on."

"Is he dead?" she asked.

"Look," Maggio said. "there was a body found, and it was burned up pretty badly, but the dental records that Avi Joseph gave me for your boyfriend matched. I'm sorry. Now I'm supposed to solve this crime and no one wants to cooperate with me. So you're going to answer my questions. You understand? Now, give me a real address."

She gave him the address of a high-rise apartment in Lincoln Park. He didn't believe her, but he wrote it down anyway.

"You got a home phone there?"

"No, we don't," she said. "We haven't had time to get it connected. You can always use the cell phone number."

"Beautiful. So what other phone numbers can I reach you at?"

"I have a phone number where I may be reached, but it's in London."

"How is that going to help me?"

She paused to give him a look that let him know she thought he was the biggest moron on the planet.

"You call. You leave me a message. I pick up the message or the message is delivered to me. Is that so complicated?"

"How the fuck do you call London?"

"I'll give you the country dialing code and the phone number you need to call. All you have to do is dial the numbers and you'll get my voice mail. I will collect my phone messages promptly."

"Where do you normally live?" he asked.

"London, but I'm from South Africa, actually."

"No lie. So is the country going to pieces since you gave the blacks the right to vote?"

She let that pass. "You have any other questions?" she asked.

"Yeah, yeah—all business, huh, babe?" he said. "Tell me about your boyfriend's business."

"He is a diamond courier."

"No, not that business. The business that got him dead."

The words were like a wet slap to her face. She recoiled in anger.

"Okay, look. I'm sorry. How about we quit playing around? I talk to you, you talk to me, no bullshit. We'll get through this okay. I need information from you to try to find your boyfriend. If he's the DOA in the morgue, I'm very sorry, but I assume you want me to catch his killer. And if he's not the DOA, then you want me to find him, don't you? So why don't we cut through the crap and work together."

She nodded.

"Who is Marcus Tatum?"

"I don't know."

"Come on, who's Marcus Tatum?'

"I don't know. I can only tell you what I know about Jacob. He's a diamond courier. That means he brings diamonds from one place to another. Doing that, he picks up large sums of money, primarily in cash. He has accounts in various banks in the cities in which he deals. He deposits large amounts of cash there and then wire-transfers the money back to Israel. What I believe happened was he started working with a guy, who I presume would be your Marcus Tatum—I didn't know his name, he didn't tell me. But I guessed that they were buying and selling drugs because, all of a sudden, we were doing two bank deposits—one wire-transferred to Israel and a second wire-transferred elsewhere."

"Elsewhere, what do you mean?"

"Suffice it to say that it went to an account that had nothing to do with the diamond business."

Maggio noticed an abrupt change in her personality. She was no longer the crumbling, crying, bereaved girlfriend. She suddenly became a cool, calculating businesswoman.

"So where was this other account?" he asked.

She smiled. "Let's just say it's in a safe haven."

"Okay, so how much money was going in there—fifty, a hundred, a hundred and fifty thousand?" Maggio asked.

"Yes, Detective. Thousands. That's why I believe it was drug money; you don't make that kind of cash in two days by selling lotto tickets."

"So what's your role in all this, honey?"

"Don't call me honey," she bristled. "My role in this is difficult to define."

"Try, will you, sweetie?"

She started to get angry but stopped, realizing it would only encourage him.

"I would make deposits. I would also make money transfers. Sometimes I would carry diamonds. I was basically there just to help him."

"What would you get paid?" he asked.

"Please, I wasn't an employee. We were in love."

"Oh, yeah, you got an engagement ring?" he asked.

She lifted her hand to show him.

"Hey, nice rock."

"You really are a moron, aren't you, Detective?" she said. "He is in the diamond business. I also know quite a bit about diamonds—I've learned a lot about them over the years. What kind of a diamond do you think I'd wear, some black rock that I got at a strip mall in Kansas?"

He smiled. "Okay, honey, calm down. So when were you going to get married?"

"We had some financial goals in place. I didn't want to have my husband running all over the world with a satchel of diamonds while I stayed home and took care of the children."

"Ah, I get it," he said. "So you were going to put together a boatload of money and sail off into the sunset. Is that it, honey?"

"We were going to put together a significant financial stake. Then we were going to make some intelligent investments and live comfortably off our investments."

"So tell me, was it just the two of you or did you have some help?"

"He had a gentleman that worked for him in a security capacity, Daniel Litwin."

"Who's he?"

"Didn't Avi Joseph fill you in on him? Daniel Litwin, I believe, worked at one time in the same capacity as Avi Joseph."

"Is that right? The Mossad just has agents coming out their ass, huh?"

"I don't know if there are any Mossad agents," she said. "Sometimes I believe Mossad is a myth. At least every time I ask a man about it, he laughs and tells me that it doesn't exist, and that if it did, he certainly wouldn't be in it. Let me ask you this, Detective, have you ever met a CIA agent?"

Maggio thought about it. "When I was in the military, I met a guy I thought was in the CIA."

"He told you he was?"

"No, people sat around and speculated he was."

"You see, Detective, that's what I'm up against. I assume, or believe that Avi Joseph is from the Mossad, just as I believe that Daniel Litwin was from the Mossad. But they wouldn't tell me that—just like your experience in the military. After all, no one is a CIA agent—they have some arcane title for some bureaucracy and happen to be attached to an embassy. Isn't that right?"

"Maybe you're right," Maggio agreed. "Tell me about this Litwin."

"Litwin was always lurking in the shadows," she said. "When Jacob needed him, he'd show up. And when Jacob wanted space, he'd be out of sight. Although I believe he was never so far out of sight that he wasn't watching us. If you catch my drift."

"What was his purpose?"

"As far as I know, he was security. After all, the nation of Israel doesn't want to have half a million dollars worth of diamonds and one of their prize sons disappearing."

"Tell me about Jacob's family," he said.

"They are a very prominent family in Israel. Not only are they big in the diamond business but also politically. You don't get a Mossad agent assigned to you just because you're a diamond courier. You have to be important to the Israeli government. You don't get it, do you? Do you honestly think that the Israeli government would send Avi Joseph over here just because some diamonds are missing? My fiancé is a very important man."

"Why?" said Maggio.

"I'm not sure," she said. "All I know is that he has very high security clearance and is in the Israeli military."

"Everyone is in the Israeli military," Maggio said.

She rolled her eyes.

"Jacob has a relative who is very high in the Defense Department. He works directly with the Defense Minister, and yet you won't see his name on any official government list. Does that make it clear to you?"

Maggio thought about it. None of this was clear to him and he wondered if Anaka was making it all up as she went along. "So he's got a relative that does dirty deeds for the Israeli government."

"Call it what you will," she said, "but Israel is a country that fights for its life every day. They have enemies on all their borders. Peace treaties are nothing but pieces of paper to them. They need strong men and women who are willing to do whatever is necessary to make sure the country survives. Mossad would assume that if Jacob's gone missing, someone trying to get to his family is at the center of it."

Maggio was beginning to see the picture a bit clearer. "Why don't they send the Mossad to do the work?"

"Please," she said, "you don't think you're the A-team, do you?"

It struck him. "So I'm just another avenue for them."

"Yes, Detective, they need you to help them, but do you honestly think that the Israeli government is going to put all their faith and trust in you? You're just one of the myriad of methods they're using to solve this problem. Sure, they need you, but don't mistake that for power on your part. If you do something for them, they'll reward you. But if you screw with them, you're done."

"What about you? How do you fit into all this?" he asked.

"Well, his family has no interest in me. I'm not Jewish. I'm not even an Israeli. As far as they're concerned, I'm just a shiksa he's using for fun and adventure until he settles down with a nice Jewish girl and comes back to the land of milk and honey."

"And?" Maggio asked.

"And they're not going to like it when we leave."

"What does that mean, 'when we leave'?"

"Well we're going to settle someplace, but it's not going to be Israel," she answered.

"Can I assume it'll be some place warm and sunny with liberal banking laws?" Maggio asked.

"That would be a safe bet."

"So where do I find this Daniel Litwin?" he asked.

"I don't know. I have been trying to find him myself, but I can't seem to locate him, and Avi Joseph won't help me."

"So how are you surviving here without your boyfriend?" he asked.

"I do have access to the bank accounts."

"So," Maggio began, "if your boyfriend ends up dead or if he never shows up, does that mean you can go to the sunny spot by yourself and make these wise investments without him?"

"I suppose it does," she said. "Does that make me a suspect?"

Maggio decided to switch gears. He pulled out Marcus Tatum's photograph. "Have you ever seen this guy before?"

"Yes, I have," she said.

"When?"

"Well, this is the man he was with when he left me."

"What?" he asked.

"Yes, he met this guy in the lobby of our hotel and the two of them went out together."

"Was Daniel Litwin with them?"

"No," she said, "he wasn't."

"Okay, why didn't you tell me this when we first met?"

"Didn't I?" she asked.

"Look, cut the crap. Did he or didn't he leave with this guy?"

"Oh yeah, he definitely left with this guy."

"When I first met you, you told me he went for a walk and left his wallet and all the rest of his shit in the room."

"Oh, I don't think I told you that," she said.

"Bullshit," he said, "that's what you said. Now, you're telling me he left with this guy? Did he have his wallet and keys with him?"

"I don't know," she said.

"Listen, make up your mind. Did he leave with this guy or didn't he?"

"Yes, absolutely he left with this guy. A large fellow, as I recall."

Maggio was being played and he didn't like it. "Who told you to tell me this shit?"

"Excuse me?"

"Excuse me, my ass. Who told you to tell me this garbage now?"

"I'm telling you what you need to know to try and find Jacob."

"You're lying through your teeth," he said. "I need you to tell me the truth, not what Avi Joseph wants me to hear."

"Look, I can only tell you what I know. You do with it what you like, but he left with this man."

"Where were they going?"

"He didn't tell me."

"Did he have anything with him?"

"Yes, he had a large briefcase."

"What was in the briefcase?"

"Well, it was the briefcase we use to carry diamonds, or the money for the diamonds."

"Okay. Was there money or diamonds in there?"

"I don't know what was in there. But he left with his briefcase. I can only imagine that there was money in it because he had been to the jewelers' building earlier that day."

"Ain't that a bitch," Maggio said.

"How's that?" she asked.

"Well, I find a body. Now I have a witness and a confession.

This murder case is coming together really, really well. And now you, the grieving widow, can run off to some tropical island with a boatload of money and live happily ever after."

"You make it sound so cold," she said.

"Oh, please, cut the bullshit, I don't like being played," he said. "I'm not sure what the game is, but I know that you and Avi Joseph are telling me the things you think I want to hear and you're pushing me into a certain direction. When I figure this out, I'm coming back for you, sister, got it?"

"You're a crude, simple man," she said. "Your mind spins these little webs of deception. You can't see that some things are just what they are. Do what you think is right, Detective."

"You bet your ass, I will," he replied. "You bet your ass."

* * *

A uniformed waiter was preparing the poolside tables for the breakfast crowd. Darcy had the pool to himself as he took a flip turn and glided under the water. He pulled himself up and began his crawl stroke—strong, compact, and efficient—heading toward the other end of the pool. His rubber watch began to chirp and he quickened his stroke until he touched the wall. He pushed back and glided backward in the water, feeling his heart race from the exertion. He threw his arms over the ropes and rested. His thoughts were on Marcus Tatum. He couldn't believe that, in this day and age, a detective would inflict such injuries on a prisoner and think that he could get away with it. As long as he had been a lawyer, he still couldn't believe that a policeman would try to cover up a beating by taking the victim to a hospital and checking him in under an assumed name. No one could be that reckless. A faint smile came across his face. My God, if he was that reckless, Darcy would have all kinds of evidence to substantiate Tatum's claims. Any judge, every judge would be forced to suppress those statements. Darcy thought about it. If it was what it seemed, he had a winner.

He popped his head under the water, slid under the ropes and did a quick breaststroke, popped under again for the last set of ropes and slid over to the ladder. He bounded out of the pool and reached for a towel. He threw a robe on, yanked off his suit, and dried his hair. He sat down at a table with a *Tribune* and a *Sun-Times* for company. The waiter came over and took his usual order—coffee, toast, oatmeal, and grapefruit juice. Darcy signed for it. He dropped both papers into an empty chair when his oatmeal arrived. He finished breakfast, dressed in a hurry, and headed off to his office, eager to work on the Tatum case.

As Darcy walked out of the club, he looked down the street again. It was a strange feeling, the memories that flooded him almost every day as he went to and from his workout. Every time he left the club he relived the morning that crazed mob gunman Anthony Benvenuti Jr. had jumped out of a doorway, gun blazing, trying to kill him. Two bodyguards supplied by Benvenuti's father, mob boss Tony the Babe, had fired back, killing the junior Benvenuti. The two bodyguards, known as John and Jim Doe, had saved Darcy's life.

He scurried into the lobby of his office building; it was almost deserted. He glanced at his watch, ten to eight. He was early. After getting off the elevator, he went through his pockets, pulled out his key chain and tried to figure out which one was the office key. Usually Irma was in by eight, but Darcy had preceded her this morning.

He pulled his coat off and threw it on the rack in his office. He stood for a moment looking out over the lake beyond the Harold Washington Library, beyond Buckingham Fountain and Grant Park. He watched a boat bounce along the lake. He was still watching the sailboat pounding across the choppy waves when he heard Irma's voice.

"Good morning, boss," she said, coming in. "You're in early."

"Good morning, Irma. Yeah, I got an early start," Darcy said. "I'm full of energy. I'm ready to go," he said with a faint smile.

"Well let's see if we can keep you going all day," she said. "I'm going to go make coffee."

Darcy turned back. The sailboat had crossed out of his line

of sight, lost behind some buildings. He sat down at his desk and pulled out his daybook. He scanned the day's events and then moved on through the rest of the week. He had a bond motion for Marcus Tatum later in the morning. He had planned to meet Collata before court, with the medical records that would hopefully substantiate their claims for the purposes of the bond motion.

He looked up at his doorway to make sure Irma wasn't standing there, then reached into a drawer and pulled out a Bible. He studied it carefully. He saw the red ribbon bookmark in the very early pages of it. He figured he must have well over a thousand pages to go. How could it be? he thought. It's such a big book, and yet so many people know every line in it. He realized he was procrastinating about reading more, and that he was coming up with excuses not to delve in any further when Kathy appeared at his door.

"Can I come in?" she asked.

"Sure, come on in."

She stopped after a few steps and looked at him. "Darcy, is that a Bible?"

Darcy was flustered for a second. "Ah, yes," he stammered. "It was a gift. Willie Mae Watkins gave it to me."

Kathy looked at him. "You have something to tell me?" she asked.

Darcy dropped the Bible into his desk drawer and slammed it shut. "I was just looking at it. Don't get any ideas," he said. "It's intellectual curiosity."

Kathy's entire body shuddered as if she had a chill. "Okay, let's get beyond that," she said. "Can I talk to you?"

"Have a seat."

"I really hate to do this," she began, "but I think I have to."

"What is it?" Darcy asked.

"I want Collata to follow Jim. He's going out Mondays and Thursdays now. He's staying out late and he comes home reeking of cigarettes. He doesn't smoke, Darcy."

"Have you asked yet where he goes?" Darcy asked.

"I ask him and he says he's out with his friends. I ask him

where and he tells me a bar. He's not a drinker. He's not a smoker. Why would he go to a bar? Why would he come home smelling like cigarettes? I'm afraid he's having an affair," she said.

"Jim would never do that," Darcy said.

"I don't know, maybe it's the job. Maybe it is this damn job, where we see everybody at their worst, where everyone we deal with is a liar—scamming, conning, and conniving. Maybe that's why I suspect him."

"Yeah," Darcy said, "that is one of the major drawbacks of this job—makes you suspicious and cynical. But, I just can't believe Jim would have an affair. Really, Kathy, I'm not naive and I know nobody's a saint, but of all people, I just can't see Jim cheating on you. I can't believe he would even think of doing anything that would hurt you that badly."

"I'd like to think that too," she said, "but I don't know. There's something not right. He's keeping something from me. I can tell. He's never kept anything from me before."

"Okay," Darcy said. "Collata will follow him and then you'll find out there was no reason for you to be upset in the first place."

Kathy sighed. "Can we do this in the most discreet way possible?"

"Absolutely," Darcy said. "As discreet as a two-hundred-and-fifty-pound bald-headed, goateed, motorcycle-riding private detective can be."

Kathy winced. "Thanks for the reassurance." She came around and gave Darcy a hug.

Darcy awkwardly sat in his chair and patted her on the back. "It's going to be okay, Kathy. There's no way that Jim's slinking around on you."

Kathy pulled back. "I'm not one of those people that can forgive and forget," she said. "I either trust somebody or I don't. Once he betrays the trust, as far as I am concerned I can never trust him again."

Eight

Collata stood in the waiting room of the Emergency Room at Northwestern University Hospital smoking a cigarette. He was getting down to the end when a security guard came over and pointed to a no smoking sign. Collata took one fast, deep drag on the cigarette, threw it to the floor and crushed it with his foot. He let the smoke seep out of his mouth and nose slowly, savoring the nicotine as it passed through his body. He had been there for twenty-five minutes waiting for Dr. Amy Wagner to take a break. Three or four times during that period, someone had come out and told him that Dr. Wagner would be with him in just a minute. He waited. That was the essence of detective work, waiting.

Collata was bored. He got tired of sitting so he stood. He watched an old white man with two-day stubble fighting the urge to nod off. Finally, he heard a voice.

"Detective Collata?"

He turned around and saw Dr. Amy Wagner. She was wearing a gray hospital jacket over a cotton button-down shirt, black pants, and clogs with gray felt trim. She had a stethoscope in the big oversized pocket on the right side of her jacket.

"Dr. Wagner?"

"Yes. How do you do?"

"I'm great," Collata said. "Is there someplace we could talk, Doctor?"

"Sure, come with me."

She led him to a small conference room where she went directly to two abandoned Styrofoam coffee cups and threw them in the garbage. "I don't know why people don't clean up after themselves," she said. "I mean, this is a hospital."

Collata said nothing, but he was already taking a liking to Dr. Wagner. She was tough. He liked that. He guessed her to be in her late forties or early fifties. She had dark hair liberally streaked with gray. She had a warm face with the appropriate number of wrinkles and bright blue eyes. He liked her. She wasn't a phony. She seemed content to be what she was, a competent, strong woman, not a girl.

"How can I help you?" she asked.

"Well, four days ago you treated a large black man who was brought here by the police under a false name."

"Oh, yes," Dr. Wagner said immediately. "I've been waiting for someone to come. I assume you are from the Internal Affairs Division."

"No ma'am. I am a retired detective and I work for the lawyer who is representing the young man."

"Ah, I see. Well, I have the reports and photographs all prepared."

"May I see them?" Collata asked.

"Of course. I made a second set just in case. After all, you can't be too careful," she said.

"Good idea."

"I'll go get them. You wait here. You want a cup of coffee or something?"

"No, thanks."

He watched her leave and glanced at his watch. She was back in less than three minutes with a large manila envelope. She bent the clasp out and poured the contents on the table.

"As you can see," she said, pointing to the photographs, "he had some serious injuries, and these injuries could not have been inflicted by anything other than a blunt object or a fist."

Collata looked at the pictures. There were bruises all over the body—four big ones on the back near the kidney, and a solid pattern of black and blue across the ribs.

"So tell me, Doctor, do you always expend this much effort with patients?"

"That's a loaded question," she said. "This young man whispered to me what had happened. I knew that I had to get the policeman out of the treatment room so I could talk with him in private and get all the information. So I asked the officer to handcuff him to the bed, told him that my patient and I needed to be alone. Nasty business."

"Yeah," Collata said. "Doctor, you realize that you will probably be asked to serve as a witness at some point."

"I understand," she said.

"And Doctor, if anyone asks, all we want you to do is tell the truth."

"What is the truth, Detective Collata?"

"Well, ma'am, we are trying to figure that out now. Our client told us that this detective worked him over really badly. And we find it unusual, to say the least, that they passed other hospitals to bring him here and that they checked him in under a phony name."

"Yes, it does seem odd," the doctor concurred. "I could only surmise that they're up to something," she said.

"Yeah," agreed Collata. "Anyway, thanks for what you did here, documenting his injuries and all."

She smiled. "That's part of the job. After all, a lot of people who come to the emergency room end up suing someone or another. That's the world we live in. Tell me, Mr. Collata, this lawyer you work for, what type of man is he?"

"Well," Collata said, "he's a great guy and he's the best lawyer in Chicago. His name is Darcy Cole. Have you ever heard of him?"

"No. But then, I wouldn't. I don't pay much attention to lawyers. As a matter of fact, I make it a point to avoid them."

Collata chuckled. "Yeah. You know what they say at the courthouse, don't you?"

"No, what?" the doctor asked.

"Well, that the courts are full of dangerous lying, thieving, scumbags—and their clients, too."

The doctor smiled. "Lawyer jokes."

"Well," Collata said, "I could tell you more, but I can see you're a busy woman and I don't want to keep you anymore. May I keep all these documents?"

"Of course, those are your copies. I have the originals for my records."

"Thank you very much, Doctor. It was a pleasure to meet you. Here's my card," Collata said, "and here's Mr. Cole's."

She took both cards and jammed them into a pocket.

"Mr. Collata, call me when you need me."

Collata smiled.

"Yes, ma'am. Thank you for your time, Doctor."

Collata walked over to his dilapidated van and ripped open the rusty door with some effort. He plopped into the driver's seat and pulled the door shut—it seemed to scream in agony as it moved. He rolled down the window and stuck his elbow out. He sat there for a while looking through the paperwork. It was a gold mine. There was no question that the detective had beaten Tatum, and they had the documentation to prove it. And the fact that the police had checked him into a hospital two districts over—under an assumed name—stunk to high heaven. Collata was thrilled, and couldn't wait to drop the envelope onto Darcy's desk.

* * *

Collata was smoking a cigarette outside the courtroom. "What's up, boss?" he said, dropping the cigarette onto the floor and crushing it with his cowboy boot.

"What do you have for me?" Darcy asked.

"I've got everything," Collata returned. "You're going to win this thing without breaking a sweat."

"Is that right? How do you figure?"

"I met the doctor over at Northwestern, Amy Wagner, good broad. She documented everything. She says that one dick brings this guy in in handcuffs, checks him in under a phony name, lies about what district it came out of, and tells the doctor that the guy had fallen or some nonsense like that. She takes one look at this guy and knows that the police lumped up on him, puts two and two together and kicks the dick out of the room while she treats him. Our guy tells her exactly what happened. She documents everything—photographs, a thorough examination, x-rays—everything, 'cause she's suspicious. She makes a duplicate of everything, figuring that if the police come around and want to shit-can everything, she's got an extra set. I show up, tell her who I am, and she says she's been waiting for me. She gives me everything," Collata said, patting his briefcase. "I've got it here."

"What kind of witness would she be?" Darcy asked. "I mean, does she have a bone to pick?"

"No, she's not anti-police or anything like that. She's just a doctor doing her job. You know, healing. She just doesn't like the fact that the police almost killed this guy."

Darcy glanced at his watch. "Listen, I have to talk to you about something." Darcy said, walking Collata into a secluded corner. "Here's the deal," he said. "I want you to do something, and I want you to do it in a very discreet manner."

Collata lit up another cigarette and blew the smoke out, keeping the cigarette between his lips, and threw his palms up. "What do you mean? I'm not always discreet?"

"Here's what I want you to do." Darcy hesitated.

Collata took a drag on the cigarette. "Well?"

"Kathy Haddon wants you to follow her husband."

"You playing me? He's not going outside the marriage, is he?"

"I don't think so," Darcy said, "but he's staying out a couple nights a week. He comes home smelling like cigarettes. When she asks him about it, he says he's been at a bar with his buddies. She just wants to know if he's being honest."

"Geez, that guy's not stupid," Collata said. "He knows he's got a good thing."

"Well, you never know," Darcy said, "I've seen a lot of

people do a lot of dumb things over the years."

"Come on," Collata said. "No way is her husband messing around on her."

"I agree. So why don't you find out and put her mind at ease."

"Darcy, the guy knows me."

"So, you're going to have to be discreet."

"Yeah, yeah, yeah. What does she want me to do? Does she want me to talk to her or is she going to give the information to you? How do you want to play this?"

"You talk to her," Darcy said, "but I want you to be, what's the word I'm looking for here. . . ."

Collata took a drag of his cigarette, blowing it out in a double stream from his nose and mouth. "You've already said discreet, so come up with something new, will ya?"

"Sensitive," Darcy said. "I want you to be sensitive. And I want you to be compassionate and understanding."

"Hey, I'm two hundred and forty pounds of love," Collata said, "I'm Phil Donahue, Alan Alda, and Dr. Phil all rolled into one."

Darcy reached over and patted Collata's ample gut. "Two hundred and forty pounds, huh?" he said. "All right, let's get in here and do this bond motion then grab some lunch," Darcy said.

"You're on."

* * *

Standing in the hallway of the courthouse made Darcy feel old. All those young faces passing him. Prosecutors, public defenders, even judges, all younger than Darcy; it made him realize just how long he'd been coming to this courthouse. Collata walked with him to the courtroom door, then opened it. Darcy watched Collata pull a cigarette from behind his ear and walk away. Darcy dropped his briefcase on the counsel table and pulled out a file and a yellow pad. He was reviewing his notes when someone tapped him on the shoulder.

"Hey, Darcy, can I talk to you for a minute?"

Darcy looked up to see Jack Karsten, an Assistant State's

Attorney, whom he'd known for years. "Sure, where do you want to go?"

"Follow me."

They walked out of the courtroom and into the hallway the sheriffs use to move prisoners in and out of the courtroom from lockup. Darcy shook hands. "Jack, how are you?"

"I'm good, Darcy. What's up with you?"

"Ah, you know, just doing my business."

"Yeah, that's what I want to talk to you about," Jack said.

Jack Karsten stood about six-foot-two. He had broad shoulders and big arms—an athletic build, but not slim. He had a very kind face and warm smile.

"You have Marcus Tatum, right?"

"Yeah," Darcy said. "You going to pick that up?"

"I don't know what I'm going to do yet," Jack said. "What kind of bond can your guy make?"

Darcy thought about it. "Half a million, ten percent to apply."

Jack laughed. "Yeah, fifty thousand dollars. I'm sure he can post that. Okay, look, if I agree to let him walk, would you give me a by-agreement date for about sixty days?"

"Why?" Darcy said.

"Like I said, I don't know what I want to do with this case," he said.

"And if I don't agree?" Darcy asked.

"Then we'll do a bond hearing," Jack said. "Then we'll go for a three-week date, I'll indict his ass and we'll take it upstairs."

"Okay, and if I agree, what's going to happen in two months?"

"I don't know," Jack said. "I want to look at this. I may do a preliminary hearing."

"A preliminary hearing?" Darcy jumped. "There's been one preliminary hearing on a murder case in this building in the past twenty-five years. Remember that one, Jack? That's when the copper shot that homeless man and they decided to put it off on the judge so the judge would look bad."

"Yeah, I remember," Jack said. "But maybe it's time to do another one. These are changing times. Maybe we need to take a better look at some of these cases before they end up on page one of the *Tribune*."

Darcy was eyeing him up and down in disbelief.

"So what do you want to do?" Jack asked.

"Well, if you want to agree with a half-million-dollar bond, I'll agree to a date, and then maybe we should talk a little bit further."

"Okay, let's do this," Jack said. "We'll do the bond hearing and I'll tell the judge that the State agrees to a five-hundred-thousand-dollar bond, ten percent to apply. Your guy posts fifty grand, you agree to a date two months out, and then we go up to my office and have a cup of coffee and chat."

"Sounds reasonable to me," Darcy said.

"Okay, I'll see you in court," Jack said.

A large glass partition separated the gallery from the courtroom. Inside the courtroom two dozen chairs were lined up neatly between counsel tables and the partition. Half the chairs were occupied with lawyers waiting for their case to be called.

Marcus Tatum was led in by a deputy sheriff. Tatum was dressed in khaki scrubs with CCDOC stenciled on the legs and on the back. On the chest were four Xs and an L. Marcus was a big boy. The clerk called the case.

"People of the State of Illinois versus Marcus Tatum, first-degree murder, Your Honor." He then handed the file to the judge.

Judge Moglin was in his early fifties with light brown hair that was thinning and receding. He had a square jaw hidden behind a goatee that was flecked with gray.

"Darcy Cole for Defendant, Marcus Tatum," Cole said, pointing to his client. "Mr. Tatum is present in open court."

Jack Karsten stepped up to the bench. "Your Honor, for the State, Jack Karsten."

"Mr. Karsten, nice to see you in court," the judge said.

"Nice to be here, Judge Moglin."

"What are we doing today, gentlemen?" the judge inquired.

Karsten spoke up. "Judge, the State would have no objection to a five-hundred-thousand-dollar bond, ten percent to apply in this case. I believe that Mr. Tatum would be able to make that bond and then we will be seeking a by-agreement date for approximately sixty days."

The judge's eyebrows rose. "Is that right, Mr. Cole?"

"Yes, Your Honor, that's my understanding."

"You're going to go by agreement?" the judge asked.

"Yes sir. I agreed to both the setting of the bond and to the sixty-day date."

"Okay," the judge said. "You guys must know what you're doing. We'll set it for, how's the twenty-eighth of next month, gentlemen?"

"The twenty-eighth works, Your Honor," Darcy said.

"I'm here every day," Karsten said.

"Okay, gentlemen, the twenty-eighth. Mr. Tatum, your bond is set at five hundred thousand dollars. That means you need to post fifty thousand dollars to be released from custody. If you do post bond, Mr. Tatum, you must appear for court. If you fail to appear in court, you can be tried in your absence. And, if you are tried and convicted in your absence, when you are apprehended you will go directly to jail. Do you understand, Mr. Tatum?"

"I do," Marcus said.

"Okay, we'll see you on the twenty-eighth. Let the record reflect it is a by-agreement date. Good day, gentlemen. Next case," the judge shouted.

Darcy took a few steps with Marcus as he was being led away. "We'll get the bond posted and you'll be out. I'll see you in my office soon."

"Cool," Marcus said. "Good job. I appreciate it."

Darcy turned and walked back out. Karsten was waiting in the well of the courtroom.

"Hey, Darcy, we need to talk. My office is upstairs, on the fourth floor."

"Gotcha," Darcy said. "I'll see you there in a few minutes."

Darcy walked out and explained to the Tatum family what

had occurred. There were hugs and smiles all around, and Marcus's mother said, "We'll get the bond posted in about an hour."

"Do you know where to go?" Darcy asked.

"Oh, yes. We know what we're doing."

Darcy smiled. "I'm sure you do."

Marcus's wife gave Darcy a kiss on the cheek. "We'll call you when we get him out."

* * *

Collata walked over to Darcy as the Tatum family left. "That was pretty sweet."

"Yeah," Darcy said. "Jack Karsten wants to talk to me."

"Karsten's a good guy," Collata said. "Straight shooter. I dealt with him a couple of times."

"Yeah, he's okay," Darcy said. "Let's go see what he has to say."

Darcy had a seat on a wooden bench after telling the secretary that he was there to see Jack Karsten. There was a big sign above her, "State's Attorney's Office Homicide Sex Unit." Jack Karsten was the boss. Jack came out without a jacket, his sleeves rolled up to his forearms, and invited Darcy in. Darcy introduced Collata.

"You remember Collata, don't you?"

"Sure I do," Jack said. "Your private investigator. You used to be a copper, right, Collata?"

"That's right," Collata said.

"Come on in. You're welcome to join us, Collata. It's up to you, Darcy."

"Yeah, we'll come in."

Collata and Darcy followed him into the corner office. Karsten shut the door and sat behind his desk, looking across to Darcy and Collata.

"Let's cut to the chase," Jack said. "I still don't know what to make of this case,"' he began. "As you know, we've been taking our lumps around here lately. The *Tribune* and television news are giving us a beating over a few cases. Having all these death penalty cases reversed, the Appellate Court is up our ass complaining about prosecutorial misconduct, and frankly, this case stinks. I don't mean that we don't have enough to convict your guy or to do a good faith prosecution, but that's only on the surface. A good faith prosecution doesn't mean because you have a confession and you have a body that you have a case. You follow me?"

"I understand," Darcy said. "The state's attorney's up for election in fourteen months and he doesn't want to be perceived as continuing the pattern of abuse and neglect that's taken place under his predecessors."

Jack smiled. "That's one way of putting it. The lead detective in this case is a guy named Maggio."

"We're well aware of him," Darcy said. "We've done our homework on him."

Collata nodded. "Yeah, we know what he's all about."

"Okay, let's move on then," Jack said. "There's no need to delve into that any deeper. Clearly, we have our questions about what transpired here. My inclination is to put Maggio on the witness stand, since he's the lead detective and he took the statement. We can do a preliminary hearing."

Darcy was pleased. "So you are serious. You're going to do a preliminary hearing in a murder case?"

"Well, you know," Karsten said, "there are a lot of counties throughout the country that actually do preliminary hearings on murder cases."

"Yeah, I've heard that," Darcy said, "but we don't live in Oz, we live in Cook County, and they're just not done. Your guys always take these cases to the Grand Jury, where we can't ask any questions. A preliminary hearing lets me ask your witnesses questions under oath. I think I'm in defense lawyers' heaven."

"Well, here's the thing," Jack said. "We have two months before the next court date. I think what we need to do is get some discovery and see where we stand."

"You're going to give us discovery before the prelim?" Darcy asked.

"Yeah," Jack said. "You're entitled to it. Just because we drag our feet in most cases doesn't mean we have to in every case. I think we need to be prepared. I need to be prepared. Our witness needs to be prepared. We'll put him on and we'll see where we stand after that. How does that sound?"

"You're a chip off the old block, Jack," Darcy said.

"Thank you," Jack said.

"I mean it. I liked your dad a lot. He was a great lawyer and a good man."

"He was a great father," Jack said. "I miss him."

The three of them looked around at each other not knowing what to say next.

"Anyway, getting back to Mr. Marcus Tatum," Jack began, "we have some issues. We have a cause of death issue, the identification of the victim, and the taking of the statement. There are a number of things we need to investigate before I'm satisfied that we're doing the right thing. So I'm going to do an investigation and I'll dump some discovery off in your lap. Then we'll see where we stand. I should have everything that I need in about three or four weeks."

Darcy and Collata stood to leave.

Collata pulled out a pack of cigarettes and offered one to Jack. "No thanks," Jack said.

"Oh yeah, you're a jock, right?"

"Former jock." He smiled. "Now I'm just trying to age gracefully—not get too fat."

"You don't want to balloon up like my friend Collata here," Darcy said.

"Solid as a rock," Collata rejoined.

Darcy reached over and shook Jack's hand, followed by Collata. "Okay, Jack, we'll see where we stand in a couple of weeks."

Nine

Collata parked his van in the near-empty parking lot of the Cook County Medical Examiner's Office, formerly known as the morgue. He stepped out of the van to a clear cloudless day and took a moment to glance at the bright blue sky. He looked up and closed his eyes to feel the warm sunlight. After a few moments, he shrugged his shoulders and began walking toward the glass double doors. As he entered the clean, well-lit lobby, his mind flashed back to his days as a homicide detective, when the morgue was a dank, smelly, cramped place in the basement of a building with leaky pipes and the odor of death. He meandered down the hall until he came to a reception area. A young, clean-cut man rose to meet him.

"May I help you?"

"Yeah, I'm looking for Dr. Kim."

"Yes, her office is on the left down the hall."

"Thank you," he said as he walked off.

Dr. Kim was seated behind a desk, her door open, looking through her glasses at a computer screen. Collata walked up to the threshold and then knocked on the door. Startled, she looked up.

"May I help you?"

"Yeah, my name is Collata. I'm a private detective. I work for attorney Darcy Cole. I want to talk to you about a homicide."

She laughed. "You'll have to be a bit more specific than that, Detective. I get a lot of homicides."

"It was originally a John Doe," Collata said. He handed her a copy of her autopsy report that included the internal file numbers for the medical examiner's office.

"Ah," she said. "Let me pull that."

She retrieved a file from a wall of cabinets. She sat back down at her desk and began reviewing the file. After a moment, she looked up.

"The transcription from the audiotapes that I created during the autopsy has not yet been completed, but I can tell you from my initial notes whatever you might need to know."

"Well, tell me how you identified the body," Collata said.

"Oh, I didn't," she said. "That was done by a forensic dentist. It was a comparison of the decedent's teeth to dental records brought from an outside source."

"Do you know how that happened?"

"No, you'll have to talk with that doctor yourself," she answered, "or get his notes."

"How about the cause of death? How did you come to that conclusion?"

"Well, originally the cause of death was inconclusive," she said. "The body was so badly damaged in the fire that I couldn't be certain. However, I used outside means to come up with a cause."

"What outside means?" Collata asked.

"I used reports and information generated by the police investigation to come to a conclusion."

"So the police tell you what they think happened, and you go along with it?"

"Not quite, Detective. The police reports indicated that the victim was strangled and then incinerated after he was killed. So the injuries from the fire would be postmortem."

"So you wrote up in your report that it was strangulation."

"Well, not quite. What I wrote up was that the precise cause of death was inconclusive, but that it could be consistent with strangulation."

"Would that be manual or ligature strangulation?"

"Well, with the condition of the body," she said, "I can't tell you with any degree of medical certainty what type of strangulation it was. I can't even be sure it's strangulation. I can only say that the death was not inconsistent with strangulation and, based on the information from the police department, I rule this a homicide."

"I see. So what you're saying is that you would not be able to come up with a cause of death if there wasn't a police report available."

"Well, I had no indication that it was accidental or that it was self-inflicted—suicide. So it would either be undetermined or homicide."

Collata was taking notes in a battered plastic notebook. "Can I ask you a hypothetical question?"

"I suppose," she said. "If I can answer it, I will."

"Well, hypothetically, if you found out that the police lied to you about their investigation and that they had no idea whatsoever how this person died, would that change your conclusion?"

"Well, since we're speaking hypothetically, if I came to the conclusion that the police officers' investigation and the comments to me were completely unreliable, then I suppose I would probably change my conclusion from death by homicide to cause of death being inconclusive or undetermined." She closed the file in front of her and held it in her hands. "The transcription of my narrative during the autopsy should be done in a week or two. I think that will be of use to your investigation, Detective."

"You've been very helpful, Doctor. I appreciate your time," Collata said. He reached in his pocket and fished through until he found a business card. He handed it to her. "In case you have any questions or you need to reach me, ma'am, or if there is something you think of that might be useful or not included in your report, please give me a call here. Also, there's a pager."

"I see," Dr. Kim said. She opened the file back up and used a paper clip to put the business card into the file jacket. "If I think of anything, I'll be happy to contact you, Detective."

Collata knew it was a false promise. With the sheer number of cases she handled, she wouldn't give a second thought to this one, unless, of course, she was called to testify. Then she would rely on her notes. Maybe one day she would open the file again, see the card and remember Collata, but barring that, he was sure he would be forgotten by the time she had lunch.

* * *

Hooker Harry was seated across from Darcy with Patrick immediately to his left. Harry was wearing a brown herring-bone jacket and tan slacks with tasseled loafers and textured socks that reminded Darcy of the funky ones so prevalent at Bulls games. "Okay, so what's the damage?" Harry asked.

"Well," Patrick said, "we got a response from the government. They're not interested in giving you immunity, but they did give us a proffer letter. I talked to the U.S. Attorney who's handling the case, Carl Stringer, the gentleman we talked about?"

"Ah, yes," Harry said. "Is he still being reasonable?"

"Quite so. He said he would be happy to have you come in and do a proffer. He would show us documents prior to our starting, documents he intends to ask you questions about, and then he'd allow us fifteen minutes to discuss them among ourselves. It's a good idea to do a limited proffer so we can get an idea of what they want. We'll stop it at any point it gets hairy."

"Where would this proffer take place?" Harry asked.

"Over at his office."

"So what's to prevent them from having a tape recorder running while we're discussing this and getting all the information behind our backs?"

Patrick smiled. "Well, it's against the Department of Justice regulations."

Harry exploded in laughter. "Oh yeah, the Department of Justice. I'm really secure in the fact that they're looking out for my best interests. Come on, I don't trust these guys as far as I can throw them. So what are these documents?" Harry asked.

"I have no idea," Patrick said, "but I'm sure as soon as we see them, we'll know what the thrust of the investigation is."

Harry looked at Patrick. "Patrick, I would like to talk to Darcy alone for a minute."

Patrick was insulted but didn't show it. He gave a wan smile and got up from his chair. "I'll be in my office."

"Darcy," began Harry, "if those documents are receipts from currency exchanges or money orders, I'm screwed. We go over there and there are money order receipts, we got to walk out and regroup." He thought for a moment, then continued. "I don't want to walk into a booby trap."

He got up and started pacing Darcy's office, eventually pausing at the window to stare out into the distance. "There's no way they know. There's no way."

"How do you know what they know?" Darcy asked.

"I'm telling you this, Darcy. I never went to the same currency exchange twice. I would go to post offices, grocery stores, drugstores, currency exchanges—never, never did I go to the same place twice in a row. I had a list of every place that sold money orders. I would start at the beginning of the list and go to the end, crossing them off as I went along. A year or two later, I'd start over again. There's no way they know. As I'd go from place to place, I'd rip the list down. There's no way, no way."

"Well, then, let's go and see what they have," Darcy said. "Let's look at the documents. Let's find out what the focus of this investigation truly is. You've been worried about this, and you want to get this behind you, right? The only way to do that is to actually do it."

Harry walked back and sat in the chair. "All right. I can't live like this. We got to get this over with. But I want you to come with me, not Patrick."

"Patrick is much more experienced in these things."

"I understand, but I want you there."

"How about this?" Darcy said. "How about both of us go? The three of us will go in there and find out what's going on. How's that?"

Harry slid his hand across the table. They shook. "Deal."

Ten

It was about ten after two, and Collata was parked in his van outside Al Maggio's apartment building. He was watching the front door and he could see the Ford Taurus parked nearby. He had checked Maggio's hours at the station—three to eleven—and was waiting to talk to him. He was getting angry. "This goofy jagoff has to be at work at three. He's still in the rack. What a pinhead," he thought.

Finally, the door to the apartment building opened and a disheveled Al Maggio ambled out. Collata popped out and slammed the door. Maggio was eyeing him as he walked away from the van. As Collata approached, a vague look of recognition appeared on Al's face.

"I know you," Maggio said.

"Yeah, Collata. You know me."

"Did you retire?"

"Yeah, I'm retired."

"When did you pull the pin?"

"A few years back. So what are you doing, Maggio?"

"I'm working Area Three. What are you doing here?"

"I came to have a chat with you."

"I don't want to talk to you," Maggio said. "So go fuck yourself."

"Ah, come on, let's talk."

"Screw you," Maggio said. "I ain't got anything to say. What are you, with IAD, OPS, what?"

"No, I'm not with any agency," Collata said. "I'm retired from the job. I'm working as a PI. I want to talk to you about one of your cases."

"Which one?" he asked.

"Marcus Tatum."

"Who?"

"Marcus Tatum. You grabbed him on the South Side and brought him to the North Side. Then you checked him into Northwestern Hospital under an alias. What are you telling me, who? You know who I'm talking about."

"I don't know nothing," Maggio said. "I don't have to talk to you. Why don't you talk to my lawyer?"

"You talk like a defendant," Collata said. "You've been doing this too long, pal. One dick can't talk to a former dick, what's up with that?"

"Up yours. We're not friends," Maggio said.

"Come on, you know me. I just introduced myself. How about if I do it again? I'm Collata," he said putting his hand out for a shake.

"Kiss my ass," Maggio said as he reached in his pocket for his car keys.

Collata leaned in close to him. "Give me five minutes of your time and I won't embarrass you later."

"What is that supposed to mean?"

"Well, I want to know something. Where did you get the dental records from?"

"I don't know. Some family member brought them to me."

"What family member?" Collata asked.

"I don't know. What do you think I am, an encyclopedia? Like I remember everything from every case."

Collata looked him in the eyes. "You don't remember anything from last night?"

"Fuck you."

"Listen, I know you got some personal problems and I don't want to get into that," Collata said. "I just want to talk about this case. Where did you get the dental records? Were they from a dentist in Chicago?"

"Some guy in London," Maggio said.

"London? They don't have dentists in London."

Maggio looked at him with a blank stare. "What are you talking about?"

"Damn, man, didn't you see *Austin Powers*?"

Maggio raised his eyebrows. He didn't get the joke about bad teeth in England.

"It doesn't matter," Collata said. "Do you know the name of this dentist?"

"No."

"Do you know who brought you the records?"

"No."

"Listen, you need to refresh your recollection on this, pal. You and I got to have a conversation."

"Forget your conversation. I got nothing to do with this case. They'll go to the Grand Jury and indict. Two years from now, they'll call me in and ask me to testify if the guy goes to trial. By that time, I'll be retired."

"I don't think so," Collata said. "They're going to do a preliminary hearing on this."

Color began to drain from Maggio's face. Beads of sweat formed on his upper lip. He was visibly shaken. "A preliminary hearing? They don't do preliminary hearings on homicide cases. They just indict them," he stammered.

"No way, pal, not this one. State's Attorney said there are too many questions. So you have a choice, you can talk to me now or you can talk to Darcy Cole under oath."

"Darcy Cole? What's he got to do with this?"

"Darcy Cole is representing Marcus. What, did you think Marcus was going to get a public defender?"

"Shit," Maggio said. "Darcy Cole is a good lawyer."

"Yeah, he's a good lawyer. That's who I work for."

Maggio tried to gather his thoughts. It looked to Collata like the rusty wheels were grinding in Maggio's head. Collata pulled out a cigarette and threw one in his mouth. He offered the pack to Maggio, who absentmindedly pulled one out. Collata drew a lighter and lit Maggio's first, then his.

"Look, I don't want to ask you too many questions," Collata said. "There are some things I don't want to ask and you don't want to tell. When it comes time to your testifying, you'll do what you got to do. I'm not interested in blowing up everything out here on the street. I want to know who you got the dental records from because I need to talk to that person."

Maggio felt trapped. He wanted to give a little bit to get a little distance.

"Some broad brought them to me. Supposed to be the girl-friend of the dead guy. The name is Anaka Vanderlinden. She's a South African broad, good-looking. You know the type—money her whole life, money forever. They can't look at a guy like me without being disgusted."

Collata didn't say what he was thinking. He just asked, "Where can I find her?"

"I don't know. She gave me some address and phone numbers. I don't know where they are, somewhere in the file. Your lawyer friend can subpoena them."

"Are they in the street file?" Collata asked.

"Sure, where else would they be?"

"You're not saving them for yourself, thinking you might be able to go and romance this broad?"

Maggio took a heavy drag on his cigarette that burned three quarters of it down. He let the smoke rest deep in his lungs before he blew it out. "Shit, she wouldn't give me a roll. I'm telling you this broad is all yachts and tennis clubs. You know what I mean?"

Collata said nothing, which made Maggio feel awkward and nervous.

"Anyway, this country club–looking broad comes in to see me one day and she says that her boyfriend is missing. I start an investigation, bing, bang, boom, I'm on Marcus Tatum. He comes into the station with me. He confesses after he realizes he's nailed on the murder. He goes off on me, and we get into a little tussle. I lump him up a little bit in self-defense, you know, nothing more than justifiable use of force to repel an attack from a detainee."

Collata nodded. "Why did you bring the guy to Northwestern Hospital? You didn't think anyone would find out?"

Maggio didn't have an answer to that one.

"You brought him in under an assumed name. You didn't think anyone would check or that he wouldn't tell anyone about it?"

Maggio looked away. "Hey, the guy got medical treatment. What the fuck do you want from me?"

"You know this is going to get ugly," Collata said.

"Hey, wait a minute," Maggio said. "I got a little more than two years and I'm out. If they indict this like they're supposed to, then I'm home free. The lawyers get in there and dick around for a couple of years—asking for discovery, further discovery, independent testing, and then they do all the motions. Two, three years later, I'm done. You know how it goes, especially when you get a judge with a heavy call that's backed up. A lawyer like Darcy Cole is going to cross all the T's and dot all the I's. They can't do a preliminary hearing on this."

"Well, they said they're thinking about doing it," Collata said.

"Who are you talking to, some snot-nose State's Attorney three years out of law school?"

Collata took a drag of the cigarette and was talking as the smoke soaked into his lungs. "No, Jack Karsten, the head of the Homicide Sex Unit. He said he's thinking about doing a preliminary hearing," Collata said, and blew the rest of the smoke out.

"I guess I got to see Karsten," Maggio said. "So where do we stand?"

"What? You mean me and you?" Collata asked.

"Yeah, what are you going to do about this?"

"What can I do? I had a conversation with you with no prover, just the two of us. Your word against mine."

Maggio nodded. "That's it, huh? That's the professional courtesy. I give you some background information, let you do your investigation, and you leave me alone?"

"Hey, come on," Collata said. "I'm not here to bury you. I'm just here to do what I have to do."

"Yeah, you got your pension and now you're working for this guy. Making a lot of money, I bet."

"Listen," Collata said. "Let me give you a piece of advice. You don't need to reach your full thirty, you don't have to reach your full age to retire. You got a lot of years in. You retire now, yeah, maybe it'll cost you a point and a half, or maybe you can't draw for a year or two because you haven't hit the age, but you lock in your pension. That's forever. You do something stupid and you mess it up—all those years for nothing. You know what I'm saying?"

"Yeah, I know what you're saying," Maggio said. "If I pull the pin and run, I'll lock in my pension, but then you'll win this case because it looks like I ran scared."

"No, forget this case," Collata said. "This guy's just one of many. You got to figure out what you're going to do with your life."

"You think I'm stupid?" Maggio said, his voice getting louder.

"You're a mess. You're drinking, doing drugs, staying up all night, living in a rat hole, driving a piece-of-shit car. You got to be making seventy grand a year with overtime. I look around and see you living like a ghetto rat. So you don't think I know what's going on?"

"Hey, fuck you. I don't need you talking to me like you're my father."

"I'm not your father. I'm just a cop who had his ass to the fire once himself. You pull out now and you walk away. You get another job and do something else. Get straight. You'll have your pension and insurance benefits for the rest of your life. Don't mess it up," Collata said. "I've seen too many guys gone because twenty-six years into it, they get their tit in the ringer and can't see a way out. Don't be stupid, man. What you got to do is take care of yourself, take care of your pension. Don't let any of these pissants screw you up."

Maggio smoked his cigarette down to the butt, dropped it on

the ground, and crushed it. Collata finished his and flicked it into the grass.

"Look, what I'm saying is this. Anyone who's been a copper knows there are certain times you need to hide. I'm looking at this case as a private detective working for a great defense attorney, an honorable man. The State's Attorney walks up to us and says that he's head of the Homicide Sex Unit, that he's going to handle this case personally and he's thinking of giving us a preliminary hearing. Was there one preliminary hearing on a homicide case in twenty-five years? To me, my friend, that's what we call a clue. I know this, when they start looking to help a defendant in a homicide case at the expense of a detective, I got to figure that detective's got to take stock of himself."

"Thanks for the advice," said Maggio sarcastically.

Collata was angry with his tone. "Hey, blow me. I'd say a word to the wise, but you ain't wise."

Maggio brushed by Collata gingerly, opened his car and threw his briefcase onto the seat next to him. He looked back at Collata. "I'll give it some thought."

"That Anaka Vanderlinden," Collata said. "I want her address or phone number, beeper, cell, I don't give a damn. Give me a way to find her."

"I'll think about that too," Maggio said as he slammed the door.

Eleven

The cab dropped Darcy off on the street some fifty feet from the entrance to the emergency room. He was wearing a gray pinstriped suit and carrying a black nylon briefcase. As he started walking toward the entrance, he noticed two Chicago police squad cars parked on the tarmac outside. There was a fire department ambulance directly in front of the entrance. Two sets of double doors swung open automatically, and Darcy entered. He walked in and greeted a nurse who was behind the counter.

"Hi, I'm looking for Dr. Amy Wagner."

"And your name?" the nurse asked.

"My name is Darcy Cole. She told me she'd be on duty and that I could stop in and she would see me when she had a free moment."

"All right," she said, "let me page her for you."

Darcy glanced around the emergency room. He saw four people—two men and two women wearing scrubs—in the midst of an intense conversation some thirty feet away. In the distance he heard a woman's voice, a doctor or a nurse, talking to an elderly patient behind a drawn curtain. It had been less than a minute when he heard someone call to him.

"Mr. Cole?"

He turned and saw Dr. Amy Wagner for the first time.

He felt as if he'd been knocked off balance. He guessed her to be in her mid- to late forties. Her eyes were bright and warm. She wore no makeup and had her hair pulled back. When she smiled, small wrinkles appeared around the corners of her mouth. Darcy liked them. They suited her. She had a natural beauty about her.

"You came at a good time," she said.

Darcy brought himself back to reality and shook hands with her. "Thank you for seeing me, Doctor."

"Let's go some place where we can sit down," she said.

They walked side by side. Darcy was annoyed to discover that he suddenly felt nervous; he tried desperately to think of something brilliant or witty to say.

"You never know what it's going to be like," she said. "Sometimes we're busy the entire shift, then other times it's like this, pretty quiet."

Darcy was thankful she'd taken the initiative in the conversation. "I suppose it's better to be busy," he said. "It goes faster."

"Yes and no. A steady stream is fine, but if it gets too busy, you have to worry about making mistakes."

They reached a room Darcy assumed was a doctors' lounge. They pushed through the door and entered.

"Would you like some coffee?" she asked.

"No, thank you," Darcy said.

"Do you mind if I have a cup?"

"Not at all."

"That was a silly question," she said. "I don't know why, but I'm feeling a bit nervous around you."

Darcy smiled, "Don't be. I just need to know about the patient you treated."

She poured herself a cup of coffee, then gestured toward the table with her hand. Darcy sat down, opened his briefcase, and pulled out his leather-covered notepad. He also pulled out Dr. Wagner's folder of Marcus Tatum's records of medical treatment. He took a photograph of Marcus' face and slid it across the table.

She looked at it and said, "Yes, that's him."

Darcy asked all the same questions that Collata had and got all the same answers. It only took a few mintues for Darcy to realize that Dr. Wagner would be a strong witness. She remembered everything that had happened, and she was very clear on details. It soon became very clear to Darcy, though, that he was interested in more than Dr. Wagner's connection to the Marcus Tatum case. He was trying to figure out a way to veer the conversation toward her personal life. He was curious about her. He felt a strong attraction to her, but he was nervous. He found himself examining her. Other than a pair of diamond stud earrings, she wore no jewelry. No wedding band. He presumed that it was because of her work, but he wasn't sure.

"So what kind of hours do you work?" Darcy asked, pulling himself away from his silent observations.

"Well, it depends," she said. "I work eight-hour shifts, sometimes ten- or twelve-hour shifts. It depends on what I want to do. I usually work about fifty hours a week. That's what I am comfortable with."

"What do you do when you're not working?" Darcy asked, and surprised himself with his forwardness.

She smiled. "What do you do when you're not working?" she asked back.

Darcy was again knocked off balance.

She said, "I'm kidding. It's a hard question to answer. I have a lot of interests." She paused and thought about it. "Let's see, I go to yoga three times a week, I exercise quite a bit, and I enjoy music. I have season tickets to the symphony."

"I used to have tickets to the symphony," Darcy said, "but I let them lapse."

"That's a pity," she said. "I also enjoy going to the art museum. . . ."

"The Art Institute or the Museum of Contemporary Art?" Darcy jumped in.

She laughed at his eagerness. "I really don't consider the Museum of Contemporary Art in the same league as the Art Institute, do you?"

"No, I suppose not. I prefer the impressionists myself."

"Oh, and I like to read. I spent most of my marriage putting together this incredible book collection. Since my kids are all out of the house now, I just started to read it," she said with a laugh.

"Is your husband a reader?" Darcy asked awkwardly.

"So you want to know if I'm single?" she asked.

Darcy felt a bit of sweat starting. "Was it that obvious?" he asked.

"I'm afraid so, but sweet nonetheless. I'm divorced," she said. "My husband moved on to greener pastures."

"Greener pastures?" Darcy said. "What would that be?"

"Don't you mean, *who* would that be? Can't you guess? He traded me in for a newer model. Some men are prone to do that, don't you know. How about you? Are you on your trophy wife?" she asked.

Darcy almost felt a blush coming on. "No, I'm afraid not."

"So, are you married?" she asked.

"No, I'm afraid not," Darcy said again.

"Are you widowed or divorced?"

"Well kind of, sort of both. My wife left me, then she died."

"Sorry to hear that," Dr. Wagner said.

A sly grin came over Darcy's face, and Amy was prompted to ask, "What's so funny?"

"Well, you know," Darcy said. "If we were to go out," he said hesitantly, "people would assume you're my trophy wife."

She started laughing. "I guess I'm lacking perspective then, huh?"

There was a knock on the door and a male nurse popped his head in.

"Doctor, we have an accident with multiple injuries on the way. We're going to need you."

"I'll be right there," she said.

Darcy stood and faced her. There was an awkward moment. He was trying to figure out a way to ask her out. He was running possibilities through his mind.

She smiled. "It was very nice meeting you," she said.

"Yes, it was nice meeting you, too. I hope to see you soon," he said.

She looked at him with her head slightly tilted to one side. "Well," she said, giving him ample pause to ask the question. When he failed miserably, standing there shifting uncomfortably, she finished her sentence. "I've got to get to work. It was nice meeting you, Mr. Cole."

They shook hands and she walked out of the room. The door shut, and Darcy was furious with himself.

Stupid, stupid, stupid, he repeated in his head. He was pacing angrily. She wanted you to ask her out, you idiot, and you stood there like a moron.

In the cab on the way back to the office, he stared out the window, deep in thought. I blew it, was all he could think. When the anger began to subside, he thought, I suppose I could call her. Just say, Hey, this is Darcy Cole. I was wondering if you would like to have dinner with me sometime. He tried to purge the thoughts from his mind. He had been awkward. He had blown a golden opportunity. The instant hope returned, he told himself, he would go back to the office and tell Kathy everything that had happened in minute detail. She'd be able to help him. She knew a woman's perspective. She knew him. She'd be able to advise him.

* * *

An unlit cigarette dangled from Collata's mouth. "So what do you want me to do?" he asked, bouncing his cigarette up and down.

Kathy sat at her desk looking across at him—his cowboy boots on her desk, his cigarette in his mouth, his hands resting behind his bald head with his elbows out.

"I don't know," she said. "I'll give you all the information on him, and I guess I want you to find out what he's up to."

Collata dropped his feet down and stood up. He went through his pockets until he found a lighter. He lit a cigarette, took a deep inhale, and then blew the smoke out through his nose. He pulled his cigarette out and rubbed the corners of his mouth with his fingers.

"I'll do it," he said. "I don't think it's a good idea, but I'll do it."

"I don't want him to see you," she said. "You know he's met you four years in a row at the office Christmas party."

"Yeah, yeah, yeah," Collata said. "I know, discreet."

"No, not discreet," she said. "I want you deep undercover. Deep, deep undercover."

"You sound like an Eddie Murphy movie," Collata said, throwing the cigarette back in this mouth and taking another inhale.

He leaned back and blew the smoke straight up into the air. Kathy wrote some things down on a piece of paper, then ripped it off of the yellow notepad.

"Here's our address. Here's his car. Here's the license plate. Mondays and Thursdays is when he goes out. He gets home from work, and he waits for me to get home, then he heads out."

Collata looked it over, folded it, and stuffed it into his shirt pocket.

"What else?" he asked.

"That's it. He's not going to be hard to follow," she said. "He's a high school English teacher, for Christ's sake."

Collata reached across the desk and patted her hand. "It is going to be okay, kid. He couldn't possibly be dicking around on you."

"I don't know, but I guess we're going to find out soon enough."

Twelve

Marcus Tatum was sitting in the reception area when Darcy walked in.

"Hey, Marcus," Darcy said, walking backward toward the office. "I'll be with you shortly."

"No problem, boss," Marcus said.

As Darcy walked into the office, Irma passed him a stack of messages. Darcy grabbed them without a missed step.

"Nothing important," she said. "The mail is on your desk—also nothing important."

Darcy had his career, which made him feel vital and engaged. Although he had dated periodically, he had never made a real connection with anyone. He included his ex-wife in that category. He spent every holiday alone and with the exception of his daughter had never been able to completely open up. There was something about Amy Wagner that gave him hope. He felt an energy and excitement when he was next to her. He had Seymour, Collata, and the gang at the office but there was always a barrier that had never been breached. It was easier for him to pour a drink and stare out of his window than to take the risks involved with real human contact. Thinking about Amy, Darcy was determined to take any risk to be with her.

He walked into his office and threw his briefcase on top

of his desk. Pulling his jacket off and hanging it behind his door, he turned and looked out over the lake for a sense of peace and comfort. It was a warm summer day, with boats everywhere. The lake was so flat, it looked for a minute like one of those cheap postcards you buy on State Street—picture perfect. But he couldn't stop blaming himself for blowing it with Amy.

He heard a knock and turned. "Kathy, come in. Come in. Shut the door behind you."

She was surprised at the sense of urgency. "What's up?" she asked.

"Sit down. I need to ask you something."

He told her about his visit with Dr. Wagner.

"I see," she said. "A little tongue-tied, huh?"

"I was retarded," Darcy said. "So what do I do now?"

"Well," Kathy answered, "there's this new thing people have been trying. It's called courting. Seems to be working miracles. And then there's this invention I heard something about. I think it's called the telephone. You pick it up. You call her at work, and you say, 'Hey, I was a little nervous the day I met you, but I really wanted to ask you out to dinner. How about it?'"

"I know what she'll say, that she doesn't date retards."

"Darcy, you weren't retarded. You were just a little nervous. She probably thought it was sweet."

"Sweet, if you're in high school," Darcy replied. "I'm eligible for AARP!"

"You want me to call her and ask her out for you?" Kathy teased. "Maybe I can just call her and say, 'Darcy thinks you're cute. Do you think Darcy's cute?' And then I could go back and forth between you two until we build up to, 'Do you want to wear his ID bracelet?'"

"Come on," he said. "I'm already beating myself up here. I need you to help me."

"Okay, first of all, is she single?"

"Well, yeah, she told me she was divorced."

"Does she have anyone in her life?"

"I don't know, I was asking her a question, and she just

busted me. She said, 'If you want to know if I am single, I'm divorced.'"

"Good!" she said. "That means she's telling you she's available."

"How's that?" Darcy asked.

"Because she would have said she was seeing someone or that she's in a relationship. She wouldn't have just said, divorced. She would have shut you down if she wasn't interested. Just pick up the phone and call her," she advised him.

"All right," he said. "Think of something brilliant for me to say, will ya?"

"You don't have to be brilliant. Just be honest. You're a nice man, Darcy. You're smart and handsome and successful—you're a great catch. Just call her up and say you'd like to take her to dinner or to lunch."

"How about a movie?"

"No," she said. "You don't take a woman to a movie on your first date. You sit there in the dark and have no conversation. Take her for coffee."

"I don't know if I can do this," Darcy said. "I don't know what the rules are anymore."

"Darcy, take her someplace where you can talk, and just be yourself. If you're going to get along, you'll have to get to know each other, the real each other."

"Okay," he said. "I'm going to talk to Marcus Tatum, then afterward I am going to give her a call."

"Attaboy, Darcy. Way to go," Kathy said. "Who knows, you might end up having fun, and fun is a good thing."

"Okay, get out of here," he said. "Send Mr. Tatum in."

* * *

Darcy ignored the chiming of his rubber watch. Today wasn't a normal routine for Darcy. Today's workout was for exorcising the demons working on his soul. He swam harder, faster, and longer, trying to punish himself for the emotional ineptitude he'd displayed with Amy Wagner. After a restless night and the drive to the gym, he still couldn't come up with the right thing to say to her. He thought about Kathy and what she'd said. He thought about what he should have said when he had the chance—like, 'How about dinner sometime?' and maybe she would have helped him out. He felt inadequate, rusty, and old. He took a flip turn and then swam another length of the pool as hard as he could, then another flip turn and an all-out assault to the end. He touched out and stopped, floating backward to throw his arms across the ropes—leaning his head back to look up at the ceiling of the pool. He wondered why mold didn't collect on the ceiling, then scolded himself for being such a moron. He still hadn't called Amy Wagner. Swimming to the ladder and climbing out, he quickly pulled his suit off, toweled dry, and put on a robe.

He sat down to breakfast and the *Sun-Times*. He couldn't concentrate so he pitched it on the chair at the table next to him—on top of the *Tribune* he'd picked up but hadn't bothered to look at. He watched as his friend, the federal bankruptcy judge, emerged from the locker room and put one foot into the water to test the temperature. The judge waved over at Darcy and Darcy nodded back. Summoning his courage, the judge dived into the pool and began a nice gentle swim to the other side, without concentration or focus. Darcy watched him paddle and picked at his breakfast until he gave up. He was restless and angry. Tired of trying to create some brilliant, witty banter, Darcy resolved to call Amy immediately. He skipped his steam, took a quick shower and got dressed.

In the elevator on the way down, three men and a woman dressed in business attire, with what appeared to be convention badges pinned to them, got on at the twelfth floor. They must have been overnight guests, Darcy thought. They were in fine spirits as they headed to their business meeting. Darcy leaned back in the corner of the elevator, trying to make himself invisible. The four of them were discussing the highlights of the previous night's festivities. From what Darcy could catch, they'd started with dinner and ended with drinks at one of Chicago's trendy clubs. Darcy had spent the night reading a biography of the late Mayor Daley. Darcy had never stayed in one of the guest rooms at the club. He added that to the list of things he needed to do sometime in his life. Finally, the elevator opened and the four guests exploded into the lobby. Darcy slinked out.

Darcy got to his office before Irma again. Walking by the reception area, he hung his coat on a hook behind the door. He turned and walked toward the window, looking out at the expanse of the lake that filled the horizon. The sun cast a beautiful glimmer on the water. Boats already in the water skimmed its surface, leaving perfect wakes behind them. Suddenly, Darcy felt a stabbing pain in his lower left back. He put his hand on it and rubbed. The pain subsided a bit and then returned, almost like a wave itself. Darcy bent over.

Jesus, he thought. He suspected his extra-vigorous swimming had pulled a muscle, and he tried to sit down. The pain intensified and he doubled over. He couldn't straighten up, so he walked over to the couch and flopped facedown onto it. The pain was steadily intensifying. He heard a guttural moan that he realized was coming from him.

This is not good, he thought. Darcy heard Irma come through the front door and heard her shoes across the hardwood floor. He heard the door open. He was gritting his teeth and moaning when Irma came to the threshold of his office.

"Darcy, are you okay?"

"No," he managed.

She rushed over to him. "What's going on?"

"Call an ambulance," he said.

Irma quickly dialed 9-1-1 from Darcy's desk. After what seemed like a standardized-test-length series of questions by the operator, Irma finally screamed, "Send a goddamn ambulance now. The man is in pain."

Not knowing what else to do, Irma got some wet paper towels from the bathroom and held them against Darcy's forehead. Darcy was curled up in a fetal position, teeth clenched. He continued moaning as the pain came in steady spurts, as if someone was poking him in the back with an ice pick. When the paramedics came crashing into the office, Irma ran out to meet them and waved them in. One of the paramedics, a short

African-American woman, leaned down to Darcy as she put gloves on.

"Can you tell me what's happening?" she asked.

He tried to explain his symptoms in between moans and grunts. She used a stethoscope to hear his heart. Then she put it on his back to hear his lungs.

"What's your name?" she said.

Irma answered, "Darcy Cole."

"Okay, Darcy," the paramedic said, "we're going to take you to the hospital."

"What's happening?" he asked.

"Well, I'm not a doctor," she said, "but I've done a lot of runs, and it sounds to me like you're having a kidney stone move on you."

Darcy rolled his eyes. "Kidney stone?"

They got Darcy onto the stretcher. They rolled him to the elevator and out through the loading dock to an ambulance waiting on Federal Street. Darcy was having something like an out-of-body experience. He was aware of what was going on, but he was strangely detached from it. He was in a zone, focused not just on the pain, but on someplace else where there was no pain.

The ambulance went north on Dearborn, over the river, then east until it pulled up to the emergency room at Northwestern Hospital—the same emergency room Darcy had visited one day earlier—the same emergency room where he had made a fool of himself with Dr. Wagner. They rolled him through the double doors and into an area where they pulled curtains around him.

A nurse ran in. "Well, Mr. Cole, welcome to Northwestern."

She was setting up an IV and talking to him at the same time. "Your secretary called and gave us all your insurance information. We understand you're having a bad time of it. I'm going to set up an IV drip. Do you understand?"

Darcy nodded.

"We're going to give you something for the pain," she said in a loud voice. "Have you ever had a kidney stone before?"

Darcy shook his head.

"Well, if that's what this is, you're in for a treat," she said. "It's going to be the male equivalent to giving birth."

She was using her finger to pat Darcy's forearm looking for a vein. She found something she liked, jabbed the needle in, and tapped it into his forearm. She pulled a couple of switches and the fluid began to drip. Then she took a syringe off a metal tray and squeezed a little juice out of it.

"Okay, I'm going to give you something for the pain," she said.

She stuck it into a y-joint on the tube that led into Darcy's arm and pumped the sedative in.

"You're going to be feeling a lot better pretty soon. I'll be back in a second," she said. "Hang in there."

Darcy's body began to feel soft and his thoughts were becoming fuzzy. He was curled up in a ball on his side and was staring at the wall directly across from him. The nurse came back and checked on him.

"How are you feeling?"

"I'm not sure," he said. "Better, I guess."

"Still feeling the pain?"

"Yes, but it feels distant, farther away."

She smiled. "How about if I kick it up a notch so you don't feel anything?"

Darcy nodded.

"Okay, here it goes," she said, jamming another needle into the same y-joint she had used earlier. She emptied the syringe into it.

"You're going to feel much better. I promise," she said.

In moments Darcy was aware that he was still there but that his body wasn't. He didn't feel anything. The pain was gone, but he remained curled in a ball on the side of his bed. The curtain flew open again and there was Dr. Amy Wagner.

"Well, well, well," she said. "Back to see me, eh? You know, Darcy," she said, "I was actually hoping for dinner, or maybe the theater, a walk, drinks, but no, this is how we end up spending our first date."

Darcy would have managed a chuckle, but he wasn't in control of his body anymore. "What's going on?" he asked.

"Well, I think you have a kidney stone. What we're going to do is take you for an x-ray and a CT scan. We're going to see if we can find that bad boy," she said.

"Are you going to be with me?"

"Oh, I'll be around. Don't worry, I'll keep an eye on you."

She motioned for help, and a young man in hospital greens came in. He pulled the IV bag and hooked it onto Darcy's bed. He used his foot to depress a pedal and said, "Let's roll, Mr. Cole," then pushed him out.

Darcy had to roll from his bed onto the table for an x-ray and then back onto his bed to go for another ride to get the CT scan. Again he had to roll off his bed and lie still while his body was scanned. Then he rolled back onto his bed and was brought back to his room. Moments later, Amy Wagner came in and threw an x-ray onto the light board. She used a pen to make an imaginary circle around a white spot on the x-ray.

"You see that, my friend?"

Darcy looked at it from his bed.

"That is a kidney stone. A big kidney stone."

"What do we do?" Darcy asked.

"Well, a urologist on duty is coming down, and he's going to tell us," she began. "With some of these, we can drop the patient into a tub of water and break it up using sound waves. Unfortunately, when we see one this big, we usually can't do that because when we break it up into little pieces, instead of one big kidney stone, we have several little kidney stones. A stone this big probably won't pass on its own, which means we're going to have to go through your urethra and remove it."

Darcy wasn't thrilled with his options. "I just want to make this clear. By urethra, you mean through my penis, right?" he asked.

"That's it," she said. "They go up with a little instrument that has, for lack of a better term, a tiny basket on the end of it. They grab the stone, pull it through, and then you're a happy man."

Just then a short, balding doctor walked in. "Hello, Mr. Cole, I'm Dr. Rosenblatt. I'm a urologist."

The doctor turned to the board and looked at the x-ray. He had the results of the CT scan with him, and he showed them to Dr. Wagner.

"Mr. Cole," he said, kneeling so he could be closer to Darcy. "We're going to have to perform surgery on you. I see no reason to wait, so let's alleviate this pain as soon as possible. Right now, you're on some pain medication. What we're going to do is take you to the OR. Through the IV you already have going, we'll administer anesthesia. The surgery is nothing more than going up through your urethra, retrieving the stone and then placing a stent. A stent is a long piece of plastic, kind of like a straw, that we leave in so that the swelling caused by irritation to the urethra doesn't cause your urinary tract to swell shut. Do you understand?"

Darcy nodded.

"Then in a day or two, we remove the stent and you're as good as new. Does that sound like a good plan to you, Mr. Cole?"

Darcy nodded. "Anything. Just get me better."

"I'll do my best," he said.

Thirteen

There was a voice in the distance. Darcy could hear it although it was too faint for him to recognize it. He didn't have any interest in the voice. He was someplace distant and foreign but he liked it.

Suddenly the voice got louder and he began to drift toward it. "Darcy, Darcy, wake up. Darcy."

Darcy opened his eyes and saw a person he'd never seen before saying his name.

"Hi, Mr. Cole. Darcy, hello. Wake up. Wake up."

He was having difficulty focusing. He was trying to identify the voice.

"Mr. Cole, you had surgery. It's time to wake up now."

Slowly regaining his senses, Darcy began to remember where he was and what had happened to him.

"Mr. Cole, are you there? Darcy, wake up."

"Yeah, yeah, I'm here," he said in a tired voice. Darcy had been in a better place. He didn't really want to come back, but this person was insistent.

"Mr. Cole, wake up, wake up."

"I'm thirsty," Darcy replied.

"Welcome back," the man said. "I'll get you an ice chip. The thirst probably is from having a tube down your throat. How do you feel?"

Darcy was still disoriented. The face before him was fuzzy.

"Are you okay? Hello, Mr. Cole. Are you there?"

Yeah, I'm here, Darcy thought, but you're really starting to get on my nerves, whoever you are. Why don't you just leave me alone and let me sleep?

"We've got to get you up," the man said. "Time to take you back to your room. The operation went well."

Darcy saw a clock on the wall. Six-twelve. He guessed it was evening. He'd gotten to the hospital sometime before eight-thirty in the morning. That much he knew. But he had apparently lost a few hours. He had the faint recollection of a happy place, somewhere better than earth. He was now conscious enough to realize he was sucking on an ice chip and that they were rolling him out of the recovery room. They rolled him onto an elevator, down a corridor and into another room. He could see a television hanging from the ceiling, a table with a telephone on it and a window with a view of the city facing west. Darcy was helped onto the bed, and a woman appeared.

"Hello. My name is Erin. I'm going to be your nurse," she said, walking over to a white bulletin board and using a grease pencil to write her name. "If you need anything, call me."

She walked over to Darcy and pulled the covers up to his chest.

"You're going to have to go to the bathroom a lot," she said, and pointed to a door just to his right. "When you do," she continued, "just roll this along with you." She put her hand on the long pole of the cart from which his IV dangled. "You're going to feel some discomfort at first, but it'll dissipate over time."

Nurse Erin showed him how to work the controls on the TV and how to call out on the telephone. Then she scurried away to get a pitcher of ice for Darcy.

* * *

It was a little after 9 P.M. Darcy was pacing around his room, pushing the IV cart. The TV was on, but he wasn't paying attention to it. He stopped and stared out over the city. Then there was a light knock on the door and Amy Wagner walked in, carrying a couple of bags.

"Hello," she said. "How are you feeling?"

"I feel like I've been beaten up," Darcy said.

"I thought you might be hungry, so I stopped by Maggiano's and picked up a couple of chicken Caesar salads and some bread."

"Bless your heart," Darcy said. "Now I don't have to eat this prison food."

Amy looked over at the tray. "Of course. He's got you on the liquid diet. I should've realized. I feel so stupid. I can't let you eat this! I'll just take it out to the nurses' station so you don't have to look at it."

"No, no! You should eat it even if I can't," Darcy protested.

"Are you sure? I'd hate to tempt you like that."

"No, really. The next best thing to eating a Maggiano's chicken Caesar salad is watching a beautiful woman eat one." He sat down, making sure to tuck his gown securely underneath him, and pulled the table over. "Voila," he said with a sweep of his hand. "Just like the table in Charlie Trotter's kitchen."

Amy smiled and reached into one of the bags and pulled out a salad and a little sealed bag of plasticware—knife, fork, spoon, and a napkin. She laid them delicately on the table, along with a baguette and a handful of individually wrapped pats of butter. Then she picked up a second bag off the floor and produced a bottle of mineral water, which she placed on the table with fanfare. "We can at least split this. Do you have ice?" she asked, smiling.

Darcy pointed over his shoulder with his thumb toward the windowsill. Amy walked over and collected the pitcher of ice and cups the nurse had provided, then poured two drinks.

"No wine?" Darcy asked.

"Ha," Amy said. "You know you can't drink alcohol here."

Darcy looked around. "That's a shame," he said. "It seems to me this would be the perfect place to drink it."

Darcy watched as Amy ate her salad. It felt so comfortable, the two of them sitting there, that he almost forgot he was wearing a hospital gown that was open in the back. Almost.

"So, why didn't you ask me out that day in the ER?" she asked without looking at him.

Darcy swallowed uncomfortably. "Wow, you get right to the point, don't you?"

"I'm too old to play games," she said. "I thought you were attracted to me."

"Oh, uh, I am. I most certainly am attracted to you."

"So, why didn't you ask me out? I gave you the opportunity."

Darcy smiled. "Why didn't you ask me out?"

"Well, I guess I have now," she said, "but why didn't you ask me first?"

Darcy sighed, "I choked. No, I panicked, blew it. I, I . . ."

"You mean, you didn't ask me out because you couldn't find the right words?" she asked, laughing.

"I suppose that's it," Darcy said.

She smiled. "Darcy, you strike me as the kind of man who is rarely at a loss for words. Look at what you do for a living, for heaven's sake! You couldn't just say, 'Hey, how about dinner' or 'Let's have a cup of coffee'?"

Darcy looked like he was in pain. "You know, it's easy to do something when you don't really care about the outcome. But the first time it becomes important, it raises the bar to a whole new level."

She looked deeply into his eyes. Darcy was having trouble holding her gaze. "Well, then," she said, "I think we should just take our time, relax, and get to know each other."

Darcy smiled. "Oh, I've got plenty of time," he said.

"So let's start at the beginning. Tell me everything," she said. "What's your first memory? Where were you born? What was your family like? Where did you grow up? How was your childhood? All that stuff."

Darcy exhaled. "Can I drink my dinner first?"

They both laughed.

Amy was wearing her hospital attire—blue scrubs and a gray overcoat with her name embroidered on the chest. A stethoscope nestled in her oversized pocket, and her photo ID tag hung from her lapel.

"How long can you stay?" he asked.

"Well my shift starts at 7:00 tomorrow morning, so I probably shouldn't stay too late, but I think I know where you'll be for the next few days at least," she said, smiling.

"Okay," he said, "you start. Tell me about yourself. Are you from Chicago originally?"

"I spent my early years in Powell, Ohio, a suburb of Columbus. My father worked at Ohio State University."

"Football coach?" Darcy asked.

"Afraid not," she said. "He was a professor in behavioral sciences and then he became a dean."

"Then where?" he asked.

"Then we moved to Appleton, Wisconsin."

"What's in Appleton, Wisconsin?"

"Lawrence University," she said. "My father became president there."

"Wow, how old were you then?" Darcy asked.

"Eleven," she said.

"So you spent most of your childhood in those two towns?"

"Basically," she said. "They were both really nice places to grow up in. In Appleton, I did a lot of outdoor sports—skiing, mostly, both cross-country and downhill. We had a boat, so I water-skied too. Oh, and running. It was a wonderful environment."

"So what brought you to Chicago?" he asked.

"Medical school."

"Ah, and you never left?"

"Well, you know, the best hospitals are usually in the big cities—they have the money to pay the best practitioners."

"So you sold out for the money, huh?"

"Not really. I had an opportunity to practice medicine at a great hospital, and I took it. Of course, the fact that I married a classmate from medical school might have had something to do with it."

"So then what?" Darcy asked.

"Well, two children and a house in Evanston. My husband worked at Evanston Hospital, and I worked at a few other hospitals before coming here. Then my husband started the male menopause thing. When we moved from a modest house in Evanston to a really expensive one in Winnetka, every month became a challenge. So my husband started working more and more hours, and so did I. I took the kids to cello practice, acting and art classes, soccer—the full catastrophe, as Zorba the Greek said. Pretty soon the money was good, but I never saw my husband. And after a while, it became clear that he wasn't working as many hours as he said he was, and that he didn't really need to go to as many seminars as he did. Finally, I learned the truth, and he left."

"So then what happened?" Darcy asked.

"He was very generous in the divorce settlement, despite the fact that his young chippy was angry with him for giving me anything. After all, I was a doctor, and our twelve years of marriage together didn't really mean anything to her. It will be interesting to see what happens when he moves on from her in a few years. And you?" she asked.

"Well, I grew up in the city, got married young, right out of college. Seemed like a good idea at the time. We had a little girl, and I put myself through law school working full-time and taking classes at night. Straight out of law school, I went to work for the State's Attorney's office. Made no money, but I was thrilled to death. I enjoyed going to work every day. I rose through the ranks there—tried some good cases against good lawyers. And then one of the premier criminal defense lawyers in the city called me up one day and said, 'I'm getting too old for this shit; c'mon, practice with me. I need young blood.' So I went to work with him. Almost five years later he died and left me the practice."

"Aha," she said. "So you were the one that sold out for the money!"

"Hey! Well, all right, the money was better. Anyway, in those five years I tried a lot of high-profile cases, and when he died, we didn't miss a beat. I mean, with the caliber of work. So, in effect, I took over his practice."

"Nice," she said. "Then what?"

"Well, I spent a lot of time on my practice. My wife had left me, so I had nothing but the practice."

"And your daughter?"

"Oh, yeah, she took her. Moved to New York."

"That must have been hard on you. Were you close to her?"

"Extremely close," Darcy said. "She was my world. I think that's why my wife made a point of going as far away as she could."

"How did your wife die?" Amy asked.

"Ovarian cancer. I'm told it was ugly at the end."

"You didn't see her?"

"No, I was cut out of her life. Her new husband didn't want anything to do with me or have me around at all. He saw me as a threat, I guess. I got to see my daughter, but more often than not, we'd arrange it without his knowing. I'd fly up and spend the day with her. As I say, it was pretty uncomfortable for everyone, dealing with his insecurities."

"I could see how he'd feel insecure," she said. "You are quite a force."

"I'm not sure I know what that means," Darcy answered. "But anyway, that's all water under the bridge."

"Water under the bridge. Boy, you sound like John Wayne when you say things like that," she teased.

"I don't know how else to see it," he said. "It's over. My daughter's grown. She's a lovely, smart, strong, independent, and successful woman. There's nothing else for me to do now except go forward. How about you? What are your children doing?"

"Well, my son is a student at the Art Institute and my daughter is at Illinois Wesleyan."

"It sounds like they're doing okay."

"I put a lot of effort into them. I went back to emergency medicine because the hours were manageable. I worked a lot of nights and weekends so I could be with them during the week, take them to their various lessons and appointments. They love me. They're good kids. And they seem to have a reasonable relationship with their father, too."

"What's his relationship like with you?"

She laughed. "What relationship? He and I are cordial to one another. I pity him a little. I mean, I don't think he'll ever be happy. Really, it was all for the best that he and I divorced. I think I was in denial for a long time, trying to keep up appearances, but now I've made a life for myself. I'm doing more to make myself a whole, fulfilled person." She sat on the bed next to him and put her arm around him, rubbing his shoulder blade. "How are you doing? Are you feeling okay?" she asked, pulling herself out of her thoughts.

"I have to go to the bathroom every twenty seconds, and it is not a pleasant experience. And I've got something that looks like one of those Chinese finger traps hanging out of my . . . well, you know."

"It is going to be okay. Everything is going to be fine," Amy said, and smiled.

"You know, I was going to call you," Darcy said.

"Yeah, I know." She smiled.

"No, I was. I talked to Kathy, one of the lawyers that works for me, and got some pointers."

"Really, and what was your plan of attack?"

"Well, after much debate, the consensus was that I should call you and say, 'Hi, this is Darcy. I would really like to go out with you. Do you think that's something you would like to do?'"

"Wow, straightforwardness. Hmm, that's a refreshing idea."

"Well, our second choice," Darcy began, "was for me to call you up and say, 'How would you like to share a bag of Doritos and some Colt 45 Malt Liquor at a cheap hotel with me?'"

She laughed. "That probably would have worked too."

They talked for hours. Finally, after midnight, Amy said, "Well, this has really been fun, but I need to get some sleep before my shift, and you need to get some rest. I never should've kept you up so late. Dr. Rosenblatt's going to kill me."

"No," Darcy answered, "I'm so glad you came, even if I couldn't eat with you. Please come visit me again."

"Try and keep me away. Now get some sleep, Darcy. A lot has happened to you today."

It sure has, Darcy thought. "Well, good night, then," he said.

"Good night!" Amy gave him a chaste peck on the cheek and walked out the door.

How am I supposed to sleep? Darcy thought, but he fell asleep before he even had a chance to start wondering when Amy would come see him again.

* * *

Darcy had been home for four days and was going stir-crazy. He called the office three or four times a day until Irma convinced him to stop. Kathy would call at the end of the day to bring him up to speed. His daughter had sent flowers and the gang at the office had sent a basket of food from a gourmet grocery store. Amy had visited him every evening after work, and they'd prepared and eaten dinner together and gone for walks. He felt strong enough now to go back to work, but Amy convinced him to stay home one more day. He'd been pacing like a caged animal and needed to get out. So he grabbed a lightweight cotton sweater and took the elevator down to the lobby.

It was a beautiful July day in the upper 70s with a slight breeze. He wrapped the sweater around his neck and tied the sleeves in front of his chest. He walked a couple of blocks and then stopped, realizing that if he kept walking south he'd end up at the office. He shook off the sense of frustration, turned, and walked west. At Clark Street, he turned north until he came to a coffee shop. He sat down at the counter and ordered a toasted bagel with cream cheese and a cup of coffee. He grabbed a discarded *Tribune* off the counter. He looked up from the newspaper to scan the restaurant. It was crowded, although not as crowded as it would be at lunchtime. Nobody recognized him or gave him a second thought. He enjoyed the anonymity, being able to enjoy his coffee without anyone needing something from him or wanting to talk to him. But then after some thought he was a bit conflicted; he liked being needed.

Inspiration struck when Darcy got to the entertainment section of the paper. Studying the list of current movies, he realized that he couldn't remember the last time he had been to one. He thought a movie with a bucket of buttered popcorn and a soda might relax him, but the inspiration dissipated when he was unable to find anything worth seeing. He left the paper along with a nice tip and went for another walk, thinking of Amy.

He meandered through the neighborhood until he came upon a huge bookstore that also had music and videos. He wandered in. He laughed his way through the true crime section—books about some horrific crime spree that glorified a criminal or distorted reality to create a hero to satisfy the writer's personal agenda—passed the mysteries, and found himself in an area called religion and spirituality. He thought he would pull a few books off the shelf and look through them. By the time he sat down at a table, he had eight books. He had an eclectic array of topics. One was the Dalai Lama speaking on happiness. Darcy had a vague memory of a loose, uncommitted Protestant upbringing. His most persistent memory, although certainly not vivid, was being in church on a beautiful Sunday and wanting to be outside playing ball or running with his friends. He remembered believing that his mother was going to strangle him, and he couldn't understand why a ten-year-old had to wear a suit.

Now he was reading a book about Judaism, looking for something to grab him. Although he had given in to Kathy Haddon's feigned horror, he had been, in fact, trying to read the Bible. He assured himself it was, in some secular way, a quest for knowledge rather than a quest for a spiritual awakening. But, there he was on a beautiful July day thumbing intently through books on Buddhism, Judaism, Hinduism, Catholicism, and other religions that failed to identify themselves as such but rather preferred the designation of spirituality. He was definitely looking for something, but he didn't quite know what yet.

His friend Seymour had been encouraging him to read the Bible or to pursue any religious endeavors that might engage him. He envied Seymour. Seymour was a relaxed, content person, happy in a long-term marriage with two children who adored him. Darcy ran the chicken and the egg argument through his head. Was Seymour happy because he had religion, or did a wonderful relationship with his wife and children enable him to believe in God? He wondered about things like reincarnation and an afterlife. Was there a heaven or hell?

When he read that the Catholics have patron saints for lawyers, criminals, and prostitutes, Darcy decided he had to buy that book. He purchased two others as well—the Dalai Lama on happiness and the one on Judaism. He walked home thinking more about Amy than God and dropped them on the kitchen counter.

Darcy felt strong. The overwhelming fatigue that had plagued him over the past few days was gone and he was ready to go back to work and to make a date with Amy. He called the hospital and tried to reach her. When that failed, he paged her and waited for a call back. Ten minutes later, she rang. He was excited to hear her voice and asked her to dinner. She agreed to pick him up after she got off her shift and told him about a restaurant she'd been dying to try.

"Sounds great," he agreed.

At about 6:30 P.M. she called from her car for him to come downstairs. He slid into the car, smiled and buckled his seat belt.

"How was your day?" she asked.

"Not bad. I relaxed, went for walk, did a little reading. How about yours?"

"It was slow. I left at six o'clock. There was nothing going on, thank God."

They went to a Thai restaurant at 4600 North, directly across from the El stop. They had chicken Satay, crab Rangoon, and shrimp puffs for appetizers. Amy's entrée was spicy chicken with green beans, broccoli, and water chestnuts, and Darcy had chicken and cashew nuts. They drank a bottle of wine he'd picked up from the liquor store next door and they watched people come and go in waves from the El station across the street. Darcy looked at Amy over his wine glass.

"I find myself thinking of nothing but you," he said. "I didn't even call my office today."

"Is that right?" she said. "Would you like me to support you now? You could just be my houseboy."

"I don't care about the salary," he said, "but I'd like to hear about the fringe benefits."

"You know what, Darcy," she said, "the thing I like the best about you is that you let me see how much you want to be with me. I love it. When I'm with you, I feel like no one else exists for you, that I have your undivided attention. It is a wonderful feeling. Thank you."

"So what can I do for you now?" Darcy asked, pleased with himself and touched. "There's got to be something else you want to do tonight."

"There is," she said. Darcy leaned in. "I want to find a quiet spot by the lake, spread out a blanket and talk."

"I can do that," Darcy said.

"Here's the catch," she began. "You have to really talk to me. Not these short John Wayne answers to questions."

Darcy smiled, then raised his right hand. "I swear," he said.

"I mean it," she said, swatting his hand down. "I now know your entire medical history but only bits and pieces of your life. I'm too old for games."

Darcy took a long sip of wine. "No games," he said.

Fourteen

Darcy bounded through the door of his office and said a hearty good morning to Irma.

"Welcome back," she said. "You look like you're in the pink."

"I'm feeling good, Irma," he returned. "What's going on here?"

"What, besides the fact that you didn't call at all on Friday?" she asked.

"Yeah, besides that."

"Well, everything is under control. Umm, you have messages on your desk, mail and a couple of things from the U.S. Attorney, but nothing earthshattering. Kathy and Patrick have taken care of most things."

"That's why they're my partners, so they can take care of the important stuff."

"Are you okay?" she asked.

"Yes, I am. Is Kathy in?"

"She is covering a status at Twenty-sixth Street. She won't be in until later."

"Send her into my office when she gets in, will ya? How about Patrick?"

"Patrick is at the Federal Courthouse."

"What does he have?"

"Just a few status dates—a nine, nine-thirty, and ten-thirty."

Darcy looked at the clutter that had accumulated on his desk during the week he'd been out. He absentmindedly looked through the mail, noting the return addresses. He turned on his computer; there was an e-mail from his daughter, which he replied to. He turned on his stereo to a classical music station and spun his chair around to stare out over the lake. For a moment, he searched for a word, and then it came to him: happy. He was feeling happy. He watched a plane take off from Meigs Field and turn toward Michigan. He was having almost giddy thoughts. He had dated before, and he had dated off and on since his divorce, but he had never felt like this. Not even when he married did he have the feelings he now had for Amy. Amy engaged him on every level. She was challenging without being competitive. She was beautiful and interesting, and he found himself thinking about her all the time. She had put a lightness into his step.

Irma interrupted his tranquillity by intercomming him. "Jack Karsten is on the line."

"Jack, my boy," Darcy said, picking up the phone. "How are you?"

"I'm good. I hear you had a bout with a kidney stone."

"Yes, I did."

"Well, you sound pretty chipper now."

"I am pretty chipper, my friend, I am. What's up? Are we doing a prelim today, or did you indict him?"

"A prelim. Are you ready to go?" Jack asked.

"A prelim—sure I'm ready to go. God bless you, Jack Karsten. You got balls."

"We'll see if I still have them after today," he replied. "I'll see you at eleven-thirty."

"You got it."

* * *

It had already become one of those hot, sticky July days that Chicago is known for. It was doubly unpleasant to be at Twenty-sixth and California, in spite of the beautiful fountain that Mayor Richard M. Daley had installed on the parkway outside the courthouse. Darcy made his way across the boulevard and up the steps to the courthouse. He flashed his ID and cut to his right to go to courtroom 101.

The two Mrs. Tatums were outside the courtroom waiting for him. "Where is Marcus?" he asked.

"He's in the courtroom," his mother replied.

"Okay, ladies, how are you today?" They all shook hands and exchanged small talk. "We're going to do a preliminary hearing," Darcy explained.

Teesha smiled. "I thought you said they don't do preliminary hearings."

"Well," Darcy said, "this will be only the second one I can remember, and I've been coming here a long time."

"That's good then," Dorothy interjected.

"It's very good," Darcy said. "But remember, the threshold for them to meet here is very minimal. So don't get overly excited."

"Well, it is a good first step," Dorothy said, and Teesha agreed.

Darcy set up at the defense counsel table. Judge Moglin had a fresh haircut. A large white Styrofoam cup was on the bench to his right. He took a big sip and carefully set it down and picked up a pen.

Karsten was alone at the counsel table but four young prosecutors sat behind him, a few rows back.

Tatum sat to Darcy's right at the defense table.

To begin, Jack Karsten called Maggio to the stand. Maggio was wearing a crumpled blue blazer and what appeared to Darcy to be the only pair of pants Maggio owned, khaki Dockers. Karsten was taking Maggio through his investigation. Maggio was fuzzy on dates in the beginning but, as the investigation progressed, he became specific and clear on each day in question. He finally got to the time at which the body was discovered and he went to see Marcus Tatum.

"Where were you when you first encountered Mr. Tatum?" Karsten asked.

"In his driveway," Maggio answered.

"What happened at that time?" Karsten asked as he flipped a page on his legal pad.

"I introduced myself as a Chicago police detective and told him that I needed to ask him some questions about a friend of his. I asked him if he'd come with me to my office so we could talk."

"What did he say to that?" Karsten asked.

"He said, 'Sure, no problem' and got into my car."

"Was he handcuffed at that time?"

"No."

"What did you do then?" Karsten asked.

"We went in my car to Area Three."

"At that time was he under arrest?" Karsten asked.

Maggio smiled. "No sir. He wasn't placed under arrest until he admitted killing Mr. Orloff."

Tatum began to mutter something but Darcy cut him off by grasping his forearm and telling him not to react.

"How did that happen?" Karsten inquired.

"As we talked I noticed some discrepancies in his story. I confronted him with these discrepancies and he told me that he wanted to tell me the truth. He then admitted that he killed Mr. Orloff, an associate of his in the narcotics business that he knew as 'the Jew.'"

According to Maggio, it was after Tatum was placed under arrest and told that he was being charged with murder that Tatum attacked him. He described the justifiable use of force to subdue him and denied that there was any physical contact between them prior to Marcus Tatum's attacking him in the interview room.

Tatum leaned toward Darcy. "That's bullshit. He's a liar."

Darcy began his cross-examination in a slow and deliberate manner. "Detective Maggio, you were never assigned this case by anyone officially connected with the Chicago Police Department, is that true?"

"Yes," Maggio said.

"You didn't work with any partners in this case, isn't that true?"

"That's correct."

Darcy then began going through some specific details about Tatum's arrest, some of which Maggio was able to recall. Many times he simply answered, "I'm sorry, Counsel, I don't remember."

The adrenaline was coursing through Darcy's body. This was what he loved. It was his time to perform, the courtroom was his and he was going to savor every second.

Darcy zeroed in on his key points. "Tell us, Detective Maggio, where did you get the dental records?"

"I got them from a man named Avi Joseph."

"And who is Avi Joseph?"

"He is a gentleman who was a friend of Jacob Orloff."

"Did he have a connection with the Israeli government?"

"I don't know," Maggio replied as he looked toward Karsten for help.

"Would he be a Mossad agent?" Darcy asked.

"I don't know. He never told me if he had any specific connection with the government, nor did I ask."

"You didn't want to know?"

"I didn't think it was important," Maggio replied, shifting uneasily in his seat.

"Well, did you ever confirm the origin of these dental records?"

"I don't understand what you mean," Maggio said.

"Did you ever contact the dentist who is purported to have created these documents?"

"No sir."

"Did you ever do anything to confirm that these records were accurate?"

"No sir, I'm a cop, not a dentist."

"Well, it seems to me that you're relying on the authenticity of these records to build your case, and yet you have done nothing to determine whether or not these records are authentic."

"Objection!" Karsten said, rising to his feet.

"Overruled," the judge returned.

"Is that a question or a speech?" Maggio said.

The judge leaned forward. "Detective, answer the question."

"No, I didn't do anything to find out if these records were authentic."

"You don't know if these records have been forged or in some way altered, do you?"

"Well, obviously not," Maggio said. "Since I've done nothing to authenticate them, that would also be true."

Judge Moglin leaned over. "Detective, this is not the time or place to cop an attitude. You are in a court of law. You are not in an interview room in an interrogation setting. Please answer the questions and leave the attitude behind. Do we understand each other?"

Maggio nodded. "Sure, Judge, we understand each other." Asshole, Maggio was thinking. But then what do you expect from a man in a dress?

Darcy continued. "When you took this alleged confession, no one else was in the room, is that right?"

"That's correct."

"No State's Attorney?"

"That's correct."

"No other detectives?"

"That's correct."

"And, in addition to that, you had no one else working on this case with you, correct?"

"That's correct," Maggio said, annoyance growing in his voice.

"The defendant, Mr. Tatum, wouldn't sign the statement you prepared, isn't that right?"

"No, he did not sign the statement."

"In fact, you wrote that statement out, is that correct?" Darcy asked.

"I wrote that statement out based on what he told me. It is a summary of what he told me."

"I see," Darcy said. "So, he told you some things, and you chose which of those things to summarize."

Maggio was getting frustrated. "I wrote a summary of what he said, Counselor."

"I understand," Darcy said. "And you selected each and every word that was in the summary?"

Maggio sat back. His mind was racing trying to figure out how to answer that. "I don't know," Maggio said finally. "I wrote out a summary of what he told me."

"Did he make any corrections on that statement?"

"No," Maggio said.

"Did he initial it?"

"No."

"Did he do anything to ratify that statement?"

"What?" Maggio asked.

"Never mind, I will withdraw the question," Darcy said. "When you first encountered Mr. Tatum, he was in the driveway of his home, isn't that right?"

"Yes, that's right."

"You handcuffed him and put him in the back of your car, isn't that right?"

"No, that's not right."

"You did not handcuff him?"

"No, I did not handcuff him."

"Did he come into the Area Three Police Headquarters in your car or his car?"

"In my car."

"Was that an official Chicago Police Department vehicle or your personal car?"

"My personal car."

"Were you on duty yet?"

"What do you mean?" Maggio asked.

"Were you on duty? Were you working? Were you on the clock at the time you met Mr. Tatum at his home on the South Side?"

"No, I was on my way to work," Maggio said.

"I see, so you were saving the taxpayers' money?"

"Objection!" Karsten jumped.

"Sustained."

"Sometime at the police station, you inflicted physical harm on Mr. Tatum, is that correct?"

153

"I used necessary force to repel an attack."

"Well, whatever way you characterize it, you struck him. Isn't that right?"

"Yes," Maggio concurred.

"You struck him a number of times. Isn't that right?"

"Yes."

"And you struck him repeatedly."

"I struck him as many times as was necessary to repel an attack. I was defending myself using justifiable force," Maggio insisted.

"Everything you did was consistent with proper police etiquette, correct?"

"I believe so," Maggio said.

"So, after you did this proper police work, you took him from Area Three, which is located at Belmont and Western, to Northwestern Memorial Hospital, isn't that right?"

"That's correct," Maggio said.

"You didn't take him to Swedish Covenant or Illinois Masonic or Weiss Memorial or any of the other hospitals that were in fact closer to Belmont and Western than Northwestern Memorial Hospital, correct?"

"I took him to Northwestern Memorial Hospital," Maggio reiterated.

"And when you got to Northwestern Memorial Hospital, you had him checked in under a name other than his own. Isn't that right?"

"I didn't have him checked in. I had him treated," Maggio said. "I had no idea what name your client was using at the time he came in."

"I see," Darcy said. "So you don't know if he used the name Marcus Tatum or some other name, is that right?"

"I have no idea what name your client was using. I don't know if your client ever tells the truth, Counselor."

"Ah, yet you want us to believe that he told you the truth when he gave this alleged confession?" Darcy asked.

"Objection," Karsten said.

"Yeah, I'll sustain," the judge said. "Move on, Counselor."

"In any event, did you become aware of the injuries you had inflicted upon him during the course of your so-called necessary force?"

"No," Maggio said.

Darcy read a list of Marcus Tatum's injuries then showed Maggio a photograph of the injured area. When he'd finished, he pulled his glasses off and stared at Maggio. "Was that an accurate list of the injuries you inflicted upon Marcus Tatum?"

Maggio was furious. He stared Darcy up and down. Fucking scumbag, he thought to himself. If I could have you for five minutes, I'd rip your heart out. He was glaring at Darcy.

The judge leaned in. "Did you hear the question, Detective?"

"I heard the question," Maggio said. "I'll take your word for that, Counselor. I don't know what his injuries were."

"Take my word for it? Does that mean you accept this list as the list of the injuries you, in fact, inflicted upon my client?"

"If you say so," Maggio said.

"Do the photographs truly and accurately depict the injuries you inflicted on Mr. Tatum?" Darcy asked.

"I have no idea who took those photos or whether those photographs are accurate," Maggio sneered.

"Well, tell me, Detective, did you use a metal rod to strike him?"

"No, sir."

"Did you ever use a plastic bag to cut off his oxygen supply?"

"No, sir."

"Did you put a plastic bag over his head and tighten it up so that he couldn't breathe?"

"No, sir."

"This statement that Mr. Tatum allegedly gave you doesn't include much detail, does it?"

"I don't know what you mean," Maggio said.

"Well, basically the statement says that he knew the victim and he strangled him, isn't that right?"

"Isn't that enough?" Maggio asked.

Judge Moglin leaned over. "Detective, I'm not going to tell you again. You know how to testify. You've testified many times and I'm not going to tolerate this attitude of yours. I want you to testify like a professional. Do you understand me?"

Maggio reluctantly said, "Yes."

Darcy continued. "In his alleged statement, Tatum doesn't describe the strangulation as being manual or by the use of a ligature, isn't that correct?"

"Yeah, that's correct."

"You didn't ask him any follow-up questions to determine whether it was a manual or ligature strangulation?"

"I suppose not," Maggio said.

"Detective, you didn't ask any other details as to how the homicide occurred or whether the body was transported after death, and if so, in what type of vehicle? You didn't do anything other than allegedly get him to say, 'Yeah, I strangled him'?"

"If you say so," Maggio said.

"That's it," Judge Moglin said. "One more comment like that and I'll hold you in contempt."

Maggio looked at the judge. "Yes, Your Honor," he said. Though he was thinking, I wish I could have you on the streets for ten minutes.

"Detective, you have no physical evidence tying Marcus Tatum to this homicide. Is that right?" Darcy asked.

"That's correct," Maggio said.

"No DNA material was discovered, isn't that correct?"

"That's correct," Maggio said. "Your boy burnt it all up."

"Well, let me ask you this, Detective. You say that Mr. Tatum burned it all up. Did you recover Marcus Tatum's fingerprints from anywhere in the warehouse where the body was found?"

"No sir."

"Do you have any witnesses putting the two of them together?"

"Not at the time of the homicide," Maggio relented.

"You never had Felony Review look at this case?"

"No."

"Felony Review is the unit of the State's Attorney's Office which evaluates cases and decides which charges, if any, would be appropriate, is that right?"

"Yeah, that's right," Maggio agreed.

"So you didn't bring in any Assistant State's Attorneys for direction on this case, is that right?"

"That's correct."

"And you had no, rather, there *is* no DNA material, correct?"

"That's correct."

"There's no trace evidence, is that correct?"

"Yes, that's correct," Maggio said, his annoyance building again.

"In fact, just so we're clear, you have nothing of any physical nature or eyewitness accounts that corroborate anything in your investigation, isn't that right?"

"Objection," Karsten said.

"Compound question," the judge said. "Ask it in another way."

"Do you have any physical evidence that would corroborate your theory that Marcus Tatum killed the decedent?"

"No," Maggio said.

"Do you have any physical evidence whatsoever tying Marcus Tatum to the decedent?'

"No," Maggio said.

"Do you have any eyewitness accounts that Marcus Tatum was ever with the decedent?"

"Yeah, there are people out there that would say they were together. Anaka Vanderlinden was the victim's girlfriend and she saw the victim and the defendant together on numerous occasions."

"Did she see them together the day of the homicide?"

"I'm not sure," Maggio said.

"Detective, you're getting close to retirement, aren't you?"

"Yes," Maggio said.

"Twenty-seven, almost twenty-eight years on," Darcy said.

"Something like that," Maggio said.

"And when you hit thirty, you will have reached your full pension, correct?"

"Objection," Karsten said.

"Where are we going with this?" the judge asked.

"Well, Judge, if the Israeli government is, in fact, utilizing Detective Maggio's expertise, I want to show bias and motive."

"I'll give a little latitude Mr. Cole, very little latitude."

"Isn't it true that this gentleman, Avi Joseph, told you that he was from the Mossad? And didn't he promise you a job after you retire from the police department?"

"No, that is not true," Maggio said.

"Oh, that's right," Darcy said. "He told you he worked for the Israeli government, isn't that right?"

"No, he never told me that."

"You were never given an official assignment from the Chicago Police Department to look into this case, isn't that right?"

"Yes, that's correct."

"And when it began, it was a missing persons case, isn't that right?"

"Yeah, that's right."

"And violent crime detectives don't do missing persons cases, do they?"

"No, they do not," Maggio agreed.

"In fact, juvenile officers do missing persons cases, isn't that right?"

"Yeah, that's right," Maggio said, stiffening.

"And the fact of the matter is that you were approached to get involved in this case very early on, before this was a homicide case, isn't that right?"

"Yes," Maggio agreed.

"In fact, it wasn't until you did all this investigative work that it became a homicide case, correct?"

"That's correct," Maggio said.

"Now, Detective, since you have no physical evidence to go on, the confession was something that was very important to proving this case, isn't that right?"

"All evidence is important," Maggio said.

"I see. And you needed to get a confession from Marcus Tatum to charge him with this murder. Right?"

"It was an important piece of evidence, but it wasn't the only piece."

"That's right," Darcy said. "You have this alleged confession. You have no physical corroboration. You have no scientific corroboration. You have no eyewitness corroboration. Excuse me, Detective, besides the alleged confession, what *do* you have here?"

"Objection!" Karsten said, rising to his feet again.

"Sustained," the judge said. "Can we move on, Mr. Cole? Remember, this is a preliminary hearing."

"So, Detective, you have a physical confrontation with a previously compliant suspect at the police station, and, as a result of this physical confrontation, you have to get him medical help, is that right?"

"That's right. I took him to the hospital."

"And when you took him to the hospital, you took him in a Chicago Police vehicle, is that right?"

"Yes, that's correct."

"And you took him alone, right?"

"Yes, I took him alone."

"No partner?"

"That's what *alone* means, Counselor."

The judge leaned in and then backed off and let it pass.

"And when you took him to Northwestern Memorial Hospital, you brought him into the emergency room as a prisoner, is that correct?"

"That's correct."

"And you were in charge of making sure he was getting treatment and was being guarded while getting that treatment, correct?"

"That's correct."

"Did you have a conversation with Dr. Amy Wagner at Northwestern Memorial Hospital regarding the condition of Marcus Tatum?"

"Not that I recall," Maggio answered.

"So let me get this straight, Detective. You bring Marcus Tatum to the Northwestern Memorial Hospital Emergency Room, bypassing three other emergency rooms on the way, and then you don't even inquire as to his physical condition?"

Karsten could have objected, but he let it go.

"I didn't care what the condition of your client was," Maggio said. "My only concern was bringing a prisoner to the hospital and bringing the prisoner back to the lockup after he was released. Once that was done and I brought him back to the jail, I didn't care at all about your client or his condition."

"Were you concerned about the injuries you inflicted upon him?"

"Objection," Karsten said.

"Where is this going?" the judge asked.

"Goes to the state of mind, consciousness of guilt, tacit admissions."

"I see. In other words, it is going nowhere. Sustained."

Darcy regrouped and moved on. "Detective, besides the woman you told us about, this Ms. Vanderlinden, you were talking to other civilians about this case. Isn't that right?"

Maggio was thinking of a response. After a moment, "Yes."

"Who else did you talk to?"

"Objection," Karsten said.

"I don't know, for what it's worth, I'll let him answer it," the judge said. "But wrap this up, Mr. Cole, this is a preliminary hearing."

Maggio stared at Darcy.

"Did you hear my question, sir?"

"Yes."

"Do you understand my question?"

"Yes."

"I'll ask you again. Besides Ms. Vanderlinden, who else were you talking to?"

Maggio looked at Karsten for help. Karsten sat there with his hands folded in front of him, a pen sticking out through them.

"Yes, I talked to another person."

"And what was the name of this person?" Darcy asked.

"Avi Joseph."

"Objection, Judge. We've been over this already," Karsten said, rising to his feet once again.

"And how would you talk to or reach Avi Joseph?" Darcy asked, not waiting for the judge to rule.

"Objection," Karsten said in a firm voice.

"Sustained. Do you have anything else, Mr. Cole?"

"One more question. Detective, did you ever have a conversation with an individual named Daniel Litwin?"

"No," Maggio said. "I have not spoken with Daniel Litwin."

"Nothing further, Judge."

Maggio stepped off the stand. He was absentmindedly crushing the manila folder that contained his notes and police reports. His hands were wringing it as if it were Darcy's neck. Darcy sat down next to Marcus Tatum. Tatum put his hand on Darcy's shoulder to assure him that he was happy with what he had done. Darcy scribbled on his notepad "Avi Joseph and Daniel Litwin" and underneath it he wrote, "Who?"

"Any other evidence?" the judge asked.

"Yes, Your Honor," Karsten said, standing in the courtroom. "We would proceed by way of stipulation. If called to testify, the medical examiner's office, specifically Dr. Kim, would testify that she examined the body and that, after reviewing dental records and identifying the decedent as Jacob Orloff, she began a postmortem examination. She is educated, trained and certified as a forensic medical examiner, board certified, and she is prepared to testify that upon completing a full-blown autopsy, she determined the cause of death to be strangulation, and that the manner of death was homicide."

"So stipulated. Mr. Cole?"

"We stipulate that would be her testimony on those limited points and for the limited purpose of this hearing today," Darcy said.

"Very well then. What else do you have, State?"

"With that, Judge, the State rests at this preliminary hearing."

"Any evidence, Mr. Cole?"

"No, Your Honor, we will not be presenting evidence today."

The judge leaned back. "Arguments?"

"We'll waive argument," Karsten said, "and reserve rebuttal."

Darcy stood to begin his argument.

"You know, Mr. Cole," Judge Moglin interrupted, "the standard here is minimal. It is only whether a crime has been committed and if there is any reason whatsoever to believe that your client should answer for that crime by way of trial. That's the sole purpose. So please confine your remarks to those issues."

"Well, Your Honor, then I will confine my remarks to those issues. I will ignore all the testimony about this alleged statement and the brutality that was inflicted upon my client in order to get this alleged statement, which my client repudiates and refused to sign. I will also point out that the only evidence tying my client to this alleged murder of this purported victim, Jacob Orloff, is this so-called statement, which was an oral statement that nobody witnessed besides this detective. Furthermore, I point out that this detective, as you learned through direct- and cross-, had no business undertaking this investigation in the first place."

Judge Moglin sat poker-faced, taking notes. He did not make eye contact with Darcy. Karsten was looking down at his legal pad as he took notes.

"Furthermore, it is frightening that an oral statement from this troubled detective, working without a partner who could have provided corroboration, is telling this court to hold Marcus Tatum, a businessman, an upstanding member of the community, to trial on a first-degree murder charge based only on this detective's word that Marcus Tatum made statements which were inculpatory in nature. Be that as it may, Judge, even if you were to say that there is a scintilla of credibility with regard to those statements as testified to by this detective, who is the decedent?"

Darcy was shifting into high gear. He was pacing in the well of the courtroom, speaking in a measured pace without notes.

"There is absolutely no credible, reliable evidence that this decedent is in fact Jacob Orloff, subject of Detective Maggio's investigation. Some mystery person hands him a set of dental records, but we have no indication as to where these medical records came from and whether there is any validity to those records. Furthermore, Judge, we don't even have a valid cause of death because, as you heard through the testimony, the only way the medical examiner was able to change this from an undetermined cause of death to a homicide was to rely on what she was told by this detective. Judge, all these things are frightening. In this country, we pride ourselves on jurisprudence based on independent corroborated evidence. We strive for justice. Do not hold Marcus Tatum to trial based on this skimpy, flimsy, fabricated set of circumstances. I ask that you find no probable cause and that this charade end at this point."

Darcy slowly made his way back to the counsel table. He unbuttoned his jacket and sat down.

"Mr. Karsten?"

Jack rose. He had an athletic body that stretched the seams of his jacket in the shoulders. He was deliberate and controlled as he strolled back and forth. His voice was measured and confident as he spoke.

"Judge, at this point, all we have to do is show that a homicide took place and that there is reason to believe that Marcus Tatum was the one who committed the homicide, and that the homicide was not justified under the law nor was there a compelling defense to excuse his behavior for committing that homicide. You have an experienced homicide detective who testified that the defendant admitted to committing this homicide. You have the remains of the decedent, and the medical examiners concur that the manner of death is homicide and that the cause of death is consistent with the statement of the defendant. Judge, at this point we've met our burden and I ask that there be a finding of probable cause."

"Well," the judge began, "it is an interesting case, isn't it? Not the run-of-the-mill shooting where one insane idiot shoots at another insane idiot, misses and strikes a ten-year-old skipping rope. Or one where, in the midst of a crap game or dope deal, one moron shoots another moron. This case is, in fact, all together different, and it is one that has all the hallmarks and intrigue of a cheap drugstore novel. However, none of that is my concern at this point in time." Judge Moglin clasped his hands together as he spoke. "As Mr. Karsten correctly points out, this is merely a preliminary hearing. Hearsay is admissible and I am allowed to take certain leaps of faith based on what I hear. And that leap of faith is that, in fact, as the detective testified, this person may or may not have made this statement and there is a homicide victim who has been identified as Jacob Orloff. Perhaps at some point in the future, Mr. Cole, you will be able to demonstrate that this is not true or that there is reasonable doubt. All of that is beyond my jurisdiction at the moment, and, as I have stated, the only thing we are here for is to determine whether or not there is probable cause. Certainly based on the evidence we've heard today, if it were at trial, things might be different. However, we're not at that juncture. Therefore, based on everything I've heard, there will be a finding of probable cause. This case is bound over three weeks from today for the Chief Judge's Assignment Call. Is there any further business?"

"No, Your Honor," Karsten said.

"No, Your Honor," Darcy said.

"In that case, I think we're done. Do we have anything else, Ms. Clerk?" The judge looked over to the clerk.

"No, Judge, that's it."

"Very well then, court is adjourned." The judge marched off the bench into his chambers.

Marcus whispered into Darcy's ear. "This dude lied his ass off."

Darcy whispered back. "We'll get him. Don't worry."

Darcy slid over to the State's counsel table where he leaned into Jack. "Well, what do you think?" he asked.

"I don't know," Jack said. "Maybe our detective is telling the truth. I suppose we'll find out, won't we?" He smiled. "I like the fact that you showed him the initial medical examiner's report with the undetermined cause of death."

"You liked that, Jack, my boy?"

"Yeah, Darcy, I liked that. I noticed you didn't take out the final report to show him during your heated cross."

"No," Darcy said. "I showed him the undetermined report while I was being nice to him. You know, lull him into a false sense of security?"

"Well, Darcy, I've been doing this for a long time," Jack said, "although not as long as you. But, having prosecuted this long, it isn't going to bother me to lose this case. It's certainly not going to bother me as much as I'm going to enjoy trying it against you."

"Oh, Jack, you're just buttering me up," Darcy said. "Do you have any DNA samples from the family?" he asked.

"No," Jack said. "Surprisingly, the Orloffs, this prominent Israeli family, haven't been able to cooperate with us yet."

"Unusual, don't you think?" Darcy asked.

"Yeah, it is unusual," Jack said. "But then you know victims don't always act the same way."

"Cling to that, Jack, cling to that," Darcy said as he began to walk away.

"You know, Darcy," Jack said, standing. Darcy turned and came to him. "I like the way you try a case, but I also like the way you can be a prick when you need to be."

Darcy smiled. "Thanks, Jack."

"Don't mention it," Jack returned.

Darcy walked out of the courtroom and found Marcus and the two Mrs. Tatums standing with Collata.

"Well, I think it went well," Darcy began. "We have him nailed down on all the minute details. And we can disprove quite a bit of it if we can prove a few lies by Maggio."

Marcus put a big meaty paw on the back of Darcy's shoulders. "I'm happy. We got a lot of things we can do here," Marcus said. "I feel good about this now."

"Don't get too excited," Darcy said. "We're not out of the woods yet. You're going to be held to trial. Here's what we're going to do, though," Darcy said, and he began to spell out the plan of attack. "We're going to do a Motion to Quash your arrest, and, if we win that, all the evidence flowing from the arrest will be suppressed. Collata, you have to find out who this Avi Joseph is."

He turned to Tatum. "Do you know this guy?"

"Nope. Never heard of him."

"Well, we'll find out. We're way ahead of where we normally are at this point," Darcy said. "We got the discovery. We had a preliminary hearing. And we got this son-of-a-bitch on paper. We'll be all right."

Darcy said his goodbyes to the Tatums, and he and Collata watched them walk away.

"What, no cigarette?" Darcy asked.

Collata reached from behind his ear and pulled one out. "Yeah, I wasn't smoking because of the ladies."

"And who said chivalry was dead?" Darcy smiled.

Fifteen

Darcy had finished a cup of coffee and was returning phone calls as he reflected on the Tatum hearing. That was yesterday. Today is today, Darcy thought. A smile crept over his face. It sure went well, though, Darcy thought.

Harry Feiger sat in Darcy's waiting room. He was wearing a navy blue pinstriped suit with a conservative red tie. Patrick stepped out to the lobby to collect Feiger.

"Harry, come on in."

They shook hands, and Patrick led the way to Darcy's office. Darcy was putting on his suit coat as Harry and Patrick walked in.

"You ready to do this?" Darcy asked as he flipped the collar of his coat down.

"You know how I feel about this," Harry said. "I don't want to proffer. I wish there was some other way."

"Yeah, I know, but this is the best way to figure out what they're looking at," Darcy said. "Let's go find out what they know."

They rode the elevator down from Darcy's office in silence, crossed the street and headed into the Federal Building. When they reached the security checkpoint, they emptied their pockets and went through the x-rays. After they picked up their briefcases on the other side of the metal detectors, they took the elevator to the fifth floor.

Darcy and Harry sat down on the hard plastic couch while Patrick checked them in. The receptionist sat behind bullet-proof glass. Behind her on the wall was a photograph of the president and another of the attorney general. They watched as various agents and prosecutors walked past them and were buzzed into the inner sanctum. After about ten minutes, the door opened and someone Darcy believed to be an agent called out their names.

"Hello, I'm special agent Rick Coyle with the FBI," he said as he shook Darcy's hand.

"I'm Darcy Cole."

"I'm Patrick O'Hagin."

Darcy turned toward Harry. "And this is, as you know, Harry Feiger."

"Hello, Mr. Feiger, nice to see you again."

Harry looked at him. "Oh yeah, you're the guy who brought me the subpoena."

"Yes sir, that was me. Would you follow me, please? Carl Stringer is waiting for us in the conference room."

They walked down a hallway. On their left was a series of small offices with windows. Each office was for the Assistant U.S. Attorney whose name appeared on a plastic plaque outside the office. Darcy paid no attention, but Patrick was reading off each name in his mind and looking into each office, keeping an account of friend, foe, or neutral. They turned a corner and entered a room with a plastic plaque outside that read, "Trial Preparation Room." Carl Stringer, who was seated at the table, rose to greet them.

"Hi, Patrick, Darcy, how are you?"

"Nice to see you, Carl."

They shook hands, and Carl was introduced to Harry Feiger. Harry sat directly across from Carl Stringer, the agent to Stringer's right. Harry was flanked by his attorneys, Darcy to his right and Patrick to his left.

"Well, let's get started," Carl said.

Stringer was a young African-American man in his early thirties, clean-cut, and slight of build. His suit coat was off and his tie loosened. He was using a plastic Bic pen to write on a yellow legal pad.

"First of all, Mr. Feiger, the reason you're here is that your attorneys have expressed an interest in your doing a proffer. A proffer is an agreement between the parties that you answer our questions or give information to us and that information and those answers are protected. In other words, we can't use them against you in any criminal proceedings. We are free however, to develop any leads we can independently from the information you give us. In addition, if you were to testify at some point and testify in a manner inconsistent with the proffer here, we may use this proffer for impeachment purposes. Now, I know that you are a lawyer and that you understand those things, but if there is anything you need expounding on, please stop me before we begin. Finally, what you need to know is that if we find out that you have been untruthful with us during the course of this proffer, we can use any or all of this proffer against you."

Stringer seemed humorless and focused. Darcy watched him and a feeling of dread began to wash over him. He sensed this was not going to go well.

"Your truthful responses to our questions and truthful information are essential to keeping this agreement. If we find out that you have not been truthful, the agreement becomes null and void, and we are free to do whatever we want with this information. Do you understand that?"

Harry nodded.

"Would that be a yes, sir?"

"Yes. Yes, I understand," Harry said, catching himself.

"Okay," Stringer said. "As you know, we gave some information to Mr. Cole. I assume you've had some time to review that information with him?"

"Yes, we have."

"Was that today or prior to today?"

"Prior to today," Harry answered.

"Well, then, let's get started."

Stringer ran through a series of perfunctory questions, asking how old Harry was, how long he'd been a lawyer, where his offices were, if he'd ever had any partners, where he kept his bank accounts, how many people worked in his firm, their names, if he'd had any employees who'd left recently, and so forth. After a half-hour of innocuous inquiry, Stringer began to bore in on some specific points.

"Tell me, sir, how many expungements have you done for individuals?"

"I don't know," Harry said. "My record keeping wasn't all that great. I would do an expungement, and afterward, I'd give the client the documents or I would destroy them for him. I didn't keep copies of the expungements. I would destroy those records or give them to the person who hired me to do the expungement."

"Don't you have any other business records?"

"Well, I have my receipts," Harry said.

"Did you report all of your income?"

"Wait a minute, Carl," Darcy objected, "that's out of line. We're not going to answer questions that are open-ended. Why don't you just ask him when he stopped beating his wife?"

Carl shot Darcy a look. "Okay, Darcy. Here's the deal. We're going to ask him questions, and he can answer them or not. Obviously, if he chooses not to answer the questions, this proffer will be less than productive."

Patrick stepped in. "You know, Carl, the proffer, as we understood it, was to be to ask about any criminal acts relating to extortion. Now you're going into a separate and distinct area, which I presume could be pertinent to other crimes."

"That's precisely right," Stringer said.

"Well, we're not prepared to go into those areas. So why don't we continue the proffer in the areas for which we are prepared. And then, we can reconvene on another date after we've had time to discuss these other issues you are raising."

Stringer relented. "Okay, we'll stick to the script, as it were," he said with some rancor and bitterness in his inflection. He asked about six individuals and the expungements that Harry did for them. He asked him how they'd met and the circumstances around each meeting. It was clear that they had interviewed these six individuals and had some basis of knowledge from which Stringer was asking his questions.

Harry seemed to relax as he answered the questions as best he could. Finally, Stringer began to sum it up.

"Well, since we can't go into other areas today, we'll have to finish here. Let me ask you one more question, though. Was it your intention to frighten these clients, Mr. Feiger?"

"No," Harry said, "I didn't have to do that. They were already terrified when I met them. They were all in the midst of a traumatic situation and they were looking for help. If any of them thought that I tried to frighten them by telling them the truth, well, then I apologize for that. What I did was do expungements, something I was very good at, and charged a fee commensurate with my experience."

Stringer let out an exasperated sigh. "Mr. Feiger, an expungement requires filling out documents, retrieving other documents, and filing them. There's no skill involved. Individuals are either statutorily eligible or they are not. If they are eligible and you fill out the paperwork, then the expungement is granted."

"That may be true," Harry said, "but so much of what lawyers do is perfunctory. People are paying for the sizzle, not the steak, my friend."

"I'll keep that in mind," Stringer said. "Okay, we'll get back to you, Darcy."

Agent Coyle interjected. "I have a question."

"What's that?" Darcy asked.

"It's for your client, Mr. Cole." He turned to Harry. "Where do you vacation?"

Darcy put his hand up. "Don't answer that question. Do you have another question?" he asked.

"Yeah. Do you have any bank accounts outside the United States?"

"Okay, as I said, we'll reconvene at another time after we've been able to question our client. Obviously, there is something here you're looking at that you did not tell us about, and which

you did not include in the materials you sent over for us to prepare for this proffer."

Stringer interrupted. "Darcy, I sent you documents as a
courtesy. You're not entitled to anything prior to a proffer."

Patrick stepped up. "Hey, Carl. This is not what we agreed
to."

"You don't work here anymore, Patrick," Stringer said. "So
you're not entitled to any more courtesy than any other lawyer.
I extended you that courtesy by giving you materials to prepare
your client. Obviously your client does not wish to fully cooperate."

"That's not true," Patrick said. "He fully cooperated with
all the questions under which we prepared him. I am not going
to walk someone in here blind. You agreed to give us parame-
ters for this proffer. Now we get here, and you want to jump
us." Patrick got up. "We'll reconvene if you think it is appropriate. But if you're going to pull this kind of crap, then we
really don't have anything to talk about, do we?"

Stringer was angry. "You're wasting my time, Mr.
O'Hagin."

Darcy stood up. "Why don't we all calm down here? This is
just miscommunication. I have been doing this a long time and
I can tell you that honorable men can have disagreements based
on misunderstandings. So why don't we calm down and talk
again next week."

Patrick was staring Stringer down. Stringer nodded.

"Okay, let's go," Darcy said as he grabbed Harry under the
elbow.

"The agent will walk you out," Stringer said, writing furi-
ously on his notepad.

They were escorted out and deposited onto the elevator
alone, just the three of them. "That fucking asshole double-
crossed us," Patrick said.

Harry was upset. "What's going on?"

Darcy smiled reassuringly. "Don't worry, Harry. All we did
was confirm what they knew already and now we know what
they're fishing for. So we have to do a little more work."

Harry looked at Darcy. "All I want is a simple plea agreement. That's all I want," he said. "I don't want to pick a fight with the United States government. I don't want them getting angry at me, and I don't want you fighting with the U.S. Attorney and leaving me to pay the price."

"That won't happen," Darcy said. "I guarantee it."

Patrick, Darcy, and Harry Feiger walked in silence back to Darcy's office. Darcy led them into his office, pausing to take his suit coat off and hang it on a hook behind his door. He sat behind his desk with Patrick and Harry in chairs in front of him.

"Well, it didn't go over very well, did it?" Patrick said.

"That's an understatement," Harry said. "Now what?"

"Well," Patrick said, "Stringer will have a target letter delivered to me. They'll turn up the heat here. They want you to work out a plea agreement."

"That's all I ever wanted."

"Yeah, but I don't think it's going to be what you'd hoped for."

"Yeah, well, I thought a diversion was too good to be true," Harry said.

"I think they're thinking about sending you to prison."

"Okay, okay, six months on an honor farm. I can do that."

"I don't think that's what they're talking about."

"My God. So you think they know everything about me."

"I don't know what they know."

Darcy leaned in. "Whoa, enough speculation. What we're going to have to do is what we wanted to do all along. Tell them to bring it on. They have to indict you. We've got to get the ball rolling, or they have to give us a plea agreement that we could do pursuant to an information."

"Jesus," Harry said. "If they indict, all bets are off."

"Well, we can handle it," Darcy said.

"Yeah, you can handle it. You wouldn't have to go to prison."

"Look," Darcy replied. "You're a lawyer, and you know how the game is played. At some point, you have to stare them down. It's put up or shut up time. Are you ready for this? We're going to have to get all our ducks in a row and get ready to fight. Are you ready for that?"

Harry looked around like a trapped animal. "I don't have a choice now, do I, Darcy?"

"No, you don't," Darcy said. "So let's do what we do best. Let's go to war."

"Patrick, would you excuse us so I can talk to Darcy alone?" Harry asked.

"Sure," Patrick said. He was used to Harry's secretiveness now. He got up and left, shutting the door behind him.

Harry looked pained as he leaned into Darcy. "Look Darcy, I know you're a good lawyer, but I also know that you have solid connections in the U.S. Attorney's Office. That's part of the reason I hired you."

"I thought you hired me for my discretion."

"Yeah, that too, but now it's put up or shut up time, as you said. I want to know what it'll cost me to make this work out."

"I don't understand," Darcy said.

"Look, I know some things happen. Everyone read the paper about the Espinoza trial you did. Audiotapes just don't go missing. The key piece of evidence in a money laundering trial just doesn't end up disappearing. And then all the crazy stuff that happened in the Lynne Tobias case. Come on, Darcy, I know you got somebody inside. What will it take to tap that resource?"

Darcy leaned back. "Sorry to disappoint you, Harry, but I don't have anyone inside. Those are just two cases that I did. Granted, some strange things happened, but I didn't make them happen. In the Espinoza trial the government made a huge mistake and lost some evidence. I was lucky, my client was lucky, but that's all it was, luck. The Tobias case was nothing more than good investigation. Let us do our jobs."

"Come on, I'm desperate here. I'll pay anything. Tell me you'll reach out for the person you have. I'll double your retainer, just don't leave me hanging here, Darcy. I need this to work out."

"I'll do the best I can," Darcy said, "but I think you have some misinformation. I don't have anybody over there who can do what you're asking. All I can do is represent you as a lawyer, and I will and am doing that. We'll do the very best we can. We'll prepare for trial and we'll go to trial, unless they submit an offer that's acceptable to you."

"Don't let me down, Darcy," Harry pleaded. Harry paused, then he looked at Darcy with a distant look in his eyes. "I'm screwed, aren't I?"

* * *

Maggio pulled into the parking lot and walked into the liquor store. He went over to the vodka section and grabbed the worst there was, a half-gallon of an off-brand that may just as well have been made in the back room of the liquor store. He wouldn't have cared. It was cheap, and there was a lot of it. He got two packs of cigarettes and asked for a pack of matches. He was looking ragged and disheveled, with two days' growth of stubble and bloodshot eyes. He hadn't slept since Darcy cross-examined him. He'd been around a long time, and he knew that the fact they did a preliminary hearing on his homicide was bad news. His plans of lying in the weeds for a couple of years while the case meandered through the system had been shot full of holes. He knew that he was in the spotlight now and that all his actions were going to be closely observed. The prospect of that frightened him immensely. His repertoire of drug abuse had broadened and, in addition to the usual, he was now smoking the glass pipe. He put the paper bag with the vodka on the seat next to him, opened the pack of cigarettes, and fired one up in the car. After backing out, he drove aimlessly through the city. He found himself drawn to a familiar area, one where the working girls walked the streets. He spotted Jasmine, one of the pros he'd pulled over before.

"Okay, Jasmine, get in the car," he said.

"No way, Maggio," she said. "If you're going to arrest me, arrest me, but I'm not giving you anymore freebies."

"Get in the car, bitch," he answered.

"Fuck you! I'm not going with you. All the girls know what you're up to. You ain't the man no more. You're just a guy with a badge, and you could have got that thing from a goddamn pawnshop," she said.

"Hey, I'm the real police and you're under arrest."

"Fine, arrest me then, but I'm not going with you."

Maggio was angry. He put his car in park and stepped out. He reached to his back for his handcuffs and realized that he didn't have them, so he approached her. "You fucking bitch. You're coming with me."

She turned and ran toward a street pole. She wrapped her arms around it and began screaming.

"Shut up," he yelled.

"Get away from me, get away from me," she screamed. "Help! Rape! Rape! Help!"

People stared at them, and cars slowed down. Maggio felt as if his head were on fire. The anger was boiling up through his chest. A couple of other girls on the street ran over to Jasmine.

"Get out of here, Maggio," one of them yelled at him. They started taunting him and screaming. "Get your little shriveled dick out of here. No one is going to suck that little thing ever again."

Moments later a squad car pulled up and activated its blue lights. By now, four working girls were surrounding Jasmine, who was holding onto the streetlight. Maggio fumbled through his pockets and pulled out his star and held it above his head. Two uniformed cops got out of the car. One, a big ruddy-faced guy with a broken tooth, came from the driver's side. A short, stocky Hispanic got out of the passenger side.

"It's okay," Maggio said. "I'm a dick. Area Three."

They came up and looked at his star. "Got your picture ID, Detective?"

"What the fuck!" Maggio swore. He reached behind the star and dug out the picture ID. He shoved it too close to the broken-tooth cop's face.

The cop backed away. "Yeah, okay, okay. What's going on here?"

"I wanted to check this whore for warrants. This one screamed, so I decided to check it out."

"Are you on duty?" he asked.

"Are you kidding? We're on duty twenty-four hours a day. This ho was a witness in a murder that we couldn't make."

Jasmine yelled, "That's a lie. This bastard wants me to suck his dick."

"All right," the Hispanic guy said. "Why don't we just calm down and walk on back to the squad car?"

"Fuck you," Maggio said. "You guys can't control the fucking streets. This didn't happen when I was working patrol."

"Yeah, yeah," the broken-tooth cop said. "You were a superstar cop and there was no crime when you were here, right?"

"How long have you been on the job?" Maggio asked.

Broken tooth wouldn't bite. "Why don't you take off? We'll clean up your mess here."

"Fuck you," Maggio said, and he turned to the Hispanic guy, "Yeah, and fuck you, too."

He looked over toward Jasmine. "This isn't over, bitch, and don't think I'll forget about all you other bitches in the blow-job mafia over there."

Jasmine held up her pinkie and kept flopping it down. As soon as Maggio got in his car and began to drive away, the girls started high-fiving each other. Maggio jumped on the gas pedal and got out of there.

He was still seething as he locked the door to his apartment behind him.

"Whores," he muttered. He reached under his dilapidated sofa and pulled out a cigar box. Inside was a little glass crack pipe. He dropped a big rock in the basket, blazed it up, and sucked the smoke deep in. His nerves were frayed, and he blew the entire rock before he got up and broke the seal on the bottle of cheap vodka. He poured himself a tumbler and sat back down to blow another rock. He pulled out a plastic film canister and popped the top off, spilling the contents onto a mirror. First he chopped up some flake, then worked it into three good lines and snorted all three. As he used his finger to clean stray bits of coke off the mirror, he caught his reflection and stared at himself.

What the fuck have I become? he thought. He took a sip of vodka and he sat back on the couch, staring into space. As the seconds passed, he became more and more disgusted and agitated with himself. He got up and paced, stopping every few steps to drink some more vodka. He pulled his .38 out of his shoulder holster and sat back down. He breached it and checked to see that he had full rounds, then slammed it shut and spun the cylinder. He looked at it carefully.

Smith & Wesson, snub-nose .38, that'll do it, he thought. He smoked one last rock and ran a wet finger in the film canister to get the last of the flake. He slugged down the rest of the vodka and set the glass on the table with his left hand. He sat back down and looked around his shabby apartment.

Who would miss me? he thought. He opened his mouth and put the barrel in. He tried to figure out the angle—Do I go up? Do I go back? He moved the gun around in his mouth, trying to get the perfect trajectory while he held the barrel to the roof of his mouth.

This will do it, he thought. Now pull the trigger. Nothing. Pull the trigger. Come on, you pussy, pull the trigger. He was talking to himself and talking back to himself. "Pull the trigger. What are you sticking around here for?"

He began screaming at himself. "Do it. Do it. Pull the fucking trigger. Come on, you piece of shit. You alcoholic, junkie, whoremonger."

And then, any courage he may have had evaporated. He pulled the gun out, set it down on the coffee table, and cried.

Sixteen

Collata was in his van again, waiting about two blocks from the Haddons' house. He watched as Jim Haddon got into his car, backed out of his driveway, and headed away from him. Putting the van in gear, he followed Jim from his subdivision in Palos Hills through a couple of other communities, and to a bar in a town he guessed was Evergreen Park. Collata watched from across the street as Jim parked his car in the rear of the parking lot, then went into the bar by himself. Collata checked his watch and started writing notes on a small notepad he'd pulled from his shirt pocket.

After a half-hour, Collata was confident that Jim wasn't coming out anytime soon, so he stepped out of the van and carefully made his way across the street. He walked across to the front of what appeared to be a restaurant and a bar and glanced through the windows to see where Jim might be. He looked at all the tables, but he couldn't see him anywhere. He didn't like it, and decided he had to go in. A glass display counter with an old metal cash register was just inside the door. To the right was the restaurant, and Collata peered in to check out the tables. Jim was nowhere to be seen. To his left was the bar. He walked in and stood frozen in the doorway. Jim was easy to spot—he was standing behind the bar pulling a draft for a customer. Collata found a spot at the bar with a stool and plopped down. Jim walked over to him.

"Collata, right?"

"You got it, Jimmy," he said.

"What are you drinking?"

"How about a Jack Daniels, rocks with a water chaser?"

"No problem."

Jim poured a heavy-handed drink and set it up next to a glass of water, both of which were on bar napkins.

"What brings you out this way?" he asked.

"An investigation," he said. "I'm following a guy and I came in here 'cause he's staying put for the moment. What are you doing here? I thought you taught high school."

"I do," he said. "But I need to make some extra money."

"Oh, yeah? Why's that?"

"Well, my tenth anniversary is coming up, and I want to get my wife one of those rings you see on the commercials."

"What do you mean?"

"You know. Those diamond anniversary rings."

Collata shook his head. "So you're working here to get a ring for your wife."

"Yeah," Jim said. "I know the owner here. His kid is a good kid. I had him in my class two years ago. He's away at college. So I'm filling in, making some extra dough. The boss is paying me in cash."

Collata threw the Jack down fast and then took a sip of water to cool the fire. "Give me another, pal. Remember, I'm a big tipper."

* * *

The cemetery entrance was off Clark Street. Collata had crossed under the El-track viaduct and taken a left on Clark off Wilson. He was heading south, not too far from Wrigley Field, when he reached the entrance. He pulled in and followed the road back, as he had been told, just past the pond. At the far end along the wall, he saw him. Maggio was sitting on the steps of a mausoleum. Collata parked his car and walked up to him. Six crushed cigarette butts lay at Maggio's feet. Number seven was in his mouth.

"Thanks for coming out," Maggio said.

Collata looked around. "Why here?" he asked.

"I used to patrol this neighborhood," Maggio replied. "I used to think this place was so special. It was like a fortress of civility amid all the roaches I had to deal with."

"What's going on?" Collata asked.

"I almost topped myself last night."

"Why's that?" Collata asked.

"Look at me, man. I'm a mess."

Collata looked him up and down. "Does that mean you're ready to change things?"

"I got to man, I got to. Can you help me?"

"Well, I'll do what I can," Collata said, "but it's really up to you."

"Yeah, yeah, I know that, but I really need your help."

"Why me?" Collata asked.

"I got no one else," Maggio said, "and I trust you."

Collata pulled out a cigarette and gingerly snatched the one out of Maggio's hand to light his up. He gave Maggio's back and joined him in a smoke in silence.

"I hit rock bottom," Maggio said finally. "Isn't that what the twelve steppers tell you? You hit rock bottom, then you're ready to do something?"

"That's what I hear," Collata said. "Although I've spent most of my life at rock bottom, so I wouldn't know anything else."

Maggio crushed out the seventh cigarette. "I'm addicted to so much shit, I don't even know where to begin."

"What do you want to do?" Collata asked.

"I want to get clean. I want to get sober. I want to be a cop again."

"Well, you've got a couple of problems you got to take care of, one at a time," Collata said. "My experience tells me that you got to go to the Department and ask for detox. You have to tell them that you're an alcoholic. If you do that, they'll leave you alone as long as you're getting treatment."

"Can I keep working?" Maggio asked.

"Yeah," Collata said, "as long as you're getting treatment and you're capable of doing your job. But you know they may want you to do inpatient."

"Fuck them."

"No, not fuck them. You need them. They don't need you. You want to get straight. You got to do what they tell you to do. It won't be easy. I've seen a lot of guys with a monkey on their back. Some of them made it, and some of them didn't. But the ones that did were determined to. You got to make getting clean and sober your priority above everything else in life. When you're ready to do that, then you can step up to the plate."

"I'm ready," Maggio said. "I'm finally ready."

Collata excused himself and went back to his car. He rummaged through a briefcase and returned with a small book put out by the Police Union listing important phone numbers for cops.

"What's that for?" Maggio asked.

"We're going to do this right," Collata said. "You're not going to go to some outside place. You're going to go through the Department. That way they pay for it, you're covered, and they can't make you do the piss test while you're going through detox. Besides, if they made you take a piss test now, you'd probably melt the glass."

"What if they find out I'm doing these other substances?"

"Treatment's confidential," Collata said. "As long as you stay in the treatment program, you're good. And by the time you get out, they have to have probable cause again to give you a piss test."

"Do you think this is going to work?" Maggio asked.

"You tell me, Al," Collata answered. He pulled a cell phone from his side and made a phone call. After a brief conversation, he hung up and turned back to Maggio. "Let's go, chief."

"What about my car?"

"Forget your car. You'd be lucky if they tow it."

Maggio thought about it. "Let me dump it in a legal spot somewhere in the neighborhood. You could follow me, then I'll jump in your car."

"Okay," Collata said, "but if you take off, I'm through with you."

"Take off? Are you crazy? I called you to help me. I'm rock bottom," Maggio said.

"I'll help you once," Collata said. "If you con me once, I'm through with you. One chance, that's it. Got it?"

Maggio nodded. "Got it."

Maggio found a parking space on a side street and climbed in the passenger side of Collata's van. "Damn, I thought I had a piece of shit for a car," he said.

"This is my undercover-mobile."

"What's your other car?" Maggio asked.

"I don't have another car," Collata said.

Maggio stared out the window as Collata turned on Lake Shore Drive and drove south to the expressway, then to Mercy Hospital. They took the elevator in the professional building and found the Substance Abuse Treatment Center. Collata stopped at the window and talked to a nurse, then sat with Maggio in the waiting room.

Seventeen

A busload of tourists emptied out onto the street in front of Buckingham Fountain. The fountain blasted toward the sky, and a plane arched over the lake on a descent toward Meigs. Detective Al Maggio smoked a cigarette as he leaned against the railing of the fountain, oblivious to the mist blowing off the spray. He was scanning the crowd, looking west and then slowly rotating around toward the lake. The light on Lake Shore Drive turned red, and dozens of tourists crossed the street and approached the fountain. In the middle of the pack, he spotted them.

Avi Joseph had Anaka Vanderlinden by the arm, looking no different from any of the other tourists. No one would have guessed that they were there to discuss a murder. Maggio watched them carefully and scanned the crowd to see if they'd brought any backup. If they had, he couldn't spot them. He finished his cigarette and flicked it into the water. When they got close enough, Joseph was the first to speak.

"Well, Detective, we're here as you asked."

"I have some questions," Maggio said. "Do you want to do this here or someplace else?"

It was Joseph's turn to scan the crowd. "How about that bench over there," he said. As they walked toward it together, Maggio pulled out a small notepad and a pen and started with the questions.

"Okay, where did you get those dental records from?"

Joseph smiled. "From his dentist, obviously."

"Yeah, yeah I know. What's the dentist's name?"

Anaka had begun to speak when Joseph lifted his hand. "I'll give you that information," he said. "What else do you need?"

"Well, I need someone from the family to identify the body. I need DNA."

"You have the dental records, why do you need the DNA?" Joseph asked.

"Well, funny thing about these prosecutors, they like to have irrefutable evidence. Maybe when Mom or Dad comes to town, we can take a quick swab of the mouth and use that. How's that?" Maggio said.

"This seems unnecessary," Joseph said.

"Yeah, I knew it would seem unnecessary to you. You seem to be offended whenever anyone asks you to do something. But we would like to have it," Maggio insisted. "By the way, I would like to have a number where I can reach the family— address, telephone number, fax, something."

"I'll get that for you," Joseph said.

"You don't have that now?" Maggio asked.

"I'll get that for you," Joseph reiterated. "What else?"

Maggio turned to Anaka. "I need to talk to you. We need to talk about the last time you saw him, and I need to get some consistency in your statement," he said, oozing sarcasm.

Joseph started to interrupt, and Maggio jumped all over him. "I know, you could work on that and get back to me on that, too, right?"

"Look, Detective," Joseph said, "you've been helpful so far. We helped you clear a murder, and when it's all over and Mr. Tatum has been convicted, we will be happy to sit down and talk to you about what your future career options are."

"How's that?" Maggio asked. "You're going to give me a job in Israel?"

"Well, you don't have much keeping you here, do you?"

"I have a lot keeping me here," Maggio said. "Like my job and getting my full pension. I intend to do all of that. I also intend to see that Mr. Tatum is successfully prosecuted. They did a preliminary hearing on this case. Do you know what that means, Mr. Joseph?"

Joseph looked away. "I don't have the faintest idea, nor do I care."

"That's the problem here, Mr. Joseph. You use people. You throw them away, and then you move on. But I'm grounded here. I live here, and I have to step up. Do you understand that?"

He shrugged. "I suppose it is some sort of American slang for your rising out of the ashes of your life and becoming a productive member of the police force."

"Listen," Maggio said. "I need the DNA samples. I need her statement. I need the family's address and phone number. I need all those things, and if I don't get them, this case is going to blow up. You got it?"

"Please, no threats," Joseph said. "Let's continue to work together." Joseph pulled Anaka up by the elbow and began to leave.

"Hey, it was nice talking to you, Anaka," Maggio said. He lit up another cigarette and watched them walk east toward the lake. They crossed Lake Shore Drive and disappeared down some steps near the walkway along the lake. "Assholes," he muttered.

* * *

Collata watched Avi Joseph and Anaka Vanderlinden walk away from Maggio. He followed them from a distance and watched them get into a car. Joseph drove the car, a nondescript sedan. Collata wrote down the license plate number and triple-checked to make sure it was right. He followed the car as it made its way north through the park and over the river. He was some distance away as Anaka was dropped off at a high-rise building at 680 North Lake Shore Drive. The building was a combination of retail on the first floor and offices and residences on the upper floors. Something about the set-up didn't ring true to him. He had a decision to make. He could follow Avi, or he could try to tail Anaka. He decided that the license plate was enough and figured that Avi would take evasive action to lose him anyway. So he'd stay on Anaka. He drove around the building until he came to the cab stand at the front entrance. He waited at a distance and in a few minutes was rewarded by the sight of Anaka stepping out of the building and into a cab. They traveled west until Dearborn, where they took a right and proceeded north. The traffic was heavy, so Collata was unable to pursue close up. He had to stay two car lengths behind but kept the taxi in sight. At Dearborn and Elm, the cab pulled into a circular driveway in front of a modern glass-and-steel building. Anaka settled her fare and hurried in, exchanging pleasantries with the doorman.

Collata smiled. Okay, honey, now I know where you live, he thought to himself, as he watched her disappear into an elevator. He circled the block until he found a place to park. He chose a fire hydrant on Elm near the Treasure Island grocery store. He felt out of place in the neighborhood. It was near north—a wealthy enclave of apartments and condos surrounded by stores that catered to the affluent. Collata discreetly showed his badge to the doorman, a white man in his early thirties who wore a uniform and hat. He made no effort to explain to the doorman that he was a retired cop. Instead, he just leaned into him. "Hey, pal, you know that doll just shot through here?"

"Oh, yeah," the doorman said. "What about her?"

"You know anything about her?"

"I know she lives with a guy in 1804," the doorman said.

"Is that right? Have you seen the boyfriend lately?"

"Yeah, a couple of days ago he was here. He comes and goes."

"When he comes and goes, does he stay here or someplace else, you think? I mean, do you think this is his main residence?"

The doorman thought about it. "I'm not really sure."

"Well, does she live here?"

"Oh yeah, she lives here," the doorman said. "She's here almost every day."

"So, what's your take on the boyfriend? Is he married?"

"Can't say, really."

"Is this just a stabbin' cabin for him?" Collata asked.

"I don't know."

Collata was a bit frustrated. "What do you know? What can you tell me?"

"Tell you this," the doorman said. "She's here all the time. He's here sometimes every day for weeks, then he's gone for a few weeks. It goes on and off like that, like the guy lives out of town and comes in to see her for a couple weeks. Or he could be one of those guys that just travels a lot on business."

"Is there any lovey-dovey?" asked Collata.

"You mean, have they ever porked in the hallway?" the doorman asked. "No, they've never done that. They seem to be happy together though. They are a couple, for sure. It's obvious that they're not brother and sister, if that's what you mean."

Collata smiled. "Do you have a phone at your desk over there?"

"Of course I do," the doorman said.

Collata pulled out a pen and business card. He flipped it over and wrote his pager number on the back. "Next time he shows up and he's going to be here for the night, you call me at this number. It's my pager. When I get here, I'll have a crisp one-hundred-dollar bill for you. Does that sound like a good deal?"

"Sounds like a good deal for me," the doorman answered.

"So, Chief, what's your name?" Collata asked.

"It used to be Danny, but I kind of like Chief now."

"All right, Chief," Collata said, handing him the card. They shook hands. "Remember, a hundred bucks."

The doorman smiled. "All I have to do is make a phone call for a hundred bucks." He put the card in his shirt pocket and tapped the top of his hat. "Don't worry, I'll call."

* * *

Collata had his feet up on Darcy's desk. He was rummaging through a stack of photographs he'd just picked up from a one-hour photo shop. He pulled out a couple of good pictures and threw them across the desk to Darcy.

"Okay, the hot tomato is Ms. Anaka Vanderlinden, and the spook is the guy named Avi Joseph."

Darcy was eyeing the photographs. "So what are you going to do with these now?" he asked.

"I'm going to go back to see my friend, the doorman, and then I'm going to run by Bank Leumi."

"Bank Leumi?" Darcy asked.

"Yeah, it's an Israeli bank. They have offices in Chicago, a big branch."

"So what do they have to do with this?" Darcy asked.

"Well the car that our hero, Avi Joseph, was driving, had plates registered to Bank Leumi."

"Is that right?" Darcy asked.

"Yeah, that's right."

"I'm going to the bank to talk to some clown—another retired copper who's the head of security."

"Yeah, you guys are everywhere," Darcy interjected.

"I never knew him before, but he's one of those guys who thinks he's part of the Blue Brotherhood. So he tells me that the car checks out and that they have a number of discretionary cars that they have to give up to the Israeli government."

"Meaning what?" Darcy asked.

"Meaning that this cat, Avi Joseph, does have some connection with the Israeli government because whenever Avi comes to town, all he's got to do is dial up the bank, say some mumbo-jumbo to the right guy, and he's got a gassed up brand-new car at his disposal. No questions asked."

"Well, you need to find the mumbo-jumbo man," Darcy said. "And you got to find out what questions to ask him so we can find out some more."

"Yeah, I know. I'm going over there now," he said. "I'll find out, don't worry. Then I'm going to grab my buddy, Detective Maggio, when he finishes his AA meeting. . . ."

"His AA meeting?" Darcy asked.

"Yeah, he wants to get clean and sober. I'm going to help him."

"You're going to help the key witness against our client in one of our cases get clean and sober?"

"Yeah, that's right," Collata said. "And you're not going to ask him anything about it."

Darcy looked away. "I think he's more than just a typical stew bum, if you ask me," Darcy said.

"One thing at a time," Collata said. "I'm going to help the guy get his life back together."

"Why?" Darcy asked.

"'Cause he needs somebody to help him, and I'm the only one he's got."

"And after you get him back to being a healthy cop, what's he going to do? Come into court and testify against our client?"

"One thing at a time," Collata said again. "You know when he gets sober, he's going to have to make amends. That means he's going to have to come clean."

"So what you're saying," Darcy began, "is you're doing all this to help our client?"

Collata leaned back and popped a cigarette into his mouth, and, using the lighter with the other hand, blazed it up. "No. That's not what I am saying. I'm talking about saving a man's life. Just back off on this one, okay!" Collata spoke as the smoke seeped from his nostrils. "I promise you, it's going to work out. I won't do anything that will hurt our client. I promise."

"If you say so," Darcy said. "Anyway, we have some time before we go to motions and trial."

Collata took another deep hit on his cigarette and relaxed as the smoke penetrated his lungs. There was a knock on the door before it opened. Collata was sitting across from Darcy when Kathy walked in.

"Well?" she asked.

"I'm going to need some more time," Collata said. "I've got nothing at the moment."

"What do you mean? Did you lose him?" she asked.

"Nope, I followed him, but he didn't do anything wrong."

Kathy was exasperated. "It has been three weeks. You have nothing for me?"

Darcy intervened. "Isn't that a good thing, Kathy?"

"I suppose so," she said.

Collata crushed out his cigarette. "Kathy, this isn't an issue, this is your life. You want me to be deadballs on, don't you?"

She sat down. "Give me one," she said, pointing to his cigarette.

Collata pulled one out of his shirt pocket and handed it to her. She lit it up.

"Oh, that's great," Darcy said. "Can we get you some cowboy boots and a motorcycle, too?"

Kathy blew the smoke out. "I need something to settle my nerves."

"I thought you quit," Darcy said.

"I did, but I'm a little tense right now, Darcy. Would you prefer I drank a quart of Scotch with a few maniacs?"

"Ouch!" Collata said. "I think she's insulting us."

Darcy laughed. "I suppose the truth hurts."

Collata's pager began to vibrate and he looked down at it. Kathy blew smoke straight up in the air and leaned back in the chair.

"Who's this?" Collata said in a frustrated voice.

"What's the matter?" Darcy asked.

"I can't read this damn number. Let me borrow your glasses."

Darcy threw his reading glasses across the desk to Collata, who then put them on and looked at the beeper again. After a few seconds of concentration, he was able to get the number and picked up Darcy's phone. Darcy could tell from hearing the end of Collata's conversation that it was something serious. He scribbled an address or phone number on a piece of paper.

"I gotta go," Collata said.

"Wait, I need a report," Kathy insisted.

"I gave you a report. He ain't doing nothing wrong. I'll keep following him. You have a deadline in mind?"

She leaned back. "Well, my tenth anniversary is coming up in six weeks. Will you have an answer by then?"

"Oh, yeah," Collata said. "Six weeks, no problem. I'll stay on his ass. That'll give me a bunch more times. If he goes out on any special night other than the nights he's been going out, you hit me on the pager and I'll follow him. Okay?"

"Thanks, Collata," she said.

"Don't mention it. Hey boss, I gotta run. Can everything else wait?"

Darcy shrugged. "Yeah, take care of business. Come back when you can, or call me later."

"Okay, I'm outta here."

Eighteen

Darcy and Patrick waited in the lobby of the U.S. Attorney's Office on the fifth floor of the Dirksen Federal Building. They had guest badges attached to their chests, and Darcy sat back on the couch with his eyes closed while Patrick paced the length of the room. As the two receptionists worked behind bulletproof glass, people came and went through two passageways, one on either side of the reception area. People were buzzed through, sometimes after producing an ID, sometimes simply after exchanging greetings with the receptionists, who obviously knew them.

After about fifteen minutes, a door popped open and Carl Stringer stood before them. "Gentlemen, come in," he said.

Darcy and Patrick followed Carl down a long hallway heading south, turned right, and ended up in an office overlooking the Plaza of the Post Office. Carl's office was identical to the other Assistant U.S. Attorneys' offices. They all had the same dark brown wood furniture and a shelf that lined the back wall. Carl had a collection of baseball hats on his shelf. Darcy guessed that collecting them had become a tradition with the prosecutors. All had patches of different agencies—DEA, FBI, ATF, Border Patrol, INS, IRS-Criminal Investigations.

About a dozen of them were displayed on Carl's shelf, and Darcy was perusing them when Carl turned to see what he was looking at.

"Oh, the hats," he said. "Got to collect them as you go along."

"What's the point?" Darcy asked without sarcasm.

"What do you mean?"

"Well, do you wear them?"

"No."

"Then why do you collect them?"

"I don't know. It's just something we do when we pick up a case with an agency. If you don't have the hat, the agent gives one to you. It's just collecting. It's something to do."

Darcy looked at Patrick. "Did you collect hats when you worked here?"

Patrick was embarrassed. "Yeah, I did."

"Well, what did you do with them when you left? Why haven't I ever seen them?"

"I left them here," Patrick said.

Carl was becoming frustrated. "Mr. Cole," he said, "can we stop talking about the hats now?"

Darcy smiled. "Sure, Carl. Please call me Darcy."

Stringer regained his composure and retrieved a file from his desk drawer. Patrick looked over to Darcy at that moment, but Darcy failed to understand what he meant to convey.

"Darcy, originally when I learned about your client, Mr. Feiger, I thought this was a nothing deal, that he may or may not have committed a crime. I didn't particularly have much interest in him. But I have since learned quite a bit more. I'm not going to insult your intelligence by starting at a primary level, so let's just skip to what's relevant here. Do you know who Pizza Joe Alfinni is?"

"I do," Darcy said.

"I don't," Patrick said.

Darcy turned to Patrick. "Joe Alfinni lives in the western

suburbs. He got his nickname, 'Pizza Joe,' because the Feds believe there was something underhanded about the way he expanded his pizza parlor business to include distribution to school districts throughout the suburbs."

Stringer leaned forward. "Actually, that's a very sanitized version, Darcy. Patrick, "Pizza Joe" Alfinni is in the mob, and he stacked the school boards in certain suburbs—Melrose Park, Westchester, Stone Park, Lyons, La Grange, Tinley Park, and about ten others—with his own people."

Darcy interjected. "He backed people running for the school board and he helped them financially. There's nothing illegal about that."

"That's true," Carl said. "He did nothing illegal in getting these people on the Board. But coincidentally, right after they made the Board, Joe Alfinni got the rights to sell pizza to their districts' schoolkids. Darcy, you know it's not the pizza thing anyway," Carl continued. "Pizza Joe Alfinni, we believe, is a high-ranking captain in the Chicago outfit, which is run by Tony Benvenuti. Pizza Joe is a major earner. Besides his legitimate businesses, he's involved in a number of illegitimate businesses—cash cows for the outfit—and here's where your client comes in: gambling, bookmaking, loan sharking and prostitution. We have a number of cooperating individuals who have been feeding us information. Obviously, we don't have enough yet to indict Pizza Joe, but it's been quite revealing. Your client could be helpful as a witness against Mr. Alfinni. Your client may be involved more than he is aware. He may be in way over his head."

Stringer continued. "First of all, your client did more than just represent prostitutes in misdemeanor and felony cases in Cook County. We have evidence that he was involved with Joe Alfinni and some of Joe Alfinni's men in the importation of individuals from countries such as Russia, Poland, and China for the sole purpose of enslaving these women as prostitutes in Chicago and other Midwestern towns. We also believe that your client went beyond just being an attorney and actually ran prostitution rings using some of these foreign women as well as American-born women. Your guy is real sharp. He'd have sex with these women first, that way he knew he wasn't dealing with an undercover agent. We have reason to believe that your client directly benefited financially, and then kicked money upstairs to Joe Alfinni. And then Joe Alfinni, of course, kicked up to the higher-ups in the outfit, including Mr. Benvenuti. As you know, we've been looking into Mr. Benvenuti for a long time now, but we haven't been able to touch him. We feel that if we can get to Joe Alfinni, he could get us Mr. Benvenuti. And one way we get to Joe Alfinni is through your client and his cooperation."

Patrick whistled. "So you're telling us that you want Harry Feiger to cooperate against Joe Alfinni?"

"Even more than that," Carl said. "We don't have enough corroboration on instances where Harry dealt with Joe that we could just take his word for it. So what we want to do is offer him an opportunity to work with us proactively in exchange for immunity from prosecution, and witness protection."

"You want me to call my client in for a meeting and tell him that you'll give him immunity from prosecution if he wears a wire and engages Joe Alfinni in conversations that will lead to his prosecution?"

Stringer was firm. "Yes. I don't care about that expungement crap. I want Alfinni."

There was a knock at the door, and the three of them turned in unison to see who it was.

"May I come in?" Ira Greenberg asked.

"Yes, sir," Carl said.

Ira Greenberg was a short, thin man with short dark hair and a pencil-thin mustache. He wore a double-breasted blue pinstriped suit and a blue on blue shirt and tie combination. For accent, he had a blue and red patterned silk pocket square folded perfectly and protruding from his breast pocket. Ira was an old adversary of Darcy's. In a previous trial Ira had gotten caught pulling a dirty trick against Darcy, one that stretched the rules of law. After an investigation, he had been mildly disciplined. "Gentlemen, do you mind if I join in on this discussion?" he asked.

"I should have seen your fingerprints all over this, Ira," Darcy said.

"I was disappointed, but not surprised," Patrick began, "when I heard you had gotten a reprimand instead of fired."

"Well," Ira said, "that's all in the past now. Can we get beyond that now?"

"We could get beyond it," Patrick said, "and we could work together, but your true colors will come out sooner or later. You're a true asshole."

Darcy put his hand on Patrick's forearm in a calming gesture.

"I suppose I deserve that," Ira replied, "but sometimes you have to be a bastard when you're going after the tough guys. You weren't here long enough to learn that firsthand."

"You condescending prick," Patrick retorted.

Darcy interrupted. "Guys, I'm not here to hash out an old fight. Obviously, you came in this room for a purpose, so let's get to it. Lay your deal on the table."

"This is it," Ira began. "We want your client to cooperate and wear a wire. If he doesn't, then I will presume either he doesn't want to or that you didn't convey this offer to him. I am concerned that there is a potential conflict here. We all know that you have a relationship with Mr. Benvenuti, and Benvenuti is the ultimate and primary target here. I will file a motion to have you disqualified as the attorney for Mr. Feiger due to this conflict of interest."

"You mean a potential conflict of interest," Darcy said.

"Conflict of interest," Greenberg said. "You're representing a man who is the target of an investigation."

"You mean Feiger or Benvenuti?"

"Cute," Ira said. "You are representing Harry Feiger, who is a potential witness against Benvenuti, and you have represented Benvenuti in the past."

"I represented Benvenuti's son, and you well know that

conflict no longer exists. I'll tell you what, Ira. Here's what I'm going to do for you."

Ira leaned in.

"I'm going to do nothing," Darcy said, "because I always do better when you're doing everything."

"What's that supposed to mean?" Ira asked.

"It means that every time you deal with me, you lose your sense of professionalism," Darcy said, "and you make a mistake. You want me, and I'm not doing anything wrong. Because of that combination, you will ultimately make a mistake. And with the reprimand you received from our last bout, maybe you'll just push yourself over the top and end up opening your own office or becoming partner at some big firm. You can count the ceiling tiles to see how much square footage you have, and make your hundred and seventy-five thousand dollars a year—working every Saturday and alternate Sundays—flying to Dayton to take depositions on an employment discrimination case and turning your life to shit."

Ira leaned in. "Don't worry about me, Darcy. I'll be fine."

"Is there anything else?" Darcy asked, turning to Stringer.

"No, that's it. You understand our offer. I'll give you a week to consider it with your client, and then I'll need to know his answer."

"You're right, it is his decision," Darcy said. "When he first came to me, he told me that if you guys were going to charge him, he wanted to take a plea—accept his responsibilities and move on. It's hard to imagine he'll want to become a snitch and testify against the mob and get relocated to some godforsaken hellhole under a new name—something catchy like John Jones or Jim Johnson or William Smith. Maybe you could help him get some thirty-thousand-dollar-a-year job where he can spend the rest of his life putting tape seals on the hood of his car and waiting for the bomb. But, like you said, it is his decision."

Darcy stood and leaned across the desk to shake hands with Carl. "Carl, it's always a pleasure." He then brushed by

Ira. "You know where to find me," he said. "I'll be waiting to hear from you with bated breath." As he reached the threshold of the door, Darcy heard Stringer rise.

"Mr. Cole, I do need to know in a week," he said.

"Yes, I know. One week."

Nineteen

Darcy pushed through the outer doors of Seymour's office. Since his secretary was not to be seen, he walked through the waiting room and directly into Seymour's office. Seymour was on the phone, leaning back in his chair, and chewing on a pen, listening to someone. He smiled at Darcy and gave him a little wave, pulling the pen out of his mouth.

"That's precisely my point," Seymour said. "If you would like for me to have another doctor examine him, I'd be happy to. But at this point, we already have two doctors who agree on the percentage of permanent disability, and your doctor said that he can't disagree. While he might *think* it's overstated, he can't say that it *is* overstated. So what's the point? Are we going to doctors ad nauseum until we come to a consensus?

"I think we should take this to a hearing in front of the Industrial Commission or we should settle it now," Seymour continued. He listened for a moment, and then smiled. "That's what I thought. Why don't you send me over the settlement agreement and we'll get this done. And you'll have one less file on your desk, okay? By the end of the week?" Seymour asked. "Very good."

He hung up. "I just made money," he said to Darcy.

"Don't you mean your client just made money?" Darcy asked.

"Well, actually," Seymour said, "he's been getting temporary disability, and now we rolled over his settlement. So we both made money." Seymour walked over to where the chess table was set up and sat behind the whites. "Are we going to have a Scotch?" he asked.

"No, I think I'll pass," Darcy replied.

"Really?" Seymour said. "Then I'll pass as well. We'll sit and play chess with clear, sober minds."

"So, what's new, my friend?" Darcy asked.

"Nothing's new with me," Seymour said. "I settled one case. I have others to work on. My family is healthy, and I am in the pink. How about you?"

"Same with me," Darcy said. "I'm in the pink. I lead an interesting life. I have a client who comes to me and says, 'I got a simple deal for you, Darcy. Just get me a plea agreement on this case. I'm pleading guilty. I'm going to do my time and get on with my life.'"

"And did it turn out that way?" Seymour asked, moving a pawn.

"Of course not," Darcy said. "Seems like this guy I thought was a nickel-and-dimer turns out to be a real bastard."

"Ah, the disappointment of humanity," Seymour said. "And what sort of bastard is this particular man?"

"He's the type of man that recruits women in countries like Poland, China, and Russia and tells them they could have a better life here. He then flies them over and enslaves them in sex rings as prostitutes. He's tied in with the Chicago Outfit, and they provide the muscle and business acumen. He kicks up the money and takes his piece. He sends all his money to an offshore account, evades taxes, and doesn't tell anyone about it. All the time, he's happily married—his version of happily married evidently meaning that he's having sexual relations with these immigrant girls right off the boat. The FBI can't get near him because every one of these broads has to give it up to Harry, and they don't have a female agent that wants to make a case bad enough to screw this fifty-something-year-old piece of shit. He comes into my office one day pissing and moaning because he doesn't have a plea agreement, saying that I got to pull my strings and do something that I can only construe as illegal or unethical, to try and help him out because he's paid me some money. But now, the U.S. Attorney's office wants him to wear a wire to snitch on a guy. And then, they want him to flip on Mr. Benvenuti."

"Mr. Benvenuti?" Seymour asked. "Why don't they just have the guy commit suicide?"

"So, as the Assistant United States Attorney is telling me this nonsense," Darcy continues, "Ira Greenberg pops into the office and starts threatening me."

"The boy never learns, does he?" Seymour muttered. "Move," he said as he moved his pawn.

Darcy moved one of his pawns. "The goofball skated with a reprimand for the crap he pulled on me the last time we tangled," Darcy said, "and now he's right back at it."

"Nope, he didn't learn anything," Seymour agreed, moving a bishop.

"I also have a murder case where I'm representing a guy accused of murdering a ghost."

"What do you mean, 'ghost'?" Seymour asked.

"Well," Darcy began, "this guy's a big shot in the black community. Owns a bunch of property, businesses, and so forth, and among those businesses are pawnshops—you know, diamonds, watches, and things like that. He hooks up with this kid from Israel who runs diamonds back and forth for the Israeli Diamond Merchant Association. The guy is traveling to London, Amsterdam, Johannesburg, Chicago, New York, and Miami. He was carrying about a half a million to a million dollars' worth of diamonds at a crack. This guy ends up missing, and they find a body that nobody can really identify, and they say my client whacked him. Except everybody I talk to on this case doesn't believe that the guy is dead. It is all a scam. The Assistant State's Attorney on this case is Jack Karsten."

Seymour interrupted. "Is that the son of the lawyer?"

"Yeah."

"It's a damn shame his father died. He was a hell of a man."

"Yeah, I told him that. Anyway, Karsten taps me on the shoulder, pulls me out and says, 'I'll give your client a bond and we're going to do a preliminary hearing.' Do you know how many preliminary hearings have been done in the last twenty-five years over there on murder cases?"

Seymour shrugged.

"One. One case, and that was a copper who was accused of shooting a homeless guy while the cop was off-duty partying with his girlfriend and his wife was sitting at home. They wanted to dump it on the judge, as opposed to making enemies in the police union before the election. You don't think my ears pricked up when I hear Karsten tell me that they're going to do a preliminary hearing and agree to a bond? Then we start investigating it, and everything gets goofier by the minute. On top of that, during the course of the investigation, I interview a doctor, this woman over at Northwestern in the emergency room—one of the most beautiful women I have ever seen. I mean, I was thunderstruck just standing in her presence. Do you know what I mean?"

"It's a beautiful thought," Seymour said. "So what happened?"

"So I get a kidney stone and I end up in the emergency room. They operate on me, and when I come to, she's there. We haven't been apart since.

"Then Kathy—you know my partner Kathy—thinks her husband is cheating on her. We have Collata follow her husband, and it turns out he's not doing a thing wrong. He's picked up a side job so he can buy her a fancy ring for their tenth anniversary. He doesn't realize that while he's earning the money for the ring, she's so goddamn suspicious she's ready to leave him."

Seymour laughed. "Wait a minute. We'll get back to that. But let's return for a moment—may we?—to this beautiful woman doctor who hasn't left your side."

"What?" Darcy asked.

"'What?' How long have I known you? And now you're telling me there's a woman in your life?"

"There've been other women in my life."

"There've been women that float in and out of your life, briefly and without mention. I only find out about them after they're gone. You clearly have feelings for this woman. So tell me. Let's go. What about her?"

Darcy used a pawn to take one of Seymour's, freeing up his rook. "Her name is Amy Wagner. She's smart, beautiful, and she really seems to be interested in me."

Seymour looked at him. "So is she a young woman or a woman your age?"

"I like the way you put that. I think she's young, but she's not that far from my age. She's probably about ten years younger than me," he said.

"Really, and what sort of woman is she?"

"She's smart, funny, interesting, and interested. She's the real deal."

Seymour sat back, stunned. "You're in love with this woman, aren't you?"

Darcy smiled. "Seymour, you have no idea what a wonderful person she is."

"How long have you been seeing her?"

Darcy ran his hands through his hair, a habit that appeared whenever conversations became too personal. "I have seen her virtually every night or every day since I was in the hospital. So what has that been, a few weeks?"

"So here's the million-dollar question," Seymour began. "With all the women in the world, why her? Why her?"

Darcy leaned forward. "How long have you been married to your wife?"

Seymour laughed. "Four score, seven years. Oh wait, that was Lincoln's line. Ah, you know, probably through ten presidents. Why?"

"Why are you with her?" Darcy asked. "Why didn't you trade her in for some young dolly?"

Seymour thought about it. "It never occurred to me," he

said. "When I look at her, she is a young dolly to me. She's beautiful, she's smart, and she's my friend. I love her."

"Aha," Darcy exclaimed. "In other words, she makes your life better."

"No," said Seymour, "she is my life. Without her, what do I have? I sit in this office, play chess with a lunatic down the hall—what do I have without her or my children?"

"So it doesn't matter what she looks like, or what her body is like. You love her, and you see her through the eyes of love," Darcy said, feeling a little uncomfortable with himself.

"I'm suddenly feeling like I'm being cross-examined, here, Mr. Cole," Seymour broke in, trying to ease Darcy's apparent discomfort.

"No, I'm just trying to prove a point in answering your questions. When you see her, you see everything that's good in the world. You see everything that makes your life worth living. And you see all your happiness, right?"

"I suppose that's right," Seymour said.

"When I'm with Amy, for the first time in my life, other than with my daughter, I realize that I can be happy. It's not just that she's easy to be with," Darcy said, "it's that every moment I'm with her, I'm happy. I feel like life is wonderful, like I am in a goddamn movie or something. I used to feel that people on the outside were looking in at me and saying to themselves, 'What an exciting life—he's got his own law firm, high-profile cases, trial work, meets interesting people.' And yet, in reality, my life seemed hollow and empty. Now, when I look at it, I realize that, yeah, it is pretty interesting, but it's only interesting because I have something else now. Law isn't the sole focus of my life anymore."

"I like this woman already," Seymour said.

"Amy Wagner," Darcy said.

"I like Amy Wagner," Seymour repeated. "Don't blow this, Darcy. I have never seen you like this before."

"Believe me," Darcy said, "they'll have to kill me to get me away from her."

Seymour slid his queen. "Check," he said. Darcy tried to

hide his king behind a blocking pawn, but Seymour slid his bishop to the far end of the board and declared checkmate. "Your chess game is beginning to regress," Seymour said. "You were more of a challenge before you were in love. I'll have to talk to this Dr. Wagner and see if perhaps she could play chess. Another game?"

"No," Darcy said as he moved his pieces back in line.

"So now what's going on with Kathy?" Seymour asked.

"Kathy's husband is a schoolteacher. He doesn't make a lot of money. He's not in one of those school districts in the North Shore suburbs that pay a decent salary. So their tenth anniversary is coming up and he wants to do something special for her. He starts going out every Thursday night, and then other nights. She thinks he's got a girlfriend because he's coming home smelling like a bar. So she has Collata follow him. Collata follows him and realizes that the guy is working as a bartender. Collata sits down at the bar, has a couple of drinks, and finds out that Jim is working to get enough money to buy Kathy one of those anniversary rings with the diamonds in it, the ones you see in the commercials, he tells Collata."

"It's too bad you can't put him in touch with the missing diamond boy," Seymour said. "Maybe he could cut a real good deal."

"Ha, I hadn't thought of that. We could tie everything together," Darcy said. "Anyway, he's out there trying to make money to buy this ring, and she's going crazy thinking that he's got something on the side and that Collata either hasn't caught him or won't tell her. Meanwhile, Collata's ducking and dodging, waiting for their anniversary to come, so Jim can give her the ring. He doesn't want to spoil the surprise—wants everybody to be happy."

"Jesus, it's like a soap opera over there," Seymour said. "You know, I was just thinking, maybe you could help this guy out with the ring and get a deal for yourself at the same time."

Darcy looked at him. "What are talking about?"

"Well, you said you never were going to let Amy go. You might as well give her the ring now."

Darcy chuckled. "Yeah, I'm going to jump into a marriage at my age. Besides, I don't know if she would want to marry me."

"Well, you won't know unless you ask."

"Well," Darcy said, "I'm not going anywhere. So if we're talking about spending the rest of our lives together, we can do it one day at a time until we get to forever."

"That's a great strategy," Seymour said. "Just don't blow it."

Twenty

Collata pulled his van into the circular driveway at Anaka's building and jumped out to see his buddy, the doorman— Chief.

"Sorry," Chief said, "the boyfriend came and went. I didn't know how long he was going to be here. I called you as soon as he came. He just left about ten minutes ago."

"With her or without her?"

"Without her."

"Okay," Collata said, reaching into his pocket and pulling out a wad of bills. He counted out five twenties and gave them to Chief.

The doorman looked down at them. "You told me it would be a crisp hundred," he said.

"What?" Collata asked.

"I'm kidding," Chief said, "I'm kidding."

Collata relaxed. "Hit me again when he's here, and I'll hit you with another hundred."

"Hey, beautiful," Chief replied.

"Only this time, he'll still have to be here," Collata stipulated.

"Gotcha. So I just can't keep calling you every day telling you he left."

"Right, though I'm not saying that's what you did this time." Collata shook Chief's hand and walked out. He jumped into his van, drove around the block and parked within view of the front door. He waited. An hour later Anaka walked out with an overnight bag. She had a brief conversation with the doorman, then the cab light over the entranceway of the building popped on, flagging any cab within eyesight.

Collata was looking from all different angles trying to figure out which was the closest cab and from what direction it was coming as he started his van. But before he could decide an orange taxi pulled into the roundabout and picked Anaka up. The cab headed out north. Collata turned the corner and started following from a distance. They rolled up to Division Street and went east, then hit Lake Shore Drive and headed north. Then the cab pulled into a driveway at 3600 North.

The doorman opened the door, and Anaka stepped out. A tall, thin man with dark, curly hair met her there and gave her a quick peck on the cheek. Then they stepped back together into the same cab, which had waited. They exited the driveway and headed south, directly toward Collata. Collata grabbed the camera with the telephoto lens already in place from the passenger seat. He focused on the oncoming cab, and snapped a series of pictures as quickly as he could. When the cab got close, he ducked down out of sight. He watched them through the rearview mirror as they disappeared heading south. Stashing the camera in its carrying bag, he locked his van and walked over to the building.

The doorman standing outside watched as Collata approached. "Hi there. The name is Collata," he said, as he flashed him his badge.

"How can I help you?" the doorman asked.

"That woman that just left in the cab—she just got here, met a guy, and then left in the same cab with the guy she met here. Do you by any chance know who the guy is?"

"Oh yeah, that's the gentleman in 1610."

"Do you know his name?"

"Sir," the doorman replied.

"Excuse me?" a confused Collata asked.

"Some of these people, you know. Some of them, you don't.

To him, I always say, 'Sir, good morning, sir. How are you, sir? Can I get you a cab, sir?' A lot of the people say, 'Call me so and so, or call me such and such,' but this prick, he's just 'sir' to me."

"I see," Collata said, "but you do know he's in 1610."

"Yep."

"The girl that comes here, who's she?"

"As far as I can tell, they're boyfriend and girlfriend. I mean, I don't know for sure, but she stays over a lot."

"I see. Um, is there someone I can talk to about seeing his apartment?"

"Well, that depends," the doorman said.

"On what?" Collata asked.

"If it's official, you can see the assistant manager. But she'll tell you to get a warrant. If it's not official, I could hook you up with one of the maintenance guys. You take care of him, you take care of me, he'll let you in for a little while."

"What's your name?"

"Mike."

"Okay, Mike, you and I could get along," Collata said.

"That's good, because if I ever get popped out on Rush Street, having too many cocktails, I'm going to give you a call."

Collata smiled. "You got it. Where's your maintenance man?"

"Hang on," he said. "I'll get him." Mike walked into the lobby and picked up the phone behind the desk. He had a short conversation and walked back to Collata. "He'll be here in a little while."

Collata reached into his pocket. His funds were getting low, but he still had a few hundred dollars on him. He pulled out a fifty as Mike watched. Mike shook his head. He pulled out another fifty, and Mike smiled. "How about your buddy?" Collata asked.

"You take care of him too," Mike said. "And by the way, I never seen you before."

"And I haven't seen you."

A short, thin Hispanic guy wearing a pair of tan pants and

a tan shirt emerged from the building. The building's address was embroidered over his right pocket and the name "Bobby" was over the left. He approached Collata.

"Okay, you the guy?" he asked.

"I'm the guy," Collata said.

"Let me see your badge?"

Collata showed him the badge.

"What do you need?" Bobby asked.

"Is your name really Bobby?"

"Hell no," the Hispanic guy said. "It's Roberto, but they don't want to have to say that around here. Makes the old people feel bad, so they made me Bobby."

"What do your friends call you?"

"Mostly Bobby," he said.

Collata was perplexed. "I thought you said . . ." He trailed off.

Bobby pointed to the nametag. "Look, people meet you, you got a nametag that says Bobby, so you become Bobby. You know what I'm saying?"

"Gotcha. What do you want me to call you?"

"Bobby works," he said.

"Okay, Bobby. I need to see unit 1610."

"I need to see your badge again," Bobby said.

Collata showed him the badge again. Bobby studied it.

"Okay," he said, "let's go."

Thirty-six Hundred North Lake Shore Drive was a two-tower building separated by an entranceway. Bobby walked hurriedly toward an elevator in the south tower with Collata right behind him. They got in. Bobby looked Collata up and down.

"You're a retired copper, aren't you?"

"That's right," Collata said. "I'm a PI."

"So I really shouldn't be letting you in here."

Collata reached into his pocket. He had less than two hundred dollars. He grabbed a hundred and sixty and handed to him. "I need the rest for lunch."

Bobby smiled. "I'm going to stay with you so that you don't take nothing."

"That's a deal," Collata said.

Bobby opened the door, and Collata walked in. Bobby closed the door behind them. Straight ahead were windows facing north with a white telescope on a tripod in front of them. There was furniture—not expensive, not cheap, just run-of-the-mill stuff—a sofa, chair, entertainment center, TV, VCR, and stereo. There was a small kitchen area with a couple of stools up against a countertop. The bathroom was small, and a bedroom had a queen-size bed and a chest of drawers. Bobby stood at the threshold as Collata carefully opened the drawers and looked through. Collata found an assortment of passports. He picked them up and sat on the edge of the bed to have a gander.

"Will you look at this?" he said out loud.

Bobby stepped forward. There was a British, French, Canadian and American passport—all with the same picture but different names. "Holy shit," Bobby exclaimed. "This guy's got some connections."

Collata pulled out his notepad and wrote down the information off each of the passports. "Well, I suppose we're going to find out who he is," he said.

Bobby was still staring at the passports.

"Do you know what this guy calls himself around here?" Collata asked.

Bobby shrugged his shoulders. "I got no clue. Ask Mike. He knows the comings and goings." Bobby started getting nervous. "I think we need to wrap this up," he said. "And if anyone sees us, you're a plumber looking at some pipes."

"Yeah, I got it," Collata said. He put the passports back together and started to deposit them back into the drawer when he pretended he heard something. He turned suddenly in the direction of the front room and whispered, "What was that?"

Bobby said, "Oh shit," and ran toward the door.

Collata quickly pocketed the passports. He closed the drawer and stepped out of the room.

Bobby came back, relieved. "It's nobody," he said. "Something in the hall, I guess. But let's get out of here."

"Yeah, yeah, I gotcha, my man," Collata said.

They stepped out and backed down the hallway to the elevator. The elevator door opened and they stepped in. As the door closed, Bobby let out a sigh of relief. "Holy mother," he said. "Who is this guy?"

"I don't quite know yet, but I'm going to find out," Collata answered. "You want to know what I already know?"

Bobby mulled it over. "No, I don't want to know nothing. I don't know you, I don't know him. I don't know nothing. Get what I'm saying?"

"I get it."

On the ground floor, Bobby scurried out of the elevator, leaving Collata to fend for himself. As Collata walked out, Mike called to him. "Sir," he said, "I need to talk to you."

Collata walked over to him.

"You expressed some interest in renting an apartment, sir?" Mike asked.

Collata went along with it. "Yeah, I'm looking for an apartment. Something on a high floor with a southern exposure."

"Here's the card of the manager of the building," Mike said.

Collata took the card and put in his pocket. "Thank you."

"Yeah, I look forward to seeing you again sometime soon," Mike said.

"Well, I hope so. I have other apartments to see, but thank you for your help. Friendly building." Collata walked out through the revolving door into the sunshine and got into his van. He pulled out the card. On the front was the name of the management service, and on the back was the name David Yale, the person who leased 1610. That would be Jacob Orloff, Collata thought. He put the card back in his shirt pocket. "Thank you, Mike," he said to himself. Then he reached into his back pocket and pulled out the passports. "And thank you, Bobby," he said as he put them in his shirt pocket with the card.

Twenty-One

The Tatum family filled the waiting room area of Darcy's office. One chair strained under the weight of Marcus Tatum. To his left sat his mother, Dorothy, and to his right, his wife, Teesha. Darcy opened the door. "Thank you for coming," he said.

Marcus stood up. "Like there's anything else more important to me than this case right now," he replied.

Teesha and Dorothy shook Darcy's hand and they followed him into a conference room. Collata was pacing the floor as they stepped in.

"You remember Mr. Collata, don't you?" Darcy asked.

Collata stepped up and shook hands with Marcus. "Nice to see you again, Marcus, Mrs. Tatum," shaking hands with Dorothy, "Mrs. Tatum," he said again, shaking hands with Teesha.

"Please sit down," Darcy said, pointing at the table. Everyone sat down.

Collata turned his chair around so his arms were resting over the back of his chair as he straddled it. "Do you recognize this guy?" he said, throwing the passport across to Tatum.

Tatum opened it up. "Yeah, it's the guy I worked with that they say I killed."

Darcy and Collata shared a glance and then looked

back at him. "So, that's him. That's the guy you called 'the Jew'?"

"Yeah, that's him," he said.

"So where did you find this passport?" he asked.

"Don't worry about that," Collata replied.

"What do I need to worry about?" Tatum asked.

Darcy and Collata stole another glance at each other. "Well," Darcy began, "here's what you have to worry about." Darcy stopped and tried to gather his thoughts. "You're sure that's the guy you're charged with killing?"

Tatum leaned in. "Yes, that's him."

"Well," Darcy said, "for a dead guy, he sure gets around."

"Meaning what?" Dorothy Tatum interrupted.

"Meaning he's not dead," Darcy replied.

"I knew it," Marcus said as he slammed his hand on the table. "I told you this cat was all the way CIA."

Collata threw a cigarette in his mouth and put his palms out with the pack of matches, a gesture to inquire if anyone objected. No one did, and he fired up. "This guy is alive, all right," Collata said, "I saw him with my own eyes."

Dorothy looked at Darcy. "What do we do now?" she asked.

"Well," he said, "it's one thing to know he's alive, and it's another to prove it. It's like proving a negative."

"So what are you going to do?"

Darcy began to answer when Collata interrupted. "I'm going to get the detective in this case—I'm going to grab him and drag him around until we find this guy."

Marcus was incredulous. "You're going to take Maggio, the cop who tried to kill me and set me up on this trumped-up shit, and you're going to bring him in."

"Who better?" Collata asked.

"The man is insane."

"Absolutely," Collata said, "but what's he going to do when he sees that Jacob is alive?"

"What's he going to do? The man's been lying for years. He'll just step up and lie."

"No he won't," Collata said. "I'm going to prove to him that this guy is alive. He's going to have to step up and square it. He has to make things right with you."

"You're crazy," Marcus said. "He's not going to do it."

Dorothy Tatum put her hand on Marcus's forearm. "Just a second, honey," she said. "Why would we do this?" she asked Collata.

"Because," Collata said, "it's one thing for me to say he's alive. Even if I could videotape him, they'd say I changed the dates of the videotape. I have to get a credible independent witness to see him. Or even better, I have to get Maggio to say that he saw him. And if Maggio says that, they don't know who the victim is. They got no case against Marcus."

"But why Maggio, why not another detective?"

"Because Maggio's the only one that Marcus 'confessed' to. Maggio's the one who can say, 'Yeah, he confessed to me, but now I know that his statement was the unfortunate product of the interrogation process, rather than the truth because I can see that Jacob is alive.' Then the case is gone, and we don't even have to go to trial."

"I'm apprehensive about doing anything that would involve Detective Maggio. Look what he did to Marcus," Dorothy said. Teesha agreed.

"Well, he owes Marcus the truth," Collata said. "I know where Orloff lives, and he doesn't know I found him. Now it's a question of finding Orloff at the right time with the right person."

"How did you find him in the first place?" Dorothy asked.

"It's just detective work," Collata said, shrugging modestly and letting his words trail off.

"I'm sure it wasn't easy for you to find a dead man," Dorothy said. "We're very happy with what you've done so far. Please continue and know that you have our complete confidence. It is just that we are very concerned about doing anything with Detective Maggio."

"I understand completely," Collata said. "But we feel we need him. I already have an independent witness who can tell us that Jacob was alive recently, or certainly long after the corpse was identified. Now I got to do a little more legwork. Like Darcy said, our goal is to get this case dismissed. There have been a lot of innocent people sent to prison for crimes they didn't commit."

"Amen to that, brother," Marcus agreed.

"One common theme among those innocent people," Dorothy began, "was that none of them could afford a real defense. People think it's racial, but it's more than that, it's financial. We have the means necessary, and we will stop at nothing to make sure Marcus is exonerated in this case."

"I understand," Darcy said.

"Do you understand, Mr. Cole?" she said. "You see, my son is successful. That success has come with the help of his wife, Teesha, and me. We have been there for him at every stretch. He is a black man in the city of Chicago. A successful black man is always a target. So you see, Mr. Cole, it's not unexpected that Marcus would be targeted for this. However, I am not going to allow the system to crush Marcus, and that is why we have retained you. I am thrilled with what you and Mr. Collata have done so far, but you know we're not done yet, and we need to continue this momentum. We need him exonerated."

"I completely agree with you," Darcy said. "We'll do everything possible."

"So you know why I don't feel comfortable with Detective Maggio being involved in this? If you use Detective Maggio and it fails, I will not be forgiving."

"I understand," Darcy said. He leaned in toward Dorothy. "I think we need him. You know, Mrs. Tatum, there's a lot of instances where doctors operate on people—they bring all their skill and expertise to the operating room. But even with all that, they can't always save a patient. Sometimes they can't because there's no way to save them. Sometimes they can't because they make a mistake, do something wrong. I can assure you that, as much as that surgeon wants to bring his acumen to the table for his patient, I want to bring mine for your son. I expect and I accept that you will examine everything I do and that if you are unhappy, you will seek out whatever remedy you deem appropriate. If you think I have committed malpractice, I'm sure you'll sue me. However, I am very comfortable that whatever I do, I will do it the right way, that I will do it well, and that you will be satisfied with my performance. I realize again that you will be scrutinizing everything, and I am comfortable with that."

She smiled. "Yes, you are," she said, "and I'm sure that you will do a great job. I just wanted to voice my concerns. What would you like us to do now?"

"I would like you—the three of you—to say nothing to anyone about our belief that Jacob is alive. It must remain in this room until we're able to get definitive evidence. I don't want to rely on a bunch of witnesses saying, 'Oh yeah, I saw him.' I need something more, and I don't want to scare him off either."

"I understand," Dorothy said, "and I promise you that it will not leave this room, at least not by us."

"Okay, let's get back to work. Feel good about this turn of events," Darcy insisted. "Remain optimistic, but cautiously so."

"You sound like a doctor," Dorothy said, and the room broke out in laughter.

"Well, I haven't lost a patient yet," Darcy said. "Let's keep it going."

They shook hands and Darcy walked them out, leaving Collata in the conference room with his steadily filling ashtray. Darcy returned and sat in a chair, stretching his arms out to the conference table.

"Everything is not about race," Collata began. "Every time you deal with a black person, they think it's all about racism."

"Isn't it?" Darcy asked.

"Hell no, this wasn't racist. This was a detective getting a bad lead and following it up. He had a hunch and made the hunch pan out."

"Isn't that racist?" Darcy asked.

"How?" Collata asked. "No one said, 'the black guy.'"

Darcy leaned back, putting his hands behind his head. "That's exactly what they said. These guys needed someone to take the fall for a homicide. So they took a high-profile black man who had some dealings with Jacob and they decided to pin it on him, knowing full well that Chicago Police would roll with it."

"Hey, every cop isn't racist," Collata said.

"What about Maggio?" Darcy asked. "Is he racist?"

"I don't know. I see him walking through a fog every day."

"Precisely," Darcy said. "His vision is impaired and yet he was willing to take this at face value and roll with it."

"Yeah, you said that already," Collata said.

"What is with you and Maggio? Are you guys buddies now?"

Collata lit up his fourth cigarette and looked away. There was an awkward silence between them. "You know," Collata began, "the guy's messed up. There's no question about it, but somewhere inside that shell is the spark of a good cop, and he wants to re-ignite it. He wants to get clean. He wants to get sober."

Darcy leaned back toward Collata. "Well I'm happy to see you're trying to help him toward redemption, but your first priority should be this case. Ask yourself a couple of questions here," Darcy began. "Why did they go to Maggio in the first place?"

Collata was looking at Darcy, trying to figure out where he was going with this. Then he shrugged. "Well, they wanted to have Jacob dead."

"Who and why?" Darcy asked.

Collata shrugged.

Darcy pointed a finger in the air. "First of all, no one is going to look for a dead man. If he comes over with a million dollars' worth of diamonds and then ends up dead, that's a million dollars' worth of diamonds that he keeps—not to mention the money he's been hoarding from all of his previous transactions. To believe Marcus, this guy's got a couple million socked away, and diamonds. Not a bad little nest egg for the honeymoon couple, huh? Next, they have a body. The body's dental records come from England. England is in another time zone.

Every time we're at work, they're asleep, and vice versa. So no one's ever going to call. They're going to accept the fact that these records were handed over. They get the records that match up to a body that's burned to a crisp. Why is it burned to a crisp? Obviously, the face and the hands are disfigured so we can't do fingerprints and we can't get an ID. So, we have to rely on the teeth. Then the grieving family won't have to be bothered to give a DNA sample. And why? Because the DNA from the family is not going to match the DNA from the deceased.

"To bring this all together, they need a patsy they can count on to do exactly what they want him to do. The patsy has to be so much of a patsy that if he deviates, they can bring the hammer down and discredit him, and no one will listen to what he has to say. Does that fit our boy Maggio? Maybe they've implied that there would be a job waiting for him after he gets done with the police—that he could live in Israel on the coast and spend all his time underneath the palm trees, sucking down drinks with little umbrellas in them—that his pension gets transferred to a bank in Tel Aviv. Are you with me so far?" Darcy asked.

"So far," Collata said. "So you think they came to Maggio with these promises and he's going to jump through the hoops for the payoff."

"Of course. It's the perfect con. They never told him they'd give him a payoff. They only gave him an opportunity, expecting his greed to kick in. Who wants a big score more than a guy who's lost every hand?"

Collata was shaking his head. "You got Maggio figured out, huh, Darcy?"

"I don't know. I'm just presenting a possible scenario. Your friend, Maggio, might be looking for the pot of gold at the end of the rainbow here. This is his out."

"Then why does he want to get sober?" Collata asked.

"Look," Darcy said, "if he decides he wants to get sober, that's great. God bless him. I hope he can pull it off. But the fact of the matter is, he's still a dope fiend and alcoholic. They're the biggest con artists around."

"What's the point of this?" Collata asked.

"The point, my friend, is that I don't want to see you get taken."

"Me?" he said, incredulous. "How's he going to run a scam on me?"

"Listen," Darcy said, "I know you want this guy to get his life together and that you're trying to help him do it. But remember why he has to get it together in the first place. He's a weak man and he's got these vices. That's a bad combination. We need him, but don't put your trust in him, and don't count on him."

Collata took a deep drag on his cigarette and concentrated as he slowly crushed the butt into the ashtray. He blew the smoke out in a steady stream and nodded as he stood up. "I get your point loud and clear," he said. "I'll be careful."

Twenty-Two

Harry Feiger sat in the client chair across from Darcy's desk. He was nervously fidgeting with a paper clip. He wore a blue blazer, tan slacks, a blue button-down shirt and a tie that brought it all together. His tasseled loafers were replaced with some brown Italian slip-ons. "How bad is the damage?" he asked, looking at Darcy.

"Oh, it's pretty bad," Darcy replied.

"Damn it! I knew it," Harry swore. "All I wanted was a simple plea. Maybe it was a mistake to call you in. Maybe I should have gotten some young kid who'd go in like a beggar."

"Oh, it has nothing to do with me," Darcy said. "It seems they think highly of you over there."

"What does that mean?" Harry asked.

"Well, they think you work directly under Pizza Joe Alfinni."

"Pizza Joe Alfinni!" he exclaimed. He didn't try to pretend that he'd never heard of him, and that was a good sign, Darcy thought. It also meant that he must have known him, and that was a bad sign. "Jesus," Harry said under his breath.

"They want you to snitch on Pizza Joe."

"Are they crazy? I snitch on Pizza Joe, they won't even find chunks of me."

"That's what they want," Darcy said. "Are you ready to do that?"

"No way. Let's go behind curtain number two and see what's there."

"I'm afraid it's not that easy," Darcy said. "I'm not Monty Hall, and we're not here to make a deal."

"What are we here to do then?" Harry asked.

"Look," Darcy began, "here's what they believe you're doing. They believe that you are importing women from Poland, China, Russia, and various other countries and that you are enslaving them into a prostitution ring. They also believe they can't get close to you because you've had sex with all of them, and none of their agents are willing to do what it takes to deal with that, nor are they allowed to under the U.S. Department of Justice guidelines."

"So what?" Harry piped. "They're mad at me for committing adultery. What do they want from me?"

"They believe,"' Darcy continued, "that you're running these girls in concert with the Chicago Outfit."

"The mob?" Harry asked. "They think I'm part of the mob?"

"No," Darcy said, "but they think you're protected by one of the Outfit guys, Pizza Joe Alfinni, and they know he works directly for Mr. Benvenuti."

"Holy shit, they want me to snitch on Tony Benvenuti. Are they insane?"

Darcy sighed. "I think they're insane. You're right. But they want to offer you immunity from prosecution and the witness protection program."

Harry laughed out loud. "Witness protection, are you serious? I'd have to live in Idaho under an assumed name and work as a clerk at a bait shop. No way," he insisted. "What do you suggest?" he asked Darcy.

"First of all," Darcy said, "I don't think they have as much evidence as they do background. They get information from people as background saying that they heard someone say you did this or that. It's not the same as having them say they saw you do this or that they did this with you. You follow me?"

"Yeah," Harry said. "You mean, they may believe something to be true, but don't have the evidence to prove it."

"Exactly. So I think they want to scare you into doing something here, and what they want to scare you into doing is cooperating against Joe and Tony."

"Look, I'm not on a first-name basis with these guys," Harry began, "and even if I were, I wouldn't give these guys up because my life isn't worth shit if I do. I have a wife and kids. My daughter is not going to be homeschooled in Idaho while her dad's out selling worms."

"Okay," Darcy said, "assuming you don't want to cooperate, then we have another option. We can tell them we're done talking to them and that we want to surrender as soon as they're prepared to return an indictment against you."

"This is just great," Harry said.

"Well, it's not bad," Darcy said. "Everyone is going to know that you're standup when you go in for a bond hearing and they're asking you to be detained. The bottom line is that even with related conduct, they have to have evidence. They can't put someone on the stand to say someone else told them something. They need some direct evidence or to bring a guy in to snitch on you. And they're not going to run up your related conduct because to bring in the snitch against you, they have to expose that snitch to the light of day and everyone in the mob is going to know who that rat is. Once they bring the rat out of the cage, his life isn't worth two cents. And, as you said, whoever it is probably has family on the outside, and you know that the people they're talking about are supposed to be heavyweights. A + B = C, if you know what I mean."

Harry nodded. "The C stands for 'C you later,' huh?"

"Well," Darcy said. "That's their theory. Last option is to tell them that you are no longer willing to talk to them and that you will wait until the indictment comes down, at which time you're going to go to trial. Then they know that they're going to have to prove everything on you and that they're going to have to burn whatever informants they have."

227

"What happens if we do that?" Harry asked.

"They have to put up or shut up."

"Shit or get off the pot," Harry added.

"Hey, whichever cliché you like," Darcy said, "but I guess you get the idea."

"Can I think about this?" Harry asked.

"Absolutely," Darcy agreed.

"Darcy, there is one more option that we haven't talked about."

"What's that?" Darcy asked.

"What if I split?"

"If you flee the jurisdiction?"

"Yeah."

"Well, as your lawyer, I have to tell you that would be against my advice. I recommend that you stay here, that you contest these allegations and we take it to trial."

"Yeah, I know, Darcy," he said, "but I'm not wearing a fucking wire. So let's change this to the hypothetical. Hypothetically, there's nothing keeping me here now, right?"

"You mean, are you free to leave? Sure, you're free to leave. There's no warrant for your arrest."

"And if I were to leave and they want to indict me, what would they do?"

"They could indict you in absentia, but in the federal system, they'd have no right to try you in absentia. So unless they can place you under arrest and bring you back to the jurisdiction, there's nothing they can do."

"So that would mean there'd be a warrant outstanding for me."

"That would be correct," Darcy said, "hypothetically speaking."

"So if I run and they want me, they'll issue a warrant and contact you."

"Not necessarily. If they don't know you're gone, they'll contact me and tell me to bring you in. But if they know you're gone, they may just indict you and get a Grand Jury subpoena to keep it sealed to the general public. Only law enforcement would know. Then one day you're passing through Miami on your way from one island to another and immigration gets a pop on you. They place you under arrest and zip you back up here. The one problem a person in this situation might have, and I am speaking hypothetically," Darcy said, "is that, if he were to go outside the United States, he would have to travel on another country's passport. He would no longer be able to travel on his American passport once they've revoked it. And they would revoke it after they've issued a warrant."

Harry stood up and began to pace. "I have a lot to think about, don't I, Darcy?"

"Yeah, you do," he said. "First of all, you have to decide whether or not you want to become a cooperating individual."

"No way," Harry declared. "That's never going to happen."

"Let me ask you something," Darcy said. "You haven't made any grand protest of innocence. Should I prepare for the possibility that there are witnesses who could prove you did these things?"

"Come on, Darcy," he said, "you don't have cellophane on your face. You're not new. We're not babies, here."

"I'll take that as a yes," Darcy replied.

"Look," Harry said. "I told you what the truth was when I met you—that I made a lot of money with the girls. I just didn't tell you everywhere I made the money. I told you that the money is waiting for me offshore and that I was willing to take a hit. You tell me what the sentencing guidelines are for humping a bunch of illegal immigrant hookers."

Darcy shrugged. "I have no way to calculate those guidelines."

"Okay, then, so the stakes are raised a little bit. Are you still in?"

"I'm your lawyer," Darcy said, "but if there are any other surprises I need to know about, I'd appreciate your telling me now."

Harry turned to leave. "Yeah, I'll think about things and get back to you, Darcy." He left.

Darcy had a sudden urge to take a shower—a long, hot shower.

* * *

It was close to eight o'clock when Darcy heard a knock outside the locked office door. He walked through the empty office, past the reception area, and opened the door a crack to see Amy standing in the hallway. He let her in, closed and locked the door behind them, and took her into his arms.

"Hello," he said.

"Hello yourself," she said and gave him a warm, short kiss.

"The highlight of my day," he said as he eyed her up and down. "You look sensational."

"You've got kind eyes."

"So what shall we do tonight?"

"I've never seen your office before, so why don't you give me a tour."

Darcy began to walk her around. "This is the nerve center of the Law Office of Darcy Cole—I'm sorry, I mean Cole, Haddon and O'Hagin, or is it Cole, O'Hagin and Haddon. I forget. In any event, this is where Irma sits. Irma runs the place."

"Ah, the faithful secretary," she said. "Tell me, does she harbor any romantic interests in you?"

"If she does, they're deep and repressed," Darcy said. "But, I like to think that all women harbor those interests in me."

"Sure you do, big guy," she said, patting him on the shoulder.

They walked down the hallway. "This is Kathy Haddon's office. Kathy has been with me since she was a student in law school. Kathy is a wonderful lawyer. She writes well, does great research, and juries love her."

"I see she has photos of her husband and children on her desk."

"Yes," he said, "there's a long story there."

"Really? Well, you'll have to tell me about that later." They continued down the hall.

"And this is Patrick's office," Darcy said, pointing to the open office.

"This man is not neat, is he?"

"No, he's not. He's a slob but he's a great lawyer. I have to kick him out of the office or he'll work all night."

She stepped in and looked around. "He's also a sports nut," she said, looking at some of his memorabilia."

"That he is," Darcy said. "He is a serious sports nut."

"No pictures of children or a wife," she said. "Is he a young man?"

"Mid-thirties," Darcy said.

"I see, so he's one of those unlucky in love."

"Well, yeah, more than you'd guess. He had someone special in his life," Darcy said, "but he got blown up in a car bomb that was meant for me."

Amy was taken off guard. "You're joking, right?"

"Afraid not," Darcy said.

"Well, let's talk about that story right now."

"It's a long story but here's the short version," Darcy began. "There was a man named Tony Benvenuti Jr. who fancied himself an old-time gangster. He was serving time in the federal penitentiary in Terre Haute, Indiana. He had his boys out settling vendettas, and I became his primary target. You see, I was his former lawyer. Actually, I was still his lawyer at the time. I was representing him on appeal."

"Oh, my God," she said. "I read about this. That was you?"

"Afraid so."

"Wow."

"And the person that was killed in your stead didn't work for you?"

"No, he was Patrick's friend."

"Ah, his partner. Poor Patrick."

Darcy pointed to his nose. "Bingo. You do remember the story. It was terrible for Patrick."

"Oh, my God!" she repeated. "You're one interesting fellow, Mr. Cole. What have I gotten myself into?"

Darcy shrugged. "I don't think there's anyone out there trying to kill me now."

"Well, saints be praised."

They strolled out of Patrick's office and into Darcy's. "This is mine."

"I like it," she said. "A corner office, two views. Hey, you can see the lake from here."

"That's one of the nicest features," Darcy said. "When I first looked at these suites, I stood in this empty office and the only thing I saw was the lake. I didn't see these other buildings then, and I wouldn't have cared anyway, as long as I could see the lake. It has a calming effect on me."

"Yes, me too," she said.

Amy walked around Darcy's office carefully checking for clues about Darcy.

"My God, you don't have any photos or personal effects in your office. I've never see anything like this."

Darcy wasn't sure what to say.

"Tell me something, Darcy, do you have anything in your office that's not work-related?"

Darcy hesitated then made his way to his desk where he retrieved his Bible from his drawer. He held it up.

"I'm trying to read it."

Amy took it from him and looked it over.

"You haven't gotten very far, have you?"

"No, but I'll get there."

They left the office and got onto the elevator. The elevator doors opened to the lobby, and he held her hand as they strolled out. They went down the hallway and headed toward Jackson Boulevard. As they passed the restaurant and bar, they saw an active and lively crowd. When they passed the security guard, Darcy gave him a slight nod, then pushed through the double doors. Amy and he walked out onto the street.

"It's a beautiful night," he said.

"Yes, it is," Amy agreed.

"Where do you want to go now?"

"No place in particular," she said. "How about you?"

"Let's walk east until our hats float."

"Sounds good," she agreed, "except I forgot my hat."

Twenty-Three

Collata sat across from St. Ben's Church with his elbow hanging out the open window of his van. He remembered St. Ben's Parish as a working-class neighborhood. Now it was yuppified and expensive. It was just west of Wrigley Field. The two- and three-flats that used to house generations of the same family had been converted into luxury condos and single-family dwellings for rich young traders, brokers, lawyers, and doctors.

At about twenty after six, he saw Maggio walk out of the church in conversation with an equally disheveled fifty-ish woman. They said their goodbyes, and Maggio ambled over to Collata's van.

"Get in," Collata said.

Without saying anything, Maggio flipped his cigarette away, walked across the front of the van, and got in the passenger seat. "What's up?" he asked.

"How was your meeting?" Collata asked.

"In-house detox, AA, NA, this sucks. A bunch of drunks sitting around talking about how powerful the lure of alcohol is," he answered. "They ought to try cocaine."

"That's all in your past now, hotshot," Collata said. "Remember, one day at a time."

"Where are we going?"

"We are going to talk to a dead guy."

"What are you talking about?" he asked.

"I saw your boy, Jacob. He's alive and well."

"Get outta here," Maggio said.

Collata pulled out the passport and handed it over. "Is this your boy?"

"Yeah, that's my boy."

"Look at the name on that."

"Who is Allen Weiss?"

"Allen Weiss, Jacob Orloff, Jacob Goldman, David Yale, Scott Berg—this dude's got more names than I got underwear," Collata said.

"That I believe," Maggio returned, smiling.

Collata realized that it was the first time he had ever seen Maggio smile. He took it as a good sign. "The boy is alive," Collata said. "He's alive. Whoever the dead guy may be, he is not Jacob Orloff, or whatever his name is. Mr. Maggio, you've been had."

"Bastard," Maggio whispered. "They played me like a fucking violin. What do we do now?"

"Well, the way I see it, being a good cop, you want to make sure the bad guy gets punished and not an innocent guy. Isn't that right?"

"Absolutely right," he agreed.

"So, that would mean that Marcus Tatum didn't whack the dude."

Maggio looked out the window. He was pale and sweat was spreading over his face. "Hey, I guess people make mistakes."

"You made a mistake," Collata said.

"I followed the evidence," Maggio said.

"You beat the evidence out of him. Did he ever say those things, or did you just tell him that was what he was going to say?"

Maggio stared out the window. "What the fuck's the difference?" he said. "It's all a blur anyway. I was coked and boozed out of my head when I did that shit. I thought I was solving the case."

"You didn't solve the case," Collata said. "You just

wrapped it up in a box. That's all you did. Now all the garbage is going to fall out, and we're going to have to start over."

"Well, what's going to happen to me now?"

"What's going to happen is that you're going to solve this case right. After you solve this case, you're going to get the credit. You're going to be a hero, and you're going to get clean and sober. And after you become a clean and sober hero, you're going to fight every day of your life to stay that way. Then you're going to have the life you're supposed to have. You're going to be a homicide dick in the city of Chicago, and you're going to coast until your retirement. Then you'll pull the pin on your own terms and retire to do whatever you want."

"Can I work with you?" Maggio asked.

Collata laughed. "Hey, if I can trust you, you can work with me. But we're a long way from that now."

"Fair enough," Maggio said. "Where we going?"

"We're going to search for a walking dead man."

* * *

Collata and Maggio sat in the van in a park across from the 3600 building. Twice Maggio left the van and walked toward a clump of trees. Each time he vomited, got some water from a drinking fountain, and returned without comment to the van. Collata had a strong pair of binoculars trained on the entrance of the building, and he periodically called Mike, the doorman, on his cell phone. On the hump of the floor between the two front seats was a camera with the biggest telephoto lens Maggio had ever seen. "See that?" Collata said, nodding his head toward the camera. "Pick it up, will ya?"

Maggio picked it up.

"You know how to work one of those things?"

"Hey, I'm a detective. I can figure it out."

"Figure it out then."

Maggio looked through the viewfinder, found the button on top, and practiced focusing on different points. "Okay, I got it," he said.

"Now, when I tell you, I want you to focus it on the front door."

Maggio looked through the viewfinder. "Okay," he said, "I'll be ready."

"See the guy in the uniform?"

"Yeah, is he one of ours?"

"No, he's not one of ours. There aren't any of ours. It's just me and you, pinhead," Collata said. "Point it at that guy. You got a good view of his face and everything?"

"Yep," he said.

"When I tell you, get a view of that front door and take a million pictures of Jacob when he comes out. You know what he looks like?"

"I've seen one picture of the guy alive, and then I saw some charcoal-broiled briquette at the morgue that was supposed to be him. What do you want from me?"

"Okay, he's going to be walking out with Anaka. There's your clue, Detective. Take a million pictures of the face of the dude next to the hot broad. You got that?"

"You want me to get her in the picture?"

"I already know what she looks like," he said. "I want you to take pictures of the dead guy. Try not to puke until after you get the photos."

"Got it."

After sitting in silence for more than thirty minutes, Maggio turned to Collata. "How do you know the broad's over there?"

"Because the doorman told me she's over there. Geez."

"Why are you so down on me, man?" Maggio said.

"It's just the way I express affection, dickhead." Collata continued, "Now pay attention. They're going to come out soon."

"Do you know what time they're going to come out?"

"You've got something better to do?" Collata asked.

Maggio thought about it. *My head is on fire. I've been puking for days and I feel like I've been dipped in ice water,* Maggio thought to himself. He looked at Collata. "No."

"Goddamn skippy," Collata said, "Sit your ass there, shut

up, and when I tell you, start snapping. That's called detective work."

Maggio gave him a dirty look. "Hey man, you're getting paid by the hour. I'm not getting paid at all for this."

Collata started laughing. "You're one brainless moron, aren't you? I'm going to save your career right here, pal, and you're sitting there wondering about whether you're going to get paid. Are you nuts? You're going to make this case; you're going to get the credit for it, and you're going to be the big star over at Area Three. You're going to get a commendation from the mayor. The chief of police is going to pin a ribbon on your chest. You think a couple of days in detox is going to get you clean? This ain't Hollywood. Every day for the rest of your life your primary goal is to get through the day without using. In a couple of weeks you'll stop feeling sick all the time, and then it gets only slightly easier. Don't quit, we'll get through this. You're going to be a civic treasure, and you're going to beef about sitting here waiting? Now shut the fuck up."

Maggio dug in his pocket for a cigarette and lit it up. "How do you know how this is all going to play out?" he asked.

"Please," Collata said, "you think these guys are all that smart?"

"They outsmarted me," Maggio replied.

"Big deal," Collata said. "I got change in my pocket smarter than you."

"Now what the fuck is that?" Maggio said. "Why are you dogging me so much?"

"Because you're a drunk. You're an alcoholic and an addict, and the minute you start cleaning it up, you want me to pat you on the back and tell you how smart you are. You got used, man. You almost put an innocent guy in the penitentiary for the rest of his life. All because you wanted to get next to the tennis-playing broad."

"What are you talking about?" Maggio protested.

"She ran you around by your dick. She came into your life and sashayed around, and you were following your sword into battle. You wanted to get next to her so bad it hurt. Somehow if you could have poked her, you would have felt better about yourself, right? Because, instead of scamming hookers, you would have been with some high-class broad. That's it, isn't it?" he asked.

Maggio stared at him in disbelief. "That isn't it. I knew that broad was out of my class the whole time."

"So what was the deal?"

"What do you mean, what was the deal?"

"Let me put it to you this way. Darcy's got a theory that they came out and tried to hook you with a job with the Israeli government, maybe help you get to your pension and then cash you out with a job with them. So you're sucking your pension and working for them someplace warm and sunny. Is that it? They told you they would stick you under a palm tree and let you drink froo-froo drinks—let you work security for the embassy or a consulate someplace."

Maggio was sheepish. "Look, I wanted something out of this, no question about it. They never promised me anything, though. They just led me on—let me believe what I wanted to believe. My hope was that I would be able to do this, solve this case like any other homicide case, and then, on the ass end, they'd protect me so I could get to my pension. Once I got my pension, I wouldn't give a damn. If they wanted to give me a job, hey, that would be great. Shit, I got nothing holding me in Chicago. They want me to work for the consulate here, I'd work for the consulate here. If they want me to go to Washington, that'd be fine, too. If they want to stick me in Israel, hey, it's warm and sunny there, like you said. Got a beef with that? But most of all, I thought that if I didn't dance for the man that he'd get me fired. I was hanging by a thread and he had a big scissors."

"So that's it, huh?" Collata said. "You were thinking there was going to be a payoff on this."

"Hey, no one ever came out and said it, but they sure wanted me to believe it. Mostly I was afraid of getting fired. I didn't want to eat dog food in my golden years."

"I see."

"Don't be like that," Maggio said. "Come on, man, look at it from my position. Look at my state of mind at the time."

"Whatever," Collata said.

His cell phone rang. "Yeah, Collata here. Uh-huh, okay, thanks. Yeah, I'll take care of you. I'll be back tonight." He hung up. "That's my boy. Your photo subject is coming with his girlfriend. They called down and asked the doorman to hail them a cab. Now get the fucking camera out."

"Hey, you want to do this yourself," Maggio asked, "to make sure we get it right?"

"No, I want you to do it so that when the pictures get developed, you can tell Jack Karsten that you took these pictures yourself. You know what I'm saying?"

"You could take the pictures. I'll still tell him that I took them," Maggio said.

"You haven't learned a thing, have you?" Collata said shaking his head. "Take the pictures and get his face."

Maggio stepped out of the van, leaving the door open, and rested the lens on the top of the door. He lined up the camera sight and kept it trained on the entrance. He spotted them walking toward the doorman, so he zoomed in, getting a nice shot of Jacob. He started pushing the button. He took five or six of Jacob's face as he walked through the double doors. He had him dead on. Jacob stood waiting for the cab as Maggio snapped away, taking picture after picture until the camera clicked empty. Maggio watched as the dead man got into the cab with his girlfriend and drove away.

"Did you get any good pictures?" Collata asked.

"I got him, man." he said excitedly.

"You never did any work like this, did you?"

"What do you mean?"

"Is this the first picture of a dead guy you ever took?"

"Fuck you," Maggio said.

"Yeah, fuck me."

* * *

Darcy stood behind his desk and watched as Irma escorted Ellen Feiger into his office.

"Mrs. Feiger, it's nice to meet you," he said, shaking hands with her. "Please sit down."

Ellen Feiger was a small-boned, almost frail woman. She had short gray hair and wore pearls over a cashmere sweater and slacks. She placed her designer bag on the floor by her feet and started wringing her hands. "I don't know where to begin, Mr. Cole," she said, her voice trailing off.

Darcy leaned into her. "Why don't you begin by telling me why you're here, Mrs. Feiger."

She looked off and then back at Darcy, tears welling in her eyes. "My husband is gone," she said.

"What do you mean, gone?" Darcy asked. A chill ran through him and his stomach knotted up. Darcy's first thought was that someone tipped Joe Alfinni off and Harry was now stone-cold. "I'm sure he just needed some time to think," he said, trying to reassure himself and Mrs. Feiger.

"Oh, no," Ellen replied. "He packed his clothes. He took some things, and he left."

"Well, have you heard from him?"

"No."

"Could he be down at your place in Naples?"

Ellen gave him a surprised look. She was confused. "What place in Naples?"

Now it was Darcy's turn to be confused. "Don't you have a place in Naples, Florida, or somewhere near there?"

"That would be news to me," she said.

"That's odd," Darcy said, "when I first met your husband, he told me that you two had a place in Florida and that he had a Florida real-estate license."

"I believe he told you that, Mr. Cole," she said, "but I don't believe it's true."

Darcy let out an exasperated sigh. "You never discussed with him the possibility of the two of you moving to Florida?"

"No."

He took a moment to compose himself. He was also aware

that it was becoming more difficult for Mrs. Feiger to speak. She had tried to continue and then stopped. Finally, she broke down and cried. Darcy offered a tissue and waited her out. After a few moments, she was able to continue.

"You see, Mr. Cole, as far as I can tell he's been planning this for some time. He liquidated all of our marital assets and now he's gone. He refinanced the house. We had it paid off. We'd been in that house for over twenty-five years, and then he takes out a home equity loan and leaves a large mortgage. He cleared out all the bank accounts, stock portfolio, and the retirement accounts, and now he's gone."

Darcy leaned back. "How could he clear out all the accounts without your approval?"

"He did it," she said, "and then he wired the money to an offshore account. From there, it was transferred again, and now it's disappeared. Mr. Cole, you can't imagine. He's left me with nothing. I have a house with a huge mortgage and no equity. I have minimal savings in my checking account, and there's nothing else."

Darcy stood up and began to pace. He stopped and looked out the window over the lake. He turned back and looked at her. "Mrs. Feiger, I am so deeply sorry to hear this. I wish I could do something to help you."

"You can find that son of a bitch," she said.

"Well, Mrs. Feiger, I have to tell you, there are a couple of problems here. First of all, it seems as if everything he told me about himself was a lie." Darcy hesitated, once again searching for the right words. When he couldn't come up with any, he went on nonetheless. "The worst part about this, Mrs. Feiger, is that I wouldn't be able to help you even if I could."

"What does that mean?" she asked.

"Well, he's my client. I can't betray the attorney-client privilege. Anything that I might have learned about him, I have to keep to myself."

"You don't understand," she said, "I'm destitute. I have no job skills. I have been a mother and homemaker for the past twenty-five years."

Darcy felt an ache deep in his heart. He was mortified. "Mrs. Feiger, if there were anything I could do for you, I would."

She reached down, grabbed her purse and stood up. "You know, Mr. Cole, my husband was a lawyer, too, and he used the law. He used that knowledge for evil purposes. I knew about his girlfriends, but he thought it would reassure me to know that they were merely minor indiscretions along the way. You know what he did, Mr. Cole? He used me. He used me and threw me out. Now I'm sure he's someplace with some young tramp, spending the money that I helped him build up over the years. You know what that does to someone, Mr. Cole? It's taking my self-esteem, my dignity, and it means that the rest of my life will be misery."

"I'm truly sorry," Darcy said.

She looked at Darcy. "Mr. Cole, I'm leaning toward believing you, that you are sorry. But then again, you are a lawyer after all, and my faith in lawyers is deeply shaken." She turned and left without shaking hands.

Darcy turned and walked toward the window. He put a hand on either side of the window jamb and pressed his face against the glass, looking down toward the street.

Darcy had been relieved that Harry hadn't been murdered. Now he wished he had. Rat bastard, Darcy thought. He ran the possibilities through his head. If Harry had been whacked, then Ellen Feiger would be financially secure.

Somewhere out there, Harry Feiger was going to enjoy the fruits of his crime while his dutiful wife was left penniless. Rat bastard was all he could say to himself.

Twenty-Four

Maggio sat in his beat-up Taurus across the street from the high-rise on the corner of Dearborn and Elm. He had an extra-large coffee from Dunkin Donuts and was on his third cigarette. August had crept into Chicago, bringing stifling humidity with it. Today was no exception. Maggio had sweated through his undershirt, leaving stains in the armpits and across the back. He hadn't eaten anything since yesterday's breakfast, which was a piece of toast and a glass of ice water. The toast stayed down, which was a small sign of progress.

Finally, Anaka appeared in the lobby of the building. She said something to the doorman and then stepped out through the revolving door. The yellow light on top of the entranceway was activated, sending the signal for cabs trolling for fares. A checker cab pulled in within moments and Anaka got in. Maggio put his car into gear and accelerated, crossing the intersection and entering the roundabout in the wrong direction so that the nose of his car rested a few feet from the cab. He jumped out in one quick move, pulled his badge, and showed it to the cabdriver, who was startled and confused. He protested that he had committed no traffic violations as Maggio ripped open the back door and put his arm around the bicep of Anaka Vanderlinden.

"Come on, sweetheart, we're going," he said, yanking her out of the car.

"Get your hands off me," she ordered.

"No way."

Maggio put his hand on the back of her head, forcing her onto the top of the cab. She leaned forward, and her arms instinctively came back. Reaching for her right wrist, he put a handcuff on it and pulled it tightly toward him as he reached around for her left wrist and cuffed it.

"You must be insane," she yelled.

He pulled out a crumpled piece of paper and pushed it in her face. "It's a subpoena for you to appear and testify today, sweetheart. I'm supposed to make sure you get there."

"You son of a bitch," she said. "I'm going to call my lawyer."

"Fuck you," he said. "You're a witness. You don't have any rights. Besides, you're not even a citizen. So shut up." He put her on the passenger side in the back seat and shut the door, locking her inside. He scooted around to his side, jumped in, and put the car into gear before he even closed his door. "Let me tell you something, sweetheart," he said. "You started something, you're going to finish it. You're going to testify today."

"What are you talking about?" she asked. "I don't know anything about anything."

"Yeah, well, you know all about this case."

She gave him a strange look. "How can this case be going to trial already?"

"It's not a trial. It's a motion to quash arrest. Do you know what that means?"

She stared at him with hate in her eyes. "A motion to quash arrest? No, I don't know what that means."

"It means they're saying that there's no probable cause to arrest Marcus Tatum. Do you know who Marcus Tatum is?"

"Yes, I know who Marcus Tatum is. He's the man who killed Jacob."

"Well, you certainly know a lot. At first, you don't know anything about it, and then, all of a sudden, you remember that your boyfriend left with him, and then, you know that this guy killed him. Do you ever tell the truth?"

"I don't appreciate your tone," she sniffed.

Maggio laughed.

"You're a crude and simple man," she said.

"You know what, honey," Maggio started, "you are so full of shit. You've been playing a game ever since you met me. What'd you think, a pretty smile and a set of yah-yahs is going to get me to do anything?" He looked at her in his mirror. "You were a lot cuter before I got to know you."

"Will you take the handcuffs off me now?" she demanded.

"Nope," Maggio replied. "I'm going to take your lying ass to the courtroom. I'm going to bring you straight back to the jury room and I'm going to cuff you to a wooden chair. When they call you to testify, I will handcuff your wrists together again. I will personally walk you up with the handcuffs on, put you on the witness stand, and then, and only then, I will remove the handcuffs. Do you understand me?"

"You truly are insane," she insisted.

"I may be insane, but at least now I'm thinking clearly," he said. He fumbled through his jacket pocket until he found his cigarettes. With one hand on the wheel he used his other hand to manipulate the pack and shake a cigarette free. He shoved the pack back into his pocket and pushed the car lighter in.

When they got to Twenty-sixth and California, Maggio drove past the staff parking lot and into the section used by the judges and dignitaries behind the courthouse. Flashing his badge at the sheriff guarding the gate, he pointed to his handcuffed prisoner. The sheriff let him through, and Maggio parked in a spot near the entrance of the courthouse. He whisked Anaka in through the back door, flashing his badge to the sheriffs at the security checkpoint, and took the elevator to the sixth floor.

Courtroom 600 was one of the large, ornate courtrooms in the complex. It had beautifully detailed woodwork and large wooden pews for the visitor's gallery. The carved jury box was thick with years and years of accumulated lacquer. He walked

Anaka through the courtroom during a recess and, true to his word, brought her directly back to the jury room. He removed her left handcuff and attached it to the wooden chair. "Sit down," he said, and she complied.

On the other side of the room and at the end of a huge table were three cops, all oblivious to Anaka's predicament. One was reading a newspaper, another, a book, and the third was doing a crossword puzzle in the *Sun-Times*. Anaka stared out the window.

"Ms. Vanderlinden," a voice broke in. Jack Karsten stepped into the jury room. "Hi, I'm Jack Karsten, an Assistant State's Attorney, and I'm prosecuting this case. I'm very sorry for the loss of Mr. Orloff."

"Why am I handcuffed?" she asked.

"I'm sorry about that. It's an extra precaution. We'll get those off you soon."

"Why am I handcuffed?" she repeated. "You're avoiding the question."

"Well, that's the best answer you're going to get. How about this? You're handcuffed because you're an essential witness to a murder case and we take murder cases very seriously around here. Do you understand that?"

"I do, but I'm a victim here," she insisted.

"Yes, ma'am," Jack replied, "I'll be sure to keep that in mind."

"You don't know who you're dealing with," she said.

"You're right. If I knew who I was dealing with—I mean, if I really knew who I was dealing with, there probably wouldn't be a need for handcuffs."

She gave him her best look of hate, which left Jack unmoved.

"So what we're going to do is put you on the witness stand. We're going to put you under oath and ask you questions. When we're done, I'll have Detective Maggio take you home. And on the way home you probably won't have to be handcuffed."

"You son of a bitch!"

"I'm disappointed," Jack said. "I was so hoping to make a good first impression on you."

"Ms. Vanderlinden," Darcy said as he stepped into the room.

She turned her head even more to look at Darcy. "Who are you?" she asked.

"My name is Darcy Cole. I'm a lawyer."

"Are you this man's boss?" she asked.

Darcy laughed. "No, ma'am, I'm a defense attorney. I represent Marcus Tatum."

"You represent the man who killed Jacob?"

Darcy smiled. "As I said, I represent Marcus Tatum, who stands accused of killing Jacob Orloff."

"Get me out of these handcuffs," she demanded.

"Ms. Vanderlinden," Darcy began. "I'd like to ask you some questions. Of course, you have the right not to answer those questions."

"Fine. I'm not going to answer any questions."

Darcy continued. "Okay, so what we'll do is put you under oath and put you on the witness stand. Then if you don't answer my questions or don't answer Mr. Karsten's questions, the judge will hold you in contempt and put you in jail until such time as you purge the contempt by answering those questions."

She turned away from Darcy and Jack and looked out the window. "You're all a bunch of bastards. My boyfriend was murdered. I'm not a citizen of this country, and this is how you treat me."

Darcy turned and left, with Jack on his heels. As they stepped out, Jack shut the door, leaving Anaka handcuffed to the chair with the three police officers who were, of course, ignoring her. It seemed like hours to Anaka, but it was only forty minutes later when Maggio came back in.

"Do you have to use the can?"

"Excuse me?" she asked.

"Do you need to use the bathroom?"

"No," she answered.

"Okay, then, come on. You're on." Maggio unlocked the handcuff from the chair and held on to the wrist that was still cuffed as he walked her to the threshold of the courtroom. He uncuffed her there, and pushed her through the doorway.

The judge saw her. "Ms. Vanderlinden, would you come here and take the stand, please?" The judge stood and, with his finger, directed her through the well of the courtroom, around the court reporter, and up into the witness chair. "Please stand and take the oath. Raise your right hand."

The clerk administered the oath, and Anaka Vanderlinden turned to the judge. "Your Honor, may I ask you a question?"

"No, ma'am," the judge said. "Please have a seat."

"Judge, I want to tell you what these men did to me."

Judge Michael McGinn had light blue eyes, white hair, and red ruddy skin. He was thirty pounds too heavy and blue veins pushed out from his nose to his cheeks.

He was known to be quick-tempered, and Anaka seemed determined to test him.

"Ms. Vanderlinden, you're a witness. You're under oath. Please sit down and answer the questions as the lawyers put them to you. Do you understand me?"

"Yes, Your Honor."

"Ms. Vanderlinden, I don't want to hold you in contempt of court. You're a witness. You're here pursuant to a subpoena, a court order to appear and answer questions. You will do that. Do I make myself clear?"

Anaka nodded, glared and sat down. Darcy rose and walked over to the podium with a legal pad. "Your Honor, I'd ask that Ms. Vanderlinden be treated as a hostile witness."

The judge looked at Karsten, expecting an objection, but there was none. "Well, Mr. Cole, I think your request is premature. Why don't you begin questioning her, and if it becomes apparent that she's hostile, we'll address that issue at that time."

"Thank you, Your Honor." Darcy was now focused on Anaka. "Ma'am, would you tell us your name and spell your last name for the record?"

Anaka answered a series of seemingly innocuous questions.

She talked about her relationship with Jacob and her travels with him. She discussed all the places they had been and painted a picture of a young couple in love—looking forward to marriage and spending the rest of their lives together. Darcy ran her through all the events leading up to the disappearance, and she milked the role of the grieving widow impeccably. Darcy held an eight-by-ten photograph of Jacob and approached her.

"Ma'am, do you recognize the man who is depicted in this photograph?"

"I do," she said. "That's Jacob."

"That's what Jacob looked like when he was alive?"

"Yes, that's right."

"And you haven't seen Jacob since his disappearance, is that right?"

"Yes, that's right," she said.

"In fact, there was a body at the morgue identified as Jacob, is that right?"

"Yes, that's right," she said.

"And that was done through dental records, isn't that right?"

"Yes."

"And do you know where the dental records came from?"

"From his dentist," she replied.

"Who is that dentist?"

"That would be Dr. Henry Lawrence in London, I believe," she answered.

"And how did those records get into the possession of Detective Maggio?"

"I don't know," she replied.

"Well, were they given to him by a man named Avi Joseph?"

"I don't know," she answered.

"Well, let me ask you this. Did you give those records to Avi Joseph?"

"No."

"Do you know a man named Avi Joseph?"

She was uncomfortable and began to squirm. "Yes, I know a man named Avi Joseph."

"Who is Avi Joseph?"

"He's a man," she answered.

"Yes, can you tell us any more about him?"

"No, actually I cannot tell you any more about him. He's a man who seemed to know Jacob. I believe that Avi Joseph had something to do with the Israeli government, but I really don't know. He never volunteered that information."

"Did you give the dental records to Avi Joseph?"

"No."

"Are you familiar with dental records?"

"I have a passing familiarity with them," she answered.

"Would that be because you once worked for a dentist?"

"No," she answered.

"Let me show you a photograph. Do you recognize who is depicted in this photograph?"

Her shoulders tightened, and she sat up rigidly. "Yes, I know who that is, it's Dr. Henry Lawrence."

"That's the same Dr. Henry Lawrence who prepared the dental records for Jacob Orloff?"

"Yes," she answered.

"Let me show you another photograph," Darcy said, walking back to the counsel table and retrieving a photograph. He made his way slowly across the courtroom back to Anaka. "Do you recognize who is depicted in this photograph?"

Anaka stared at the photograph, her mind racing. She looked up at the judge without saying anything. She looked at Darcy and then back at the judge. Finally, in a quiet voice, she said. "That's me with Dr. Henry Lawrence."

"And this would be a photograph from a brochure about his dental clinic. Is that right?"

"Yes," she replied in a meek voice.

"You used to work for Dr. Henry Lawrence. Isn't that right?"

"Yes," she said, her voice getting even softer.

"You were a dental hygienist and office manager for Dr. Henry Lawrence. Isn't that right?"

"Yes," she answered.

"And you were in charge of keeping track of the dental records, isn't that right?"

"Yes."

"And it was you who got these dental records that were used to identify the body, isn't that right?"

"Yes," she admitted.

"Now, let's talk about these dental records. Dr. Lawrence had many patients, didn't he?"

"Yes," she said.

"And he would count on the records to be able to determine what work was previously done on any individual patient, isn't that right?"

"Yes."

"And he would look in the mouth of the patient and he would be able to tell whether it was his work or someone else's work, right?"

"I presume so," she replied.

"But in terms of records, he wouldn't remember what he did to each individual patient, would he?"

"I don't know what he would do," she answered, looking around the courtroom for help. Karsten did not seem so inclined.

"And so, if you put x-rays or records in a file other than their own, you could confuse whose records they actually were, couldn't you?"

"I suppose that's possible."

"Tell me, was there a patient of Dr. Lawrence named Daniel Litwin?"

"I don't know."

"Let me refresh your recollection, Dr. Lawrence had a security clearance to work on members of the Israeli government who were stationed or working in London. Isn't that true?"

"I don't know."

"Yes, you do," he said. She was taken aback. Darcy walked back to the counsel table and picked up a folder. "Ma'am, you know that Dr. Lawrence had a contract to do the dental work for Israeli nationals attached to the Israeli government working in London. Isn't that right?"

"Yes," she admitted.

"And you know because you did the paperwork billing the Israeli Consulate for those people, right?"

"Yes."

Darcy crossed his arms in front of himself.

"At some point you and Jacob became lovers?"

"We were more than that. We were going to be married." She practically spat out the words.

"You helped him with his business, correct?" Darcy asked.

"Yes," she replied.

Darcy put the folder back down. "Jacob Orloff and you would have to process large sums of cash. Isn't that right?"

"Yes," she said.

"And you also had to carry large amounts of diamonds worth hundreds of thousands of dollars. Isn't that right?"

"Yes."

"Did Jacob Orloff ever use any other name besides Jacob Orloff?"

"No," she replied.

"How about Allen Weiss? Did he ever use the name Allen Weiss?"

"No," she said.

"Jacob Goldman? Did he ever use that name?"

"No."

"David Yale? Did he ever use that name?"

"No," she said, her anger rising.

"How about Scott Berg? Did he ever use that?"

"No."

"Do you know whether Jacob Orloff had any passports from any countries other than Israel?"

"No," she replied.

Darcy walked back to the table and picked up a folder. He then approached Anaka Vanderlinden and laid a number of passports in front of her. "Please, Ms. Vanderlinden, look at each of these individual passports and tell me after you've had a chance to inspect them whether you know the person."

She picked up each one of the passports, each from a different country, and when she finished, set them down. "Okay," she said.

"The photographs in all of those passports are of Jacob Orloff, are they not?"

"Yes, they appear to be," she said. "But I've never seen these before."

"But each of those passports has Jacob's picture in it?"

"Yes," she said.

"And each one of those passports is for an individual with a name other than Jacob Orloff. Is that correct?"

"Yes," she said.

"And each is from a different country. Isn't that right?"

"Yes."

"Tell me what Jacob Orloff did for a living prior to being a diamond courier?"

She looked at Judge McGinn. "Do I have to answer this?"

"Yes, you do," he replied.

"He worked for the Israeli government. I don't know what he did, but prior to that he was in the Israeli Army."

"Did he work in the intelligence community?" Darcy asked.

"Perhaps," she said. "I'm not entirely sure."

"Did he work for the Mossad, the Israeli secret police?"

She looked at Darcy. "I don't know. I don't know if there is really a Mossad. I don't know that I've ever met anyone who worked for Mossad. These people don't just come up to you and say, 'Hi, I'm a spy.' So no, I truly don't know if he worked for the Mossad or in Intelligence. I just know that he worked for the Israeli government prior to his working as a diamond courier."

"Tell me, Ms. Vanderlinden, what is Jacob Orloff's real name? Do you know?"

"It's Jacob Orloff."

"Do you know where he got all these other passports?"

"No."

"Do you know how he got these other passports?"

"No."

"But you do know that you haven't seen him since the day

255

he disappeared, which, according to you, was the day he left to meet Marcus Tatum. Is that correct?"

"That's correct," she said.

Darcy walked back to the counsel table yet again and rummaged through his papers until he pulled out another file folder. He approached her. "Ms. Vanderlinden I would like to show this photograph. Do you recognize who is depicted in this photograph?"

"Yes," she said.

"And that would be a photograph of you and Jacob. Is that correct?"

"Yes."

"And that's Jacob Orloff, the decedent in this case?"

"Yes."

"Ms. Vanderlinden, do you know when this photograph was taken?"

"No, I don't," she said.

"Well, Ms. Vanderlinden, would it surprise you if I told you that this photograph was taken two days ago?"

She sat back in her chair, trying to retain her composure.

Judge McGinn leaned forward. "Let me see that photograph," he demanded.

Darcy walked over and handed it to him. The judge studied it for a few moments and then gave it back.

"Ms. Vanderlinden, answer the question," he demanded.

"I'm sorry," she said, a little dazed. "What's the question?"

"Why don't we cut to the chase?" Darcy said. "You know Jacob Orloff is alive, don't you?"

She stared at him, saying nothing. She had been broken and was now confused.

"I'll ask you again. Jacob Orloff is alive, isn't he?"

She looked at the judge and back at Darcy. Tears rolled down her cheeks, and she obviously felt trapped. The judge stood up to get a better look at her. "Ms. Vanderlinden, answer the question, please."

"No," she said. "Jacob is not alive. This is a trick photograph."

"Is that you in the photograph?"

"Yes," she said.

"Is that Jacob?"

"Yes, but this is a trick. Jacob is dead."

Darcy took the photograph back from Anaka. He walked back, dropped it on his table and then walked around to stand behind his chair. He looked at Anaka and the judge, back and forth. He turned and looked at Karsten. He felt like a pitcher who had just struck out the side. "Your Honor, I tender the witness."

Marcus reached over and grabbed Darcy's hand and began shaking it profusely. Darcy pulled his hand back and patted Marcus on the shoulder. Karsten stood up.

"Your Honor, may we have a sidebar?" he asked.

Karsten and Darcy joined the judge off to the side near the corner of the courtroom. The court reporter set up her machine in the middle of them. Darcy and Karsten stood with their backs to the courtroom and leaned in close to the judge, whispering so that only the court reporter and the judge could hear them.

"What's up, Mr. Karsten? What do you need?"

"Well, Judge, in light of that testimony, I have grave doubts about being able to proceed in good faith with this prosecution. I have the opportunity to cross-examine her. I would like to have a continuance so I can do some investigation prior to my cross-examination. I don't know if Mr. Cole has an objection to that."

Darcy leaned in. "I have no objection to that. Mr. Karsten has been nothing but professional throughout this entire case, and I think that I should show him the same courtesy he has shown me."

"That's just great. The two of you are in love, and your witness has been committing perjury since the moment she sat down. How much time do you need?" the judge asked.

"How about a week?" Karsten asked.

"Is that good for you, Darcy?"

"Yes, Judge."

"Okay, since both sides are in agreement, that's what we'll do. Nothing will surprise me in this case now— preliminary hearing and a hearing on motions within two months," the judge said in a bemused voice.

He went back to the bench, and the court reporter set up in her usual spot. Darcy sat next to Marcus, and Karsten stood behind the chair.

"Judge, I would like you to instruct this witness that she is under subpoena and that if she doesn't return for cross-examination, a warrant will be issued for her arrest. She will be placed in custody pending a hearing on a rule to show cause why she should not be held in contempt for ignoring the subpoena."

"Okay," the judge said. "Do you understand that, Ms. Vanderlinden?"

"No," she replied.

"We're going to stop here and continue one week from today. You are under subpoena. If you do not return, I will issue a no-bail warrant for your arrest, and that warrant will mean that when you're caught, if you're caught, you'll be taken to jail. A hearing will be held to see if you will be held in contempt of court. Contempt of court means that I can sentence you to jail. Do you understand that?"

"Yes," she agreed.

"Okay, one week continuance. This court is adjourned." The judge stood and bounced into his chambers.

Maggio stepped into the courtroom from the back door and walked over to Anaka. "Okay, honey. Give me your wrist. We're going to handcuff you again."

"You son of a bitch." She glared at him.

"I'll tell you what," Maggio said. "I won't handcuff you if you promise to be nice."

"Fuck you."

"Okay." He popped a handcuff on her left wrist and twisted it in a rough manner behind her back, reached for her right and joined it up with the other handcuff. "Come on, honey, we're going to talk to Mr. Karsten." Maggio escorted Anaka toward the counsel table where Karsten was getting his things together.

"Take her up to fourteen. Get her printed and bring her to my office," he said.

"What?" she replied, obviously shaken.

"Listen, Ms. Vanderlinden, you're about three seconds away from being locked up. So if I were you, I would say very little," Karsten said.

"Come on, honey," Maggio said, and he pulled her out of the courtroom.

Jack had his sleeves rolled up, his tie loose and was drinking a diet soda when Maggio brought Vanderlinden into his office. "Here's the deal, young lady," Karsten began. "You're going to go home. If you're not back next week, then there will be a warrant issued for your arrest, and I will spend the rest of my life looking for you. You got it?"

"I understand," she said. "I'm going to call the Consulate as soon as I get home." Her voice was a weak monotone. She looked drawn and defeated.

"Absolutely," Karsten said. He reached to the corner of his desk, pulled a card from a wooden holder, and slid it across to her. "Here's my name and phone number. So when you're pitching a bitch, make sure you give them my name."

She left the card sitting on the corner of the table and stood up. "Take me home, Detective."

"Yes, ma'am," Maggio sarcastically agreed.

"And by the way," Jack said, "you can take the handcuffs off of her now."

Maggio pulled her out of the office and into the hallway. "I'll take the cuffs off, but don't think I won't smack you if you act up," he warned her. "I don't care if you're a woman. To me, you're just a scumbag." Maggio took the handcuffs off and she rubbed her wrists.

"You're a son of a bitch," she snarled.

"Does that mean you don't want a ride?"

"Fuck you, I'll take a taxi."

Maggio stood there laughing as she walked away. "Honey, you're not going to get a cab here. This is Twenty-sixth and California. There are no cabs here. You are in Chicago's armpit."

Twenty-Five

The Mallers Building on South Wabash was once known as Jewelers Row. It wasn't until the late eighties that the Mallers Building dismissed its human elevator operators and moved up to automation. It was a building where traditions died hard. Small jewelry shops filled the building from the first floor all the way to the top—family-owned jewelers, each with his own specialty. To get into any of the jewelry stores, you had to be buzzed in from the inside. Not just anyone was allowed in. Despite the high-tech security—surveillance cameras and double-locked doors—there still was an old-fashioned trust among tenants. It was not uncommon for one jeweler to lend another jeweler diamonds or gold with no collateral, just a handshake. A system of barter and trade had made most of these people wealthy over the years. While most of the jewelers were Jewish, many ethnic groups and religions were represented, and they maintained an easy harmony together.

Meyer Brownstein's shop was on the seventh floor. A third-generation jeweler with a specialty in diamonds, he had the clearest, finest-cut diamonds in the building. He did an enormous trade in engagement rings and earrings. The bulk of his sales went to jewelry stores in the neighborhoods, where they would sell at retail prices. Meyer would sell to them at wholesale with a healthy commission.

Jacob had been dealing with Meyer for seven years. They had become friends and soon their relationship developed beyond business. They'd begun having dinner together after the shop closed. Jacob arrived late this evening. It was four o'clock on a Friday, the eve of the Jewish Sabbath, and Meyer was ready to close so that he could make it home before sundown. He had a little more time these days because of the late sunset in summer. So he had agreed to do business with Jacob and grab a quick bite with him before going home. Meyer buzzed Jacob in and Jacob set down his catalog briefcase and wrapped Meyer in a big bear hug.

"Hello, my friend," he said.

"Hello, boychik," Meyer replied.

"Where is your beautiful wife?" Jacob asked.

"She went home," Meyer said. "We're alone. Let's do this business and then go eat."

Jacob smiled.

"What do you got for me?" Meyer asked.

"It's been a good month, I've got plenty."

"Let's see your merchandise. I'm in a buying mood."

Jacob walked over toward the door and flipped the sign hanging in the door to 'Closed.' He threw the deadbolt so that even the buzzer wouldn't let anyone in. "I have some nice stuff," he said. "I think we should be extra careful."

"Good point," Meyer said. "There are thieves everywhere."

Jacob pulled a box from his briefcase and opened it. He began removing small envelopes of folded waxy paper. Each packet contained several diamonds. "Here you are, my friend. I got halves, three-quarters, .80, carats. What do you want?"

"Let's look big first," Meyer said. "You got any three's?"

"Three carats?" Jacob asked. "My, my, business must be good." He rummaged through and pulled out an envelope. I got three, I got five, I got six. What do you want?"

"Let's see them," he said. They went through the merchandise—diamonds, from the tiny to the obscene. Meyer was very happy at what he saw. "I'll tell you, my friend, let's talk prices."

"What do you have?" Jacob asked.

Meyer went to the safe and opened it up. He came out with a large bag. He pulled a list out of the bag. "This is what I need," he said, showing the list to Jacob. "These are for the people who have paid me in advance. They're waiting for me to find the diamond they want."

"Wow, that's quite a list," Jacob said. "There must be a hundred forty, hundred sixty thousand dollars' worth of purchases here."

"You're correct," he said. "Would you let me hold that four and that five?"

"Are you kidding?" Jacob asked. "I can't let you hold those. They're too much."

"I'm going to sell one, and when you come back next month, I'll give you the diamond or I'll give you the money."

"Let me think about it," Jacob said. "What do you have?"

"This list," Meyer began. "I collected a hundred and thirty-five. I want you to sell to me for a hundred and fifteen."

Jacob laughed. "I can't do that. What am I, giving them away?"

"Please," Meyer said, "you've made so much money off of me. I need a little."

"How about a hundred and twenty-five?"

Meyer grabbed his chest. "Are you trying to kill me? Hundred and twenty?"

"Okay, a hundred and twenty," Jacob agreed. "Now, what about for you?"

"Can I keep the four and the five?"

"You can keep one of them if you buy enough of the others."

Meyer took the four-carat diamond and put it down on a black felt display atop a glass cabinet. He took a 10x jeweler's loupe, put it to his eye and examined the diamond. "It's beautiful," he said. "Let me see the five."

Jacob handed him the five and Meyer examined that with the jeweler's loupe. "Flawless," he said, "a beautiful stone."

"Do you have a buyer for that?" Jacob asked.

"I might," he said. Meyer looked out toward the door. "Let's go in back and count some money."

Jacob grabbed his briefcase and followed Meyer into the back. Meyer poured out piles of money onto a work table. Jacob pulled the curtain shut behind him and reached into his briefcase. He pulled out a Browning 9mm with a silencer on it. "I'm sorry, my friend," he said.

Meyer looked up. "What is this?" he asked.

Jacob aimed and fired, striking Meyer in the forehead. Meyer crashed to the floor and Jacob kicked him over onto his back. He stepped away so the blood wouldn't splatter on him and fired another shot into Meyer's heart. Carefully unscrewing the silencer, he returned it and the Browning to his briefcase. He gathered up all the money and stuffed it back into the bag, then rifled through Meyer's safe, taking the best gems he could find. He went through Meyer's pockets as an afterthought, removed a substantial wad of cash and dropped it, along with the rest of the booty, into his briefcase. He snapped it shut and looked around.

Jacob knew Meyer didn't have security cameras. He also knew that Meyer's wife, the only person who ever worked with him, wasn't there. He walked back out into the store and unlocked the front door, stepped out into the hallway, and pulled the locked door behind him. Jacob walked down the stairs one flight and waited for the elevator.

It was close to five o'clock on a beautiful summer day in Chicago when Jacob exited the Mallers Building onto Wabash Avenue. He stepped out into pedestrian traffic, blended, and then disappeared into the early rush-hour crowd.

* * *

Patrick was seated at his desk typing away at his computer. Maggio and Collata were pacing behind him, both smoking. Patrick coughed. "Are you two trying to kill me? Put those damn things out."

Collata walked over to the window and pulled it open a good eighteen inches. "There. There's plenty of air for you."

Patrick turned toward him. "It's ninety-five degrees with ninety percent humidity out there. The air is so thick that you're pushing the smoke farther up my ass. Can you please put the cigarette out?"

Collata looked at him. "Listen, Tinkerbell, we need these cigarettes. Do you understand? Without these cigarettes, the two of us would be drinking. And neither one of us should be doing that, do you understand?"

"You drink all the time, Collata," Patrick replied.

"Not with my friend here," Collata said, gesturing toward Maggio.

"Whatever," Patrick said.

"What the hell," Maggio said as he leaned over Patrick's shoulder to look at the computer screen. "What is that?"

"Fundraising for the Palestinian cause," Patrick said. "They've gone Internet. Now every anti-Israel group has its own website."

"How do you know about this stuff?" Maggio asked.

"Well, the websites I know about because—" he began.

Collata interrupted. "He does all his chicken hawkin' on the Internet."

"Funny," Patrick retorted. "As I was saying, when I was a federal prosecutor, I had to prosecute this guy who was raising money for Palestinian terrorist groups."

"I don't get it," Maggio said. "Why shouldn't he raise the money? What's raising money have to do with terrorists?"

"Well, we were able to prove that the money went directly to people who committed acts of terrorism."

"It's not that hard to follow," Collata interrupted. "Who cares? Just get to this website. Let's start seeing something."

They found a page that had hundreds of pictures of men and women on it. "What's that?" Collata asked.

Patrick's nose scrunched up as he squinted to read the screen. "Just a minute," he said. After a few minutes, Patrick began scrolling through hundreds of faces with captions underneath their pictures. "This is a list of purported Israeli spies." he said.

"No guff," Collata said, "how did they get that?"

"Who knows, and who knows if it's accurate? But let's see

if we can find something on your boy, Daniel Litwin, or Avi Joseph."

It was close to eight when Collata paid the pizza delivery man and put the two pizzas, salads, and sodas on the conference table. Maggio, Collata, and Patrick sat down for a late dinner and were meting out slices when they heard someone walking in the hallway. Collata reached down and pulled a snub-nose .38 out of an ankle holster. Holding it to his side, he stepped into the far corner of the conference room and pointed Maggio to the other corner. Patrick left the table. The footsteps got louder, then stopped. They then picked up again, growing still louder as they moved closer toward the door of the conference room. The door opened, and Darcy poked his head in.

"I'm glad you guys are still here," he said, smiling.

Collata sat down and holstered his gun. Patrick went back to the table and picked up a slice of pepperoni pizza.

"What's up?" Collata asked.

"You guys been listening to the news?"

"No," Collata said, "we've been spending our time on the Internet trying to find Avi Joseph or Daniel Litwin on the anti-Israel terrorist websites."

"Any luck?" Darcy asked.

"None," Collata said.

Darcy looked over at their meal. "That looks disgusting," he said.

"What brings you down here?" Collata asked, ignoring his comments.

"Well," Darcy began, "some poor old lady got nervous because her husband didn't come home from his jewelry shop at the Mallers Building."

"So?" Collata asked.

"So, all the diamonds have been cleared out and her husband got one in the head and one in the heart."

"No shit?" Collata said.

"No shit."

"What does this have to do with us?" Maggio asked.

"That's why I'm here," Darcy said. "Don't you get it,

Collata?" Darcy continued. "You know my theory. You know who did this hit, don't you? Jacob Orloff."

"What do you mean?" Maggio asked.

"The whole purpose of faking his death is so he can skip off into the sunset with the diamonds and the money, and nobody will look for him," Darcy said. "So he has one last hit. Dollars to doughnuts says he was doing business with this dead guy and he took him out before he left. My bet is that he's getting ready to jump on a plane tonight to never-never land with his little hotsie-totsie."

Collata looked at Maggio. "Let's go."

"Where are we going?" Maggio asked.

"We're going to make an arrest. You're going to be a hero, remember?"

Collata and Maggio headed toward the door as Darcy went over to the table and sat down. Darcy reached over for a can of diet soda, popped it open, and took a sip. "Hey, Collata," he yelled out, as Collata and Maggio were leaving the office.

"What?" Collata replied, returning to the conference room door.

"Be careful, my friend."

"You got it."

They headed out again. "Hey, Maggio," Darcy yelled.

"What?" Maggio asked, coming back again.

"Be careful, and listen to Collata."

"You got it."

Twenty-Six

Collata was pushing the van north on Dearborn with Maggio in the passenger seat. They passed luxury condos and million-dollar brownstones. None of the beautiful people gave the speeding van a second glance. "You ready to go, big man?" Collata asked.

"What happened to pinhead?" Maggio asked.

"You graduated."

Collata handed Maggio a small key and used his thumb to point simultaneously over his shoulder. He directed him toward a box in a cabinet in the back of the van. Maggio retrieved the box and opened it.

"Damn," Maggio said as he checked out the black Gloc 9mm. "You like these German guns?"

"I like the clip," Collata said. "I don't like the idea of getting into a gun fight and having to reload a revolver."

"Gun fight?" Maggio asked. "You think these guys would shoot at us next?"

Collata took his eyes off the road for a moment. "You bet your ass they would," he said.

"These guys have been planning this scam for a long time, and they've done a pretty good job so far. Besides," Collata continued, "this asshole probably has diplomatic immunity. He could shoot your eyes out and still get on a plane to Israel."

"No way," Maggio said. "I thought diplomatic immunity was a myth, you know, cop bullshit. Diplomatic immunity for killing a cop?"

"Diplomatic immunity for anything."

They pulled into the driveway of Anaka's building. Collata took the 9mm from the box and put it under his seat. Danny, the doorman, was at his desk flipping through the paper. "Hey Chief, working late?" Collata asked.

Danny looked up. "Double shift, my man."

"Good for you. Is she here?"

"She just left."

"Alone?"

"No, with our hero."

"Really? Notice anything about her?"

"She was carrying a big bag like she was going on a trip."

"Anything else?"

"Nope. No cab though. He picked her up in a Lexus."

"Did you see which way they went?"

"They came out of the roundabout and headed north."

"You're a good man," Collata said.

Collata reached into his pocket and pulled out an assortment of bills. He handed them to Danny. "I'm a little light, but I will be back to make it up to you."

"God bless you," he said. "You have any interest in any of our other fine tenants?" he asked.

"Not at the moment," Collata said, laughing as he walked out the door. "See you later, Chief."

"See you later, boss man."

Collata jumped into the van and put it into drive.

"Anything?" Maggio asked.

"They're on the move. Headed toward Jacob's apartment."

"Let's go."

Maggio pulled out his gun and checked it. He was loaded and had some extra bullets, but he wasn't strapped like Collata. His nerves were frayed and he felt weak. He was operating on pure adrenaline now. They rode in silence until they got to the 3600 Lake Shore Drive building. They pulled onto the apron in

front and Collata ran into the building. He encountered a uniformed doorman he'd never seen before.

"Hey, is Mike here?"

"No, he's off."

"How about Bobby? Is he here?"

"I don't know. You could call him on his cell."

The doorman wrote a number on a piece of paper and
handed it to Collata. Collata walked back to his van and pulled
out his cell phone. On the third ring, Bobby answered the
phone. "Hey, remember me? It's your friend. I looked at that
apartment 1610. You know, I'm the plumber."

"Oh, yeah," Bobby said. "What can I do for you?"

"I need to get back up there."

"I don't know," Bobby said. "I'm off, man. I finished work
a couple of hours ago."

"How long will it take you to get back?"

"Two minutes," Bobby said, "with the right motivation."

"Trust me, I'll take care of you."

"What's the deal?"

"All I want is for you to open the door and leave."

"Can't do that."

"Yes you can. I'll be with the real police this time."

"Oh yeah?"

"Yeah. You're just saving us time to get a warrant."

"All right, I'll be there in two minutes."

Collata had the nine on his lap with the van pointed so it
faced the doorway. Maggio surveyed the situation.

"Is there another doorway?" he asked. "A back door out of
there?"

"They're not going to use the back door," Collata said. He
pointed to their left. "That's the garage entrance. They're either
going to take their car or they're going to come out the front
door and get a cab. That's our choice. Either way, we'll see
them. They don't know we're looking for them."

"Are you kidding?" Maggio said. "After our little honey's
day in court, you don't think she's got her antennas up?"

"Screw her," Collata said. "We'll get her."

They watched people coming and going, mostly well-dressed older people, leaving for dinner reservations at some elegant restaurant or for the opera. Collata turned to Maggio. "Listen to me: she's a dangerous broad. Don't think just 'cause she's a woman she won't put a cap in your ass."

"I got it."

"No, you don't," Collata retorted. "What's the good of being clean and sober if you're dead?"

"I got it," Maggio repeated.

"Just be careful."

"What do you want me to do?" Maggio asked. "I'm a cop."

"That's right," Collata said. "Remember that. Now you go in first. I'll cover your ass because you're the cop, and I'm just a private dick."

They watched a pickup truck roll up and park next to them. Bobby got out, still in his work clothes.

"You never seen this guy's face," he said, pointing to Maggio. "Show him your badge, Al."

Maggio pulled his badge out.

"We want you to let us in apartment 1610 again. Just unlock the door and get out."

"Are they there?"

"Yep."

"You going in there to arrest them?"

"Yep."

"All right, man, come on."

Bobby exchanged greetings with the doorman and pointed to Collata and Maggio behind him. "They're with me." He walked them to the elevator. When they stopped at the sixteenth floor, Bobby stood by the elevator and as quietly as possible found the key to 1610. "I'm opening the apartment, and then I'm getting out of here," he whispered.

"You got it."

"Where's my money?"

Collata looked at Maggio. "What do you got on you?"

"Are you kidding?" Maggio asked.

"All right, look," Collata said to Bobby, "I guarantee it. I'm going to take care of you, but I can't do it right now. This is important. Let me slide. I promise you I'll be back."

"You better," Bobby said.

They walked down the hall, trying not to make a sound until they reached 1610. Bobby put his key in and gently turned it until he heard a little clicking sound as the door unlocked. Collata put his hand on the doorknob and opened the door less than half an inch. He nodded for Bobby to leave. Bobby walked backward down the hall and pressed the elevator button anxiously. They waited until he got on board and the doors of the elevator closed. Collata pulled out his gun. He held his nine in his left hand and the doorknob in his right. He looked at Maggio and gave a slight nod. Maggio returned the nod and moved up even to Collata. Collata pushed the door open, and Maggio ran in with his gun out. Collata followed him.

"Freeze, motherfucker," Maggio screamed as he entered the apartment.

Jacob was in the far corner of the apartment against the windows, pulling something off a bookshelf. Maggio could only see him from the side and couldn't see Anaka at all. Maggio rolled along the wall pointing the gun at Jacob. "Don't make any quick moves, pal," he warned.

Jacob put his arms up and slowly turned around.

"Don't fuck around. I'll kill you a second time, asshole." He slowly walked toward Jacob. "Put your hands on the bookcase and spread out. Turn around slowly."

Anaka stepped out of the bathroom, which was directly behind Maggio. Raising a Walther PPK, she fired two rounds before Collata grouped four in the middle of her chest. She fell back, and her gun dropped to the floor. She made a gurgling sound and gasped for air, and then her eyes became fixed and dilated. Collata went over and picked up her gun by the end of the barrel. Maggio was down.

Collata kept his gun fixed on Jacob. "Don't move, dickhead," he said.

Jacob began to shimmy slowly along the wall.

"I said, don't move," Collata yelled.

Jacob waited and watched as Collata moved toward Maggio. That was his opening. He sprinted out the door.

"Shoot him," Maggio screamed.

But Collata stayed with Maggio.

"Get him," Maggio moaned.

"Forget it," Collata said.

"I'm gonna die," Maggio muttered.

"You'll be okay," Collata said

"I'm not gonna be okay. I've been shot."

Collata helped him sit up and then pulled his shirt back. He used a kitchen towel to apply pressure to the wound. "You're going to make it, big guy."

After Collata put a call in to the police dispatcher, he walked back over to Anaka and felt for a pulse. There was none. He walked over to the catalog case and opened it up. He took out a box and began to go through packages of diamonds. He found one with "1.04–1.08" written in pencil in the upper right-hand corner. He unfolded the packet gently, pulled out five diamonds, and folded the packet back up before putting it all back into the catalog case. He put the diamonds in his left pants pocket and returned to Maggio. Maggio was weak and was starting to drift off.

"Stay with me, pinhead," Collata said. "Stay with me."

It took about five minutes before Chicago's finest responded in droves. The paramedics worked on Maggio as Collata talked to some detectives. Jacob's description was being broadcast on police radios as detectives' questions were answered by Collata. Evidence technicians took photographs and measurements of the apartment and Collata backed off when the paramedics had Maggio ready to roll.

"I'm going with him to the hospital," he said. "Do you want to come with us and finish this there?"

Detective Stamos, an old friend of Collata's, looked around. "Yeah, whatever. You know what I got to do," he said. "When you finish at the hospital come by the Area." He pulled out a card and put his beeper number on it. "Page me, and I'll meet you there."

"You got it," Collata promised.

"Or," he continued, "page me and we'll sit down at dinner and finish the paperwork."

"Better yet."

Detective Stamos looked at his colleague on the gurney with the paramedics working on him. Maggio wore an oxygen mask and was hooked up to an IV. Stamos couldn't resist. "So he was super cop here, huh?"

"You'd have been proud," Collata said. "Did everything right."

"No shit?"

"That's right," Collata said. "First through the door."

"I guess that's something," Stamos said. "Maybe when he comes back, he'll have a partner."

Collata pulled out a cigarette and lit it up. "Hey, I've seen a lot of guys come and go. This guy, he's going to clean up his act. He'll be okay."

"I hope so," the detective said. "I'm a family man. I'm real careful about who my partners are."

"He'll be okay. Watch him, you'll see."

"I will. Call me."

The elevator ride down was tight. Collata stood next to Maggio, looking straight into his eyes. "You know what, pal? You did a good job."

"You too," Maggio said faintly through the oxygen mask.

"Keep your strength. The doctor's got to fix you up."

Twenty-Seven

They were in court. Marcus Tatum wore a bright peach-colored suit with matching shoes. Darcy was in blue pin-stripes. Marcus sat to the left of Darcy at the counsel table. Jack Karsten got up and began walking toward the bench. Darcy pushed back from his chair and followed him.

"What do you want to do today, Counsel?" the judge asked.

Karsten leaned against the bench. He took a glance toward Tatum and then toward Darcy. "Your Honor, at this time, the State would enter a motion *Nolle Pros* on the charges against Marcus Tatum. We seek to have him discharged and have the information in this case dismissed."

The judge looked out toward Marcus. "Mr. Tatum, would you stand, please? Mr. Tatum, today is a beautiful day for you. When you walked into court this morning, you were charged with first-degree murder. Your life was hanging in the balance. As of this moment, you are a free man. All charges against you have been dropped. Sir, you are free to leave. Any further motions, Mr. Cole?"

"None, Judge."

"Mr. Tatum, the bond will be returned to you in six to eight weeks by a check from the Clerk's office. I wish you the best of luck, sir."

Marcus beamed. "Thank you, Your Honor."

The judge went stone-faced. "Please don't thank me for doing my job," he growled.

Darcy walked Marcus out where he was enveloped in hugs from Teesha and Dorothy Tatum. "I take it you heard that the case has been dismissed," Darcy said.

Dorothy Tatum planted a big kiss on Darcy's cheek, leaving two lipstick marks. As Darcy talked to the Tatums, Karsten walked past him and through the double doors. He looked back over his shoulder.

"Take care, Darcy. See you again."

"You got it, Jack. We'll see you later."

Jack walked toward the elevators but ducked down the stairs before getting to them. He disappeared as the gray metal door slammed behind him.

Marcus pumped Darcy's hand. "I love you, man. Thank you, thank you. You saved my life. I love you, man."

"Thanks. Now why don't you go celebrate with your family."

"You got that right," he said. Marcus was overcome with emotion and couldn't help himself. He threw his big arms around Darcy and hugged him. "I love you man," he shouted. "I love you."

Darcy walked him back toward Dorothy and Teesha. "Ladies, take care of him. Keep him out of trouble, will you?"

"Thank you, Darcy," they said.

"Good luck."

* * *

Darcy made his way to the parking garage and drove back to his office. He was feeling pretty good about things. He tried calling Amy, but couldn't reach her. She wasn't working, which meant she could be at yoga, piano lessons, or out for a run. He walked through an empty waiting room and into his office. "Hello, Irma," he said.

She gave him a quizzical look. "What were you doing?" she asked.

"I was at Twenty-sixth Street. Tatum case got dismissed."

"Really?" she said.

"What's up with you?" he asked.

"Go look in the mirror."

He walked over to the sink and looked at his reflection in the paper towel canister. "Oh," he said out loud. He wet a paper towel and used it to rub the lipstick marks off his cheek. He threw the soiled paper towel into the garbage and walked back to his office. Collata was sitting in the chair directly across from his desk with his feet up, smoking a cigarette.

"What, you didn't break out the Scotch yet?" Darcy asked.

Collata lifted a hand from his lap and produced a glass of Scotch with two ice cubes. "What did they do?" he asked.

"They dismissed."

"Congratulations."

"How's your buddy, Maggio?" Darcy inquired.

"He's going to make it. He's got a busted collarbone. He's going to be IOD for a while, injured on duty."

"Really?" Darcy said. "They made it a duty injury?"

"Yep, since he was out fighting crime. They said it was okay, even though he wasn't on the clock."

"That's mighty big of them. How's he doing otherwise?"

"Hey, he's gonna be fine. Darcy, I wanted to tell you something."

"What's that?" Darcy asked.

"I grabbed Kathy's husband Saturday morning. Took him for a ride."

"Oh yeah, where did you go?"

"To a jeweler."

"That so. Just in time for his anniversary, huh?"

"Yep," Collata said, taking a hard drag of his cigarette. "You should have seen the piece of shit diamonds he had."

"Bad, huh?"

"Yep. I had to help him out a little bit." Collata was about to continue when Kathy burst into the room.

"You," she screamed at Collata and pointing a finger at him.

"Uh-oh," Collata said.

"Stand up, you son of a bitch."

Collata stood up, waiting to see what was going to happen. Kathy threw her arms around him and gave him a big hug and then kissed him on the cheek. "I love you," she said.

"I know," Collata said, sitting back down and taking a belt of Scotch. Kathy slid into the chair next to him.

"Look at this," she said, throwing her hand out onto the desk. "My husband got me this beautiful anniversary ring. He was out working to make money for me, for us."

"How about that?" Darcy said.

"And this big guy knew all the time," Kathy said, hitting Collata's shoulder with her hand. "That's why he jerked me around, Darcy. He didn't want to ruin the surprise." She turned back to him. "You're nothing but a big softie."

Darcy admired the ring. "Boy, that's a beaut. He must've busted his butt for that."

"He did, and I'm so grateful to you guys for not spoiling the surprise. You're right, I do have an amazing husband."

"When did he give it to you?" Darcy asked.

"Last night."

"I bet that was the best anniversary ever."

"You know, Darcy, I'm so happy and so very lucky. I have a wonderful husband, a great family, and a great boss."

"That's very kind of you to say," Darcy said. "So why don't you go back to work now?"

"Oh, I see, I'm getting you two macho guys uncomfortable with all my gushing. Okay, I'll leave you to your Scotch." She got up to leave.

"Could you shut the door on your way out, too?" Darcy asked.

"Absolutely, sir," she said, curtsying and shutting the door firmly behind her.

"Those are some nice diamonds," Darcy said, looking over at Collata.

"They are," he said.

"Her husband couldn't make that much money tending bar if he was at Gibson's at happy hour every day of the week."

"I helped him out," Collata admitted.

"I bet you did," Darcy said. "Of course, that wouldn't have been from the evidence collected in this case would it?"

"Of course not. They fell off the back of a truck."

"You are a big softie," Darcy said, "I think I'm going to have a drink with you."

Collata walked over and poured two fingers of Glenlivet neat and dropped it onto Darcy's desk. Darcy picked it up, and they clinked glasses.

"To my old friend, Collata," Darcy toasted, "may you never change."

* * *

The new police headquarters at Thirty-fifth and Michigan was clean and neat. While it lacked the character and history of its predecessor at Eleventh and State, it had all the accoutrements of modern police work. Darcy and Collata walked down a long hallway and entered an auditorium named after a former superintendent of police. The crowd was settling down and cops in their dress blues were everywhere. They sat in the back and scanned the sea of blue onstage until they found Maggio. His hair was cut short now, and he was clean-shaven with a healthy glow. Besides the fact that his arm was in a sling, there was nothing to distinguish Maggio from all the other proud officers onstage.

The mayor gave a brief speech about the heroes of Chicago who came to work every day, risking their lives for the citizens. He then turned it over to the superintendent of police, who gave a short speech following the thin blue line theory, his men and women being the thin blue line protecting the good citizens of Chicago from evil. Then the deputy superintendent began the awards ceremony. There was an impressive parade of brave men and women. Those who had saved people from burning buildings, who had shootouts with desperadoes, and finally, they got to Detective Maggio. He was presented with the Mayor's Commendation, an award for heroism and bravery above and beyond the call of duty. He had been singled out from eleven thousand men and women the politicians liked to refer to as Chicago's finest.

At the reception that followed, Darcy and Collata skipped the cake and coffee and walked straight over to Maggio. "Hey, big man, congratulations," Collata said, shaking hands with Maggio, who had extended his free arm.

"To tell you the truth," Maggio said, "I think I'd like to go back to pinhead. Mr. Cole," Maggio said, reaching out his left hand again to Darcy.

"Just call me Darcy."

"I've wanted to tell you that I'm sorry about the circumstances under which we met," Maggio apologized.

"Don't worry about it," Darcy replied. "It's okay. Congratulations on your award."

He nodded his head. "Couldn't have done it without your boy here."

"It's nice to see you back on track."

"I'm going back into an inpatient treatment center. This time for twenty-eight days."

"That's great," Darcy said. "Hope all goes well."

"It will," Maggio said. "I have to make it work. It's been a living hell. I've dropped twenty pounds. My body is all out of whack but it's still better than what my life was. I have to beat this. I have to."

Collata smiled. "I'm going to kick his ass if he falls off the wagon."

"You see," Maggio said, "it's those warm fuzzy feelings that endear him to me."

"Hey, we're here, aren't we?" Collata returned.

"That's right," Maggio said. "You're the only ones who are here for me. Thank you. So," he continued, "Avi Joseph's car was found at the airport in Toronto."

"Really? I think you were right," Collata said to Darcy, "Avi Joseph wasn't there for Jacob or Anaka. He was there for Daniel Litwin. Avi was looking for Litwin. If anybody was Mossad it was Litwin and Avi."

"So you figure Daniel Litwin was the stiff that was burned up?" Maggio asked.

"It's my guess," Collata said. "Litwin was most likely a tough guy in the Mossad and Avi Joseph came to see what had happened when they lost contact with him."

"That would explain why Avi Joseph wasn't surprised when the dental records matched," Maggio said. "It would have been a lot simpler if Avi just told us what was going on."

"I'm not buying any of this Mossad nonsense," Darcy said. "Jacob was just a criminal who murdered and stole. Avi was probably from the insurance company that's on the hook for the missing ice."

"No way," Collata said, practically jumping on Darcy's words. "Avi was Mossad. He's going to find Jacob, recover the diamonds and smoke the kid."

"Why wouldn't he just have killed Jacob here? Why get me involved?" Maggio asked.

"He had to be sure about Jacob," Collata said.

"He should have taken care of this himself," Maggio said.

"He couldn't," Collata said. "He had to let this shit play out."

"What about Jacob? Any word on him?" Maggio asked.

"Nothing. He's long gone," Collata said.

"You should have shot him."

"Maybe," Collata said, "but I was more concerned about you."

"Thanks for being there for me, Collata," Maggio said. "It meant a lot."

"You just get better. You've got a long life ahead of you."

"I do now," Maggio said.

POSTSCRIPT

The limousine stopped outside the terminal at American Airlines. The driver got out, popped the trunk, and handed the bags to Darcy. Darcy settled the bill, and he and Amy went through security.

"This is very exciting," she said. "Three days at the Four Seasons in New York."

"I'm looking forward to it," Darcy replied.

"What do you want to do first when we get there?" she asked.

Darcy smiled. "You mean what do I want to do next?"

Walking to the gate, Darcy stopped at a newsstand and bought a *New York Times*. They checked in and took a seat.

Darcy folded the newspaper and smiled as he looked into Amy's eyes.

He threw the *New York Times* on her lap. "See that article?"

"Yes."

"Read it."

She read an article on the front page about a terrorist trial in New York. Some international terrorists had been arrested and were being tried in the Federal District Court in Manhattan. Halfway through, she stopped.

"Yeah, so?"

"Keep reading it," he said.

She finished the front page and folded the paper over to finish the article on page seventeen. When she was done, she handed it back to Darcy.

"So?"

"Well, I thought that while we were in New York, you might want to meet my daughter."

"I thought your daughter lived in Chicago."

"She does," Darcy said. "But she's on assignment in New York."

Darcy pointed to the article. "See, the prosecutor Anna Minkoff, that's my daughter."

"You must be very proud. That's great," Amy said.

"I am. I am very proud. She was one of the top prosecutors in the Chicago office and when this terrorist trial broke, the Justice Department handpicked her from prosecutors all over the country to try the case. They picked her, a guy from New York, and another guy from Boston. The three of them are trying this case."

"So is she going to have time to meet us with this big trial?"

"She'll meet us on the weekend," Darcy said. "I can't wait to introduce you two."

"Well, I hope she likes me," Amy said.

"She's going to love you after all the wonderful things I've told her about you."

"Well, you keep saying nice things like that and you increase your chances of seeing me naked on this trip."

"Oh my," Darcy said.

ABOUT THE AUTHOR

Larry Axelrood practices law in Chicago and is a former prosecutor in the State's Attorney's office in Cook County, Illinois. He is a member of the National Association of Criminal Defense Lawyers and a graduate of Indiana State University and the Chicago Kent College of Law. A native Chicagoan, Axelrood and his family live in Evanston.